Your Speech *Betrays* You

Decree & Declare

BY SPECIAL SCALES

Published By: JOY Inkz
Cover Design: Joy Osborne
Editor: Kim Matthews
Author Website: www.iamyou.network

CONTENTS

Foreward   *iv*

Acknowledgments   *v*

Introduction   *vi*

The Origin   10

Mind Cancer   23

Mind Maintenance   31

Mind Muscle   38

Coronary Artery Disease   44

Congestive Heart Failure   51

Heart Transplant   55

Mouthing Off   58

Mouth Management   67

Mastering the Mouth   73

Decree & Declare   76

About the Author   81

FOREWORD

As I look back on the many things that the Lord has allowed you to conqueror, I believe your greatest win comes from the hidden abilities that you have embraced. These gifts will create and open many doors for you. Your authentic pour causes The Kingdom of God to collide with this hidden treasure. You have now entered into a season that will unlock and decode the many obstacles that the people of God suffer through. Your perseverance and pure heart have given you access to the people. That comes from being yielded.

You have just broken generational wealth open for your bloodline and every stench of poverty is OVER. You have come into a place where the ground must obey when you tread upon it. You are most worthy to look at this first of many completed assignments and say: *"I did it!"*

As your Apostle, I have had the opportunity to see you fight. Even when you never said a word, I watched you triumph after many days of warfare and now you see the fruit of your labor.

Thank you for trusting me in this journey and letting my voice be relevant as I witness you ASCEND.

With great love and adoration in my heart; I say to you, "Daughter, welcome to the place you were called. You haven't seen anything yet!"

The Curse Breaker IS Here!

I Love You, Daughter

Blessings,
Apostle Shantay Ligons

ACKNOWLEDGMENTS

First and foremost, I have to acknowledge my God, the Father for his patience, longsuffering, and love. I struggled with my identity for so long that when I finally had an understanding that I was his and nothing else mattered, my life and everything I've done and will ever do, will forever be a small extension of his grace and mercy.

I would like to acknowledge my children, Antonio, JohnPaul, and Trinity, who have been with me since the start of this journey. They are made up of the best parts of me. They are a consistent encouragement and reminder to never quit. I love them with every fiber of my being.

To my grandmother, Mildred Lee Lamb Payton, who groomed, nurtured, labored, and warred on behalf of my soul, you were the epitome of an example and I couldn't have asked for a better blueprint. I love you so much and I pray I am making you proud.

To my Apostle, Shantay Ligons, one of the best human beings this side of heaven, who pushed and pushed and pushed... LOL to make certain that this book was accomplished, thank you from the bottom of my heart.

Your Speech Betrays You!
Decree & Declare

Welcome to the first day of the rest of your life!

As you dive into this book, it will be necessary to brace yourself for the level of application, strategy and discipline that is required to master the powers of decreeing and declaring. It seems easy enough, right? You just speak a thing, and it happens. It sounds simple, but of course, it is not that easy. Honestly, if it were that simple, life would be a lot simpler. It is simple because we do not take the power of our words seriously enough.

Listen carefully. This is a full-on war for some. Why is this such an issue? What exactly is decreeing? What really is declaring? How does it affect my life? Is it truly that important? There are so many questions. Let me help you find the answers to them all.

I am here to help you to navigate the seasons of uncertainty in life better than before. Contrary to popular belief, it takes more than just twenty-one days to create good habits. This is a life-long journey. Although there is definitely hope, regulating your speech must be accomplished spiritually.

Scripture says in Proverbs 6:2 you have been trapped by what you say, ensnared by the words of your mouth. That means your words can set detrimental limitations in your life. How does this happen? The words that we speak are groomed, through experiences, failures, ups and downs, the good, bad and ugly of life. We do not just speak haphazardly, but every word has an origin – a place where it was created.

Pay close attention. Your world is about to be flipped upside down but in the best way possible. You are about to embark upon a journey into the word of God that will search the realms of your mind and x-ray the intricate details of your heart. This journey will reveal that the mind and heart are the GPS to the mouth. The spirit of God searches for the intent and motive of everything you speak. Yes, everything! When you are lost in life, frustrated with seasons, angry at the world, hurt by situations, disappointed by circumstances, rejected by those who said they would always be there, abandoned by loved ones, or even happy, excited, or zealous, (and the list goes on) you will be tempted to speak through these feelings and emotions, spaces, and places in time. What you will learn is that the safest place to speak is out of and according to... the word of God.

There were many seasons when I hated my life and did not like what I saw. I am talking about seasons of depression, suicidal tendencies, brokenness, perversion, bitterness, people-pleasing, and self-sabotage among other things. I was in a park one day with my oldest son. An older guy who was there with his grandchildren walked up to me and asked how I was doing.

To which I responded, "I'm still here."

This stranger said something to me that I will never forget. He said, "Well, the good lord woke you up this morning. The rest, after that, Dear, is up to you. So, choose wisely."

At that moment, I honestly didn't know how to feel but I was also intrigued at the same time. All in one sentence this man had placed the responsibility of where I was in that moment squarely on my shoulders. If I am honest, and I will be, I did not like it at all. How was it possible that I had been looking all this time for the reason life was what it was and all along the answer was in the mirror? The reality was it was, indeed, true, and that same reality is staring you in the face right now.

WHATEVER YOU DON'T CHANGE, YOU CHOOSE! His statement was powerful because I was motivated to do something. BUT WHAT? I had developed a zeal to change, but HOW? I needed to start, but WHERE? I had so many questions with no clear direction. When I looked over my life and where I was, it became clear that I was living out everything I groomed myself to believe. My words and thoughts were my reality! My mindset, my mouth had become my greatest enemy. I was literally imprisoned and held captive, facing a life sentence without the possibility of parole, as a result of my own words.

I have had quite an interesting journey in life. It was at this point that I realized I had been merely existing and not really living. I was not sure about much, but I was sure that I would not settle for that. Because I wanted to live, I was about to take a life-altering journey. If you choose to join me on this excursion, I must warn you that it will NOT be easy. Expect the "Me vs. Me" war to come. Expect to be betrayed by your very own heart and deceived by your very own thoughts and speech. The truth is that you will be walking out of an old season, cycle, and story into a place you thought was impossible to reach. You must learn to master the one thing that is constant, Change! Embracing change will be the wisest decision you make on this journey. It will help you shift the trajectory of your life. The word of God does not fail, and neither will you. This is the season to DECREE & DECLARE!.

Chapter 1

THE ORIGIN:
"Learning To Talk"

Before we ever learn to talk, we first learn to listen. From the time we were born, before we thought to even form words, we learned the nature of communication by the things that we felt, experienced, expressed, and heard around us. The book of Genesis documents the beginning of creation. One of the most powerful lessons of our lives is found in the very first verse of the very first chapter of Genesis. "In the beginning God created!" Ever wonder why "In the beginning God created" was the very first thing in scripture?

Why out of all the life lessons, wisdom, and instructions would he start by demonstrating the power of decreeing and declaring with a simple statement? He gives us the powerful tool of talking our way out of or into a thing. Why is that so powerful and what does it have to do with you? Glad you asked. What's intriguing is that Genesis 1:27 says we are made in God's image and likeness.

Being made in the likeness of God means we possess the qualities of being like God in our nature, personalities, spirits and minds.

As we journey through the first chapter of Genesis, we see the repetitive statement of "God said, 'Let there be…' and there was." As God created the entire universe in these texts, he teaches us a powerful lesson of authority and power in our profession and confession. This lesson demonstrates a power that will ultimately change the world around us just as God had done.

One of the first things we need to learn about the power of our professions is that they shape, form, and make up the sum total of the world in which we live. God said let there be, and there was. He saw that it was good. It seems simple enough, right? Wrong! If we are honest with ourselves, sometimes we profess and it becomes, but it is NOT good!

Let's take a journey, if you will, into your own personal life for just a moment. Think about how many days you wake up and say, "Today isn't my day. I'm broke. I hate this life. I'll never get ahead. Every time I move ten steps forward, I get knocked back twenty steps back and there's nothing that I can do about it." I know It seems a bit extreme. I mean, NO ONE does that! Truth be told, all of us have made these statements or worse at some point or another because of circumstance. When things in our life begin to go in the opposite direction of what we desire, what is our natural response? Better yet, ask yourself, what is your response? Most of us, without thinking properly, begin to come into agreement with the things that we see, instead of using our words to command the outcome we desire.

Let's look back into scripture. Genesis chapter 1 verse 2 it says, "And the earth was without form, and void; and darkness was upon the face of the deep. And the spirit of God moved upon the face of the waters." This indicates that God did not see everything that he desired to see. The words "without form and void" illustrate that for us. He literally began with nothing at all to resemble what he desired, but he spoke to the need or lack and created what he desired by the power and authority of his words.

There is something particularly important that we have missed. Having the creative ability to be able to speak into nothing and create something means that there has to be nothing first! Whoa! This statement can go either way, because it means at some point we have to suffer lack or be without in order to see the power of our words. On the other hand, if everything is without form and void, with the right mindset, we are in the right place! Life becomes a blank canvas, and we hold the paintbrush. This gives us the opportunity to operate in the likeness of our Father.

Oftentimes we become discouraged at the thought of having to start from nothing, but if we mirror the Father's example, the possibilities that arise are endless. The creative ability that lies within us to produce what we cannot see should be the basis by which we all live. Now that we understand what we were created to do, let's lay some groundwork.

We first must understand the responsibility of accessing that type of power and influence. When power is given over to ignorance and immaturity, it can be very destructive. Although we have the power to speak things into existence, it does not always mean that we should. So initially we must be careful.

Beginning will be difficult because we are learning to talk all over again. Learning to talk starts in the mind. There must be an understanding that if the mind ain't right, the mouth ain't right. Before we say anything, it always starts as a thought.

Our thoughts create the meditations that provoke our speech.

So, how do we mentor our meditations and train ourselves in healthy thinking? I will show you how to take things that you are contemplating and search scripture to find solutions to your thoughts and meditations. You MUST think about what you think about! Ask yourself if this is healthy or toxic thinking. You will then find scripture to help you replace destructive mind patterns with the word of God. It will take work, but the alternative is to continue these patterns of destroying the seasons ahead.

You don't want to continue sabotaging your future. When I first started on this journey, I noticed that I didn't have the faith in myself to believe in the power that my words possessed. I realized that there were components of necessity, and the greatest component was faith. I would soon learn that it was the key to it all. I was struggling In my identity in Christ, confining myself into a mindset of either believing I was not deserving of what the scripture said or questioning whether the principle actually worked at all. So, I searched for scriptures on faith and confidence in him (sarcastically). I had struggled with simply believing who I said I was, it was definitely going to be a task trying to convince myself AND other people that I was actually who God said I was.

The first scripture I found was Philippians 1:6 – "being confident of this very thing, that he which hath begun a good work in you shall perform it until the day of Jesus Christ:" When I first heard it, all I did was hear it. I did not understand meditating on scripture or dissecting scripture to gain a greater understanding. While I read it over and over, there was no correlation to me. I simply could not identify with it. I just wasn't there.

I was growing and grooming during a time when everybody was on some sort of a journey. Many seeking to establish good habits were being taught that doing something for twenty-one consecutive days could create or break habits in life. Well, I already had the bad habits. It was about time I created healthy ones. So, I decided that I would begin to study scripture.

Initially, I have to admit, it was just repetitive. Then one day it began to really resonate with me. My circumstances created an issue that required me to believe beyond my abilities. I was looking for a job. I had bills piling up. My kids were running low on things, and I desperately needed to work. It just so happened that I had an interview the same day. When I read the scripture on that particular day, it went a little differently for me because of my circumstances. There was desperation and belief attached to it that time. I did not realize it at the time, but that was scripture too. In Matthew 21:22 it says, "And all things, whatsoever ye shall ask in prayer, believing, ye shall receive."

Believing that God can and will has everything to do with what we can obtain from him. Everything we receive from him is by faith even down to our salvation. Belief is the key. Hebrews 11:6 says, "But without faith it is impossible to please him: for he that cometh to God must believe that he is, and that he is a rewarder of them that diligently seek him." I needed to believe this would happen for me and my desperation caused me to be put into a position where my faith was provoked by my circumstances. My choices were to believe in God or go back to what I knew.

So, let's take a look at Philippians 1:6. I woke up that morning and actually allowed myself to think through this scripture. "Being confident in this very thing, that he (God) which has begun a good work in you will perform it until the day of Jesus Christ." Suddenly, this scripture had a whole new meaning. How many times had I searched for other things to provide, nurture and reveal to me things about myself that I desired to know? I had been on an endless journey before – searching for answers in tangible people, places, and spaces while ignoring the one who created me.

It all started to make sense. It was like breaking a nail and going to the tire shop to have it repaired. Surely, I would look foolish, and the employees at the tire shop would think I was crazy. It became clear to me that I had been looking for help in the wrong places. The fulfillment and confidence I desired could only be found in the one who created me. Obviously, I had never found it anywhere else and truthfully, I NEVER would.

I began looking at things very differently, often wondering how I had not seen this all along. I tapped into the knowledge that whatever and whoever I was and was meant to be, God knew because he created me. Finally, I discovered that if I wanted to see this thing called life through, clarity would come from what I believed about the one who started it all. By day seven I was addicted to this scripture and so many more. I memorized it so it was no longer necessary for me to look it up. I was able to recite it. It wasn't just in my mind. I meditated on it. I sat and thought about all the possible things that this God who had created the universe might have placed on the inside of me and what those gifts would look like as they manifested in my life.

I realized that not only was I no longer stressed, worried, anxious, depressed about anything, but I also believed my faith had produced my new job! Maybe this method of speaking what I wanted to see was working out for me after all. If I could tap into all of that with just one scripture, imagine what else I had missed in the word of God.

I kept running into a particular phrase during my search for freedom: Decree & Declare. It piqued my interest and I want to know exactly what it was. By definition, a decree is an official order by a legal authority. In Hebrew decree means to divide, separate, and destroy. For example, to decree "I am blessed" establishes blessing while separating that blessing from any opposition of the enemy. It all made sense. God is the legal authority and whatever he speaks is binding.

We, as individuals, have to find a way to establish in the earth the power that was given to us by the governing authority (GOD) to Decree Oh, it was on now! Next up was the word declare and by definition declare means to acknowledge possession verbally or publicly. The origin of the word declare is a mix of Hebrew and Greek words that mean to make known. The word appears repeatedly in the Psalms of David in the form of boasting, praising, and proclaiming; essentially telling everyone of God's decrees. I set out on a mission to discover what else the Word could do for me with the power of declaration and decree. Not only was I able to see the manifestation of my words, but I also felt the confidence.

The way I started to view myself changed. The way others treated me even began to change because of the confidence I had in the one who created me. The greatest part about it all was I no longer had to defend who he said I was or what I could have or do. My creator would do that for me, too.

I was learning to talk as an adult. I was starting over. It was both frustrating and hard some days, but I desperately needed this change in my life. My faith and confidence grew, and I started to believe in the God in me but there was so much more that needed to be tackled. I didn't realize it at the time, but I hadn't even scratched the surface. Because things in my life had changed for the better, I was on cloud nine. I didn't know a test of my faith was on the way.

I had been sharing my journey with a very close friend of mine and she was skeptical. She questioned whether it was really all in my mind. About a month later I went to work, and I WAS FIRED. My entire world was shattered. I was so disappointed and discouraged. That disappointment and discouragement quickly turned into anger. I felt like everything I had spoken into existence was crumbling.

My heart was broken, and I was disappointed. We must be careful where we allow disappointment to take us. It is important to understand that disappointment has an assignment; it will force us into a place of decision. Will we resort to what we know, or will we continue to believe God for what we cannot see? Our future is often forfeited because of what was not resolved our the past.

The first thing I did was resort to my former mindset. Feelings of doubt and confusion overwhelmed me. Had I really tapped into the power of faith or was I so desperate to believe in something that I created a false reality? My uncertainty was evident by the words that came out of my mouth: "I KNEW THIS WOULDN'T WORK!" I digressed and found myself in a bad space, but there were seeds inside of me that would not let me rest. The scriptures I had rehearsed would not let me rest.

There was a war going on inside of me between the flesh and spirit. I had not tapped into something good that didn't work; I had planted a seed in my soul. No matter how I tried not to believe, it wouldn't go away. The shift had already occurred. The bible says in Hebrews 4:12 "Indeed the word of God is living and active, sharper than any two-edged sword, piercing until it divides soul from spirit, joint from marrow; it is able to judge the thoughts and intentions of the heart." The word of God was alive in me. Of course, I hated that I had lost the job, but I still believed in the power of his word.

I had experienced the power; not just talked about it. It was in my veins. My feelings were hurt, and I was numb, but that word in me was living. I may not have had the job, but there was no denying what I felt in the depths of my soul in the days following my termination. I couldn't unconvince myself of the fact that I felt safe in him. This thing was all real, no fluff or fantasy. As disappointed as I was, I couldn't shake it.

Despite my disappointment I kept believing and applied for another job. There was scripture to encourage me in my disappointment. Even though life wasn't going my way, I could still trust him. It was all a part of his plan. After all, He is God. Romans 8:28 says, "And we know that all things work together for good to them that love God, to them who are called according to his purpose." As I began to meditate on this scripture, I realized that even though life was not designed to cater to me and my desires, I serve a God who could even do what I deemed as bad work for me. I resolved that even though low places would come, I did not have to live there. It was my choice!

I began to search the word of God yet again. I wasn't certain what I was looking for but somehow, I knew that it would be obvious when I found it. (It made sense to me). One day I was pondering this entire process. It was remarkably similar to the process a baby goes through when learning to talk. They don't start talking and using the entire English language in a single day. It takes time. Babies start by identifying their providers i.e., Mommy or Daddy. Then they move on to their needs: eating, drinking, hunger or pain. Based on their needs, they develop their vernacular accordingly. I seemed logical for me to do the same thing.

What did God's word have to say about provision, feelings, sickness, heartache? There was literally something in scripture about it all. "But my God shall supply all your need according to his riches in glory by Christ Jesus." (Philippians 4:19 – Provision) "For we have not an high priest which cannot be touched with the feeling of our infirmities; but was in all points tempted like as we are, yet without sin." (Hebrews 4:15 – Feelings) "But he was wounded for our transgressions, he was bruised for our iniquities: the chastisement of our peace was upon him; and with his stripes we are healed." (Isaiah 53:5 – Sickness) "Come to me, all you who are weary and burdened, and I will give you rest." (Matthew 11:28 – Heartache)

Honestly, I was gaining more control over my mind and meditations. I had not perfected it, but I was literally looking for a scripture for every little thing. One thing was still bothering me though and I couldn't lie about it. The disappointment I experienced was eating away at me. How could I get God to agree with what I wanted? Yeah, I know. I was young and still a babe in Christ. I often sat around and thought about why God did not just let me have that job I lost. I ran across 1 John 5:14 one day and was given a different perspective. It said, "And this is the confidence that we have in him, that, if we ask anything according to his will, he heareth us." His will! What was that? Why hadn't I run across this scripture first, Lord?

This scripture puzzled me. What was the purpose of asking God for things if I would end up with what he wanted anyway? It was a selfish way of thinking but a very real and honest question. That was very human of me. The more I read, the more I began to understand about the Father. I started reading stories about great men and women of the Bible who did extraordinary things. Feelings of inadequacy arose. I felt like I couldn't possibly attain all that they had. After reflecting on all of the mistakes that I had made in my life, I concluded that his will is what's best for me. After all, I had not made all the right decisions when left to my own devices.

I looked at the men and women in the Bible stories as super-heroes or individuals with supernatural capabilities, but in reality, they were human, just like me. Jesus by his authority and power told Lazarus to come forth from the dead, A prophet named Elijah called fire down from heaven to consume bulls and declared a drought over the land by his own authority. It all seemed a bit extreme. I just wanted a decent job and positive change in some areas of my life. I had no idea what I was really getting into, but I wasn't looking to change the entire world. I just wanted to change my world.

Let's take another look at 1 John 5:14. This time having confidence in the fact that when we pray according to his will: that he hears us. I learned that if I pray in agreement with God, I don't ever have to second guess whether or not heaven hears me. Now, back to the job that I lost. Is it possible that the reason I could not keep the job was because it wasn't part of God's will? There were lessons God was trying to teach me, including just because something is good does not mean it is God.

"Many are the plans in a man's heart, but it is the Lord's purpose that prevails." (Proverbs 19:21) Permitting this change to take place on the inside of me meant I would have to fully accept everything that God allowed; having faith that he is trustworthy and knows what is best for me. I had two issues with this reality. First, I did not trust anyone to that capacity, especially God because he allowed things beyond my understanding. Second, every incident of my life – good and bad, ups and downs, happy and sad – was the result of his will. I was in a rough but necessary place. I was forced to examine my life. My areas of concern had nothing to do with a job or relationship, a career or children. What got me was the years of rejection, abandonment, molestation, rape, anger, loneliness, and domestic violence. That job was the least of my worries now. GOD ALLOWED ALL OF THIS TO HAPPEN TO ME, AND IT WAS IN HIS WILL.

In reality, not only was God expecting me to fully accept all of this as his will, but I was also expected to come into agreement with him concerning it. How could I possibly do that? I was hurt from childhood traumas. I felt God had abandoned me. The truth was I did not trust him. He created me, but I did not ask to be here. I was emotional. How could he have let some of these things happen? Surely, it could not have been God's will to hurt me or to allow other people to hurt me.

What had started as a way to a better life through the power of declaration quickly became a reality check for me. I did not trust the one that created me. My past kept me from willingly coming to an agreement with him about my future. I was in a fight to use the power of declaration but there was a war going on between my meditations and my heart. The word was doing the work on my mind, but my heart was so wounded that it was hard for me to fight through the pain. Although I had read scripture concerning the deceitfulness of the heart, the war continued.

For months I reflected on this. I wanted to fully trust God, but I honestly did not know how. The Bible said, "Trust in the Lord with all thine heart; and lean not unto thine own understanding. In all your ways acknowledge him and he shall direct your paths." (Proverbs 3: 5-6) Learning to talk was more than the act of speaking, it was murder of the carnal mind, will, and emotions. It was heart surgery. When I began to search my mind and heart, the prognosis seemed increasingly hopeless. If I'm honest, my mind and heart were both winning this war, yet I was repeatedly reminded of the time I lost that job. Because I feared going back to that old mindset, I revisited Genesis 1:27. This was my opportunity to use my faith as an GPS to what God desired for me. This was my moment to take something void and formless and create what God desired. I was up for the challenge, but the hard work was just beginning

Chapter 2

MIND CANCER:
"Chemotherapy & Radiation"

Now that you understand to a certain extent how powerful your tongue can actually be, let's deal with you! Have you ever actually contemplated why it is that you speak the way that you speak? A lot of us pattern the frequency of what we heard growing up. This is the origin of many issues. The Bible traces our words from the mouth to the heart and from the heart to the mind. So, let's start there!

Based on your environment growing up, you developed a culture. Culture is and can be defined as the way of life of a group of people. Their behaviors, beliefs, values and priorities are a deposit of experiences and attitudes that they accept generally without thinking about them. These behaviors are passed along by communication and imitation from one generation to the next. Culture is so powerful that it shapes our mind and meditations. It tutors us on how to perceive everything and teaches us how to think, act, and respond.

Culture can be good and bad. When cultural beliefs are healthy, the outcome yielded is positive. Unhealthy traditions can result in a lifetime of unhealthy cycles and habits. For example, I grew up in a less than ideal household. One of my parents was overly aggressive and had been groomed by rejection and abandonment issues. My second parent was passive-aggressive with anger, self-esteem and identity issues. Imagine what the culture of this household was like and all that it entailed. The atmosphere lacked ambition, drive, and positivity.

Every word spoken in this environment was riddled with sarcasm and belittling, and very little love was shown. Now consider how that frames the mind. My culture molded me. My toxic culture led to my toxic thinking patterns, behaviors, and ways of life. Without even understanding exactly what was happening, I developed a way of living and thinking that limited the realms of possibility in my life. I, like most people, became a product of my environment.

The framework of my thinking was solely predicated on my surroundings. As a result of that, something I like to call "cancer culture" was created in my mind and meditations. What do I mean by that? When you live your entire life in certain environments, they become the only reality that you comprehend or understand, and you do not seek to understand other ways of life. This "cancer culture" cuts you off from opportunities to grow.

Why would I use cancer as a metaphor? Cancer starts small and undetectable. As it grows it spreads rapidly with the agenda of invading everything in its path. Mind meditations operate in a similar fashion. When negative seeds are planted or negative narratives are painted, we concentrate on them. Concentration produces focus and focus is the driveway to meditation. You don't have to take my word for it. Philippians 4:8-9 says "Finally, brothers and sisters, whatever is true, whatever is noble, whatever is right, whatever is pure, whatever is lovely, whatever is admirable – if anything is excellent or praiseworthy – think about such things. Whatever you have learned or received or heard from me, or seen in me – put it into practice. And the peace of God will be with you." What is found in this passage is what you have experienced all of your life without realizing it.

Let's dig into this scripture. Culture is displayed all throughout this text. It lists the characteristics, every positive attribute, and then charges you to do things that have been learned, received, heard from and seen. It specifically instructs you to put them into practice. After which, it assures you that the God of peace will be with you. One of the things that I have learned is that my meditations can cause me to move into a place of chaos or tranquility based on my level or lack of thinking. What this scripture is attempting to do is reshape the culture of your mind.

Isaiah 26:3 declares that "You will keep him in perfect peace, whose mind stays on you, because he trusts in you." This is yet another scripture for us to consider as it pertains to our meditations. Not only that, here is another correlation between peace being a matter of your meditations. I began to see a pattern of why the things I think on are of such importance, and I also began to see why my anxiety and stress levels were so high. Joshua 1:8 says "This book of the law shall not depart from your mouth, but you shall meditate in it day and night, that you may observe to do according to all that is written in it: for then you shall make your way prosperous, and then you shall have good success." Now not only did the word equate my mind and meditations to peace when it is properly stewarded, but also attributed it to prosperity and success.

For many years bad things shaped my mind, and I often wondered during this process how long it would take me to replace all the bad thoughts with good thoughts. At this point in my life, I was almost 30 years old with three children. I was separated and heading down the road to divorce. I was seeking liberation from this "cancer culture" while simultaneously trying not to duplicate that culture within my own home. I wanted better for my children.

Day by day I targeted an area where I struggled and attempted to find something in the Bible that could help me eat away at my erroneous thought life. Acquiescence - merely accepting my past reality – had somehow landed me in this rut. The thing about being in a rut is you can't help but look up. I ran across Romans 12:2 "And be not conformed to the things of this world: but be ye transformed by the renewing of your mind, that ye may prove what is that good, and acceptable, and perfect, will of God." All along I had been conforming and now it was time to transform my thoughts.

Listen, I had some days that were worse than others. There were days that I wanted to quit. There were days I didn't even want to hear scripture; I just wanted to settle for my reality. Most days I didn't wake up fully motivated, but the thought of putting my life on repeat for another 30 years was more than a notion. That was really all the motivation I needed. No matter how many times I wanted to give up or became frustrated, I had to see it through.

Eventually I got the hang of it all, but it seemed as though things were not changing. One day I received a phone call about a friend of mine. That call shifted my whole mind into another gear. She had committed suicide and I could not for the life of me understand why. She appeared to be a young student enjoying life. I was unaware that she had been in a serious battle with depression. This devastated me because I had dealt with depression and suicide. Her story could have very well been my story. Her family members openly discussed her extensive struggle with her thoughts, mood swings, and medications. She had simply been trying to regulate her mind, to regain control over her thoughts and meditations. This made me realize that depression is also a result of "cancer culture" and the ultimate goal is suicide.

Depression is defined as a mood disorder that has the ability to affect the ways you feel, think, and behave. I was no longer just learning about the word, but I now knew possible danger of the mind. If it is improperly managed, the carnal mind is powerfully dangerous. "For those who live according to the flesh have their minds set on the things of the flesh, but those who live according to the spirit, the things of the spirit. For to be carnally minded is death, but to be spiritually minded is life and peace. Because them carnal mind is enmity against God; it is not subject to the law of God, nor indeed can be. So then those who are in the flesh cannot please God." (Romans 8: 5-8)

Ultimately, the pills did not work for me, or my friend. There are individuals who suffer from clinical depression and need medication. I would never neglect the responsibility of being empathetic to those with mental illness. Not only was I heartbroken about my friend, but I was also able to see how severe this issue was. Everyday there are individuals fighting silent wars while dealing with this "cancer culture mentality." My friend's suicide made it evident to me that everyone does not win the war. Suddenly, this was not just about changing my life anymore; it became a matter of life and death to me. I had been fortunate enough to find the radiation and chemotherapy to cure this cancer and everyone is NOT afforded this opportunity.

If we look at this issue as cancer and we attack it the same way physicians do, radiation will be necessary. Let's just say that radiation is the word of God, and the culture of our minds are cancerous. Radiation is given in high doses targeting the area where the cancer is growing. It kills cancer cells and /or slows their growth by damaging their DNA. Cancer cells whose DNA is beyond repair stop dividing or die. When the damaged cells die, they are broken down and removed by the body. I know this is a lot to process but if you don't understand what you're up against you won't have the adequate tools to fight this cancer.

If radiation (the word) works in high doses then the scripture works in high doses as well. The higher the dose the greater the probability that the cancer (poor mind and unhealthy meditations) will be divided and die. If we want to take it a step further, in the natural when someone takes high doses of radiation it causes their flesh to deteriorate resulting in death, which is the same thing it does to the flesh from a spiritual perspective. The more of the word we take in the more of the word of God we put out. The more radiation we take the more cancer is destroyed.

The Bible teaches us that the word of God is like a seed. Jesus teaches us a parable about how the word works and is broken down. In Luke 8:5-8 it says "A sower went out to sow his seed: and as he sowed, some fell by the wayside; and it was trampled down, and the birds of the air devoured it. And some fell upon a rock; and as soon as it sprung up it withered away, because it lacked moisture. And some fell among thorns; and the thorns sprang up with it and choked it. And other fell on good ground, and sprang up, and yielded a crop a hundred fold." Jesus explains the meaning of the parable in Luke 8: 11-15. "The seed is the word of God. Those by the wayside are the ones who hear; then the devil comes and takes away the word out of their hearts, lest they should believe and be saved. But the ones on the rock are those who, when they hear, receive the word with joy; and these have no root, who believe for a while and in a time of temptation they fall away. Now the ones that fell among thorns are those who, when they have heard, go out and are choked with cares, riches, and pleasures of life, and bring no fruit to maturity. But the ones that fell on good ground are those who, having heard the word with a noble and good heart, keep it and bear fruit with patience." So, now I pose this question to you based on this parable: which of these illustrations best describes your relationship with word of God? For me, all of them do. During different seasons of my life, I have fallen into all of the categories.

Although transforming my mind was a new task for me, the word of God was not a new subject matter to me. I recall being the individual for whom the seed had fallen by the wayside. I would go to church to be motivated. I would hear the scriptures and it would be just enough to encourage my heart. But the moment something didn't go the way I desired for it to go, here comes the enemy to take the word out of my heart. Because of my unbelief, what was once my lifeline had been deflated. Lack of faith killed the seed.

I grew up in an environment that encouraged me to believe in what was tangible, to believe in what I could actually see. Attaching faith to my words was a far-fetched concept, so the word stayed on the surface never actually taking root. I also remember a season when I was the person for whom the seed fell on the rock. What I considered a solid foundation was a barrier to growth. I received the word with joy because it was beneficial to my current state, whether relationally, financially, or spiritually. However, every time temptation came, I would fold like a napkin. Because the word had no root, there was no nourishment for maturation.

My lack of maturity caused me to only believe for a while. When the time of tests or trials arrived, the word fell away because it had fallen on rocky ground. The plants withered because they had no moisture. So, for me rock was being a person who followed Jesus and believed his message, but never actually got around to doing anything about it.

The seed that fell amongst the thorns was most familiar to me. I was the "Thorn Patch" personified. Being overcome by the stresses, cares, trials, and tribulations of life and being lured in by materialism and lust, left no room for God in my life. I created idols out of everything God allowed me to access by the power of his authority and not Iong after that, I began to worship those things over him.

Question: Which type of soil are you in this season?

If you didn't find yourself in the "Good Soil" category, make yourself a doctor's appointment for another round of radiation (scripture). I know that this may be a lot to digest and I'm sure that those of you who are reading this book have realized by now that your mind and meditations have been an enemy to you. There is no need to be embarrassed or defensive. We all have destructive thinking that needs to be evicted. My suggestion to you is do not stay in that rut. Fight for what you desire to see in your life.

Chapter 3

MIND MAINTENANCE:
"Routine Check-Ups"

In light of what we have learned, we should have a greater understanding of what a cancerous mentality looks like. We must take a look at what is required to maintain the mind, meditation, and thoughts. Have you ever tried to clear your mind when thoughts seem to consistently overtake you? Well, so have I, and it was not easy. If clearing the mind is a task, imagine the even greater task of maintaining that clarity of mind.

What does the blueprint for clarity of mind look like? Maintaining the mind takes strategy and discipline. As you consistently exercise the strategy and execute the discipline, it becomes easier to regulate the mind. Have you noticed that whenever you try not to think about certain things, people and experiences, those are the thoughts that haunt you? They replay over and over in your mind like movies. How do you make it stop? I know you were probably expecting this, but the answer is STILL scripture. It has always been the answer and it will always be the answer.

The strength of maintaining the mind comes from the scriptures. Philippians 4:8 says "Finally, brethren, whatsoever things are true, whatsoever things are honest, whatsoever things are just, whatsoever things are pure, whatsoever things are lovely, whatsoever things are of a good report; if there be any virtue or if there be any praise, think on these things." Why would we be mandated to focus on these things? Because they have the power to strip our minds of thoughts that can be poisonous and detrimental to our mindset.

The greatest fight definitely comes in the maintenance of that place of peace in your mind after you feel it has been secured. The flesh is at constant war with the spirit. This is a journey not just a process. There will always be a war taking place against the sanctity of peace of mind. Not only is it our responsibility to guard the mind, but we must also protect it from anything harmful at all costs.

Let's talk about mind maintenance and what that looks like for us. Examine the scripture found in 2 Corinthians chapter 10. Verses four and five say, "(for the weapons of our warfare are not carnal, but mighty through God to the pulling down of strong holds;) casting down imaginations, and every high thing that exalts itself against the knowledge of God, and bringing into captivity every thought to the obedience of Christ." Often in Christianity these verses are associated with spiritual warfare, and that is exactly how we will use it. If we don't pay close attention to the verbiage in this scripture, most of us will miss the symbolisms like "imagination" and "bringing into captivity every thought." This passage refers to a war taking place in the mind. Since I have concluded that my mind is a war zone, it would be wise to level the playing field.

Most individuals do not realize that the mind needs to be guarded and protected. While we have always been told that the mind is one of the most powerful tools and resources we have, some of us don't think deep enough to understand that anything powerful needs protection. Allow me to give you some examples. As we dissect this scripture, we pull key words like weapons, which are used for protection, to guard, and to defend. When we look at the mind from this perspective, it helps us to understand the importance of protecting, guarding, and keeping the mind, meditations, and thoughts.

The word of God is likened to a sword that carries the power to protect the mind from any seeds that have been planted to corrupt the patterns of thinking. Hebrews 4:12 says, "For the word of God is quick, and powerful, and sharper than any two-edged sword, piercing even to the dividing asunder of soul and Spirit and of the joints and Marrow and is a discerner of the thoughts and intents of the heart." Maybe you have heard the slogan, "A mind is a terrible thing to waste." I agree. If the mind is not maintained, waste is inevitable. So, what do we do about the protection and guarding of our mind and meditations from the thoughts that come to plague, distract, and discourage us? We are to do exactly what Paul teaches us in 2 Corinthians 10:4-6. We guard the mind.

The first thing we must acknowledge is that though we walk in the flesh, we do not war after the flesh. What does that mean? It means that a helmet is not going to solve the issue of warfare against the mind. This is not a natural war, and we cannot use natural things to protect us. Paul teaches an immensely powerful lesson in the first clause of the passage. He tells us that the weapons of our warfare are NOT carnal. Why is that important to know? Well, if we're going to guard and protect, we have to know how.

We must know how to fight and who to fight.

Carnal can be defined as anything pertaining to the flesh as it relates to the natural. We first learn that the wars that we fight are spiritual and CANNOT be resolved naturally. Because we are human beings, our first response is mostly natural. We have the tendency to resort to the world's way of doing things. So, as it pertains to war we attempt to fight, guard and protect, but we try to do it naturally. The rules of the world are not effective in the kingdom. It has to be God's way.

Apostle Paul reminds us that the wars we fight are spiritual. This has to be reiterated so we understand that there are weapons used in this war. We are not fighting empty-handed. Now understand that even spiritually, it is never wise to bring a knife to a gunfight.

This is exactly what we are doing when we attempt to fight spiritual battles carnally. From this scripture we conclude that the war we are fighting is not with fists, knives or guns. This brings up many questions. What are we up against? What are our weapons?

The answer is found in Ephesians 6:12. "For we wrestle not against flesh and blood, but against principalities, against rulers of the darkness of this world, against spiritual wickedness in high places." Would you ever attempt to punch a ghost? Of course, NOT! Let's deal with who we're fighting. We war in our minds against the enemy, and with ourselves. Now warring with the enemy can sometimes be tricky because the enemy can be people, places, or things. For example, the enemy will use anyone who allows themselves to be used. He even uses those that are the closest to us sometimes. They can plant seeds of rejection, jealousy, or doubt.

We must be able to take the meat and throw away the bones. What does that mean? Never take anything too personally. Realize first that a majority of the things said to us by others are reflections of that person, and not us. The fact of the matter is that people can only give what they have to give and sometimes it is not good. We become affected so much by individuals because of the ties, obligations, and connections that we have with people. We take their words as if they were written in RED, like the words of Jesus. Then we allow our worlds to be shaped and framed by what others have said. We become prisoners of their words, ensnared by them. Let me free about 100 people reading this right now. Just like your words have an origin, so do theirs. Just like the origins of your words, their words need examination, too.

Most people physically live out things that people have said without fully understanding the power we relinquished over to them by receiving or coming into agreement with what they said. For example, my mom was very opinionated on how things should be. When I would do anything outside of what her mind processed as right, I would be called dumb and stupid. After hearing that long enough, I began to believe it. This led me down a path of not feeling like I was enough. I downplayed my abilities because I was made to feel like I was dumb and stupid. I lacked the knowledge necessary to distinguish the difference between her damage and my reality.

How can places become an issue of warfare for us? Easy. Places we have encountered along life's journey can be mental triggers when we have dealt with trauma, abuse, or PTSD. Places can cause us to replay things in our minds and leave us tormented by moments if we do not confront and heal from past traumas. Some individuals never grow beyond the traumas that they experienced as a child. Many get to 50 and 60 years of age still having the mentality and mindset of a 12-year-old, because of the traumas left unresolved. I remember like yesterday the day that my grandfather passed away in my grandmother's house. Until her house was remodeled, fear and anxiety that would come over me when I visited. Her house became a place of loss, grief, and sorrow for me. I associated that house with those emotions, causing me to become fearful. Whether I wanted to believe it or not, my mind was affected, and it shaped my way of thinking for the worst.

We have touched on people and places a bit. Now let's touch on things. Things also have the ability to frame your mind. This topic is very broad, but I can touch on a few. Somewhere along the way we equated things with our own value and began to believe the lie that we are only as valuable as what we have in our possession. In the world we live in today, designer things are what everybody wants: the nicest car, house, clothes, etc. This places us in a bind and materialistic things become our God. We begin to see principalities show up in our life like greed, pride, and gluttony. That causes us to prioritize things over the savior. What does this have to do with the war in the mind? Everything starts IN THE MIND!

We can also become attached to things that hold sentimental value because our mind makes us believe that we are able to capture a piece of a moment in time, causing soul ties. Believe it or not, soul ties are all in the mind. The soul is the sum total of our mind, will, and emotions. When these are not properly navigated, we allow ourselves to come into toxic covenants and ties. We will now journey into how we war within ourselves.

Most of us are our own worst critic. We war within ourselves because nobody knows more about us than we do. Life will deal us some very unfair circumstances, and to add insult to injury, we do an amazing job at making mistakes. Let's talk it through. I will be our example, of course. Not knowing my worth, I have found myself in relationships that had one agenda for me…destruction! I have shortchanged myself in jobs, college, and life decisions in general. If the decisions I made were not problematic enough, I wrestled with the one thing that causes us to war and that is REGRET!

We live years of life in regret and regret can eat away at us like cancer. When we are unable to move past the mistakes we have made, it can most certainly leave us in a war of should have, could have, would have in our minds. This will lead us on a never-ending journey to resolve things we can do absolutely nothing about. Feelings of hopelessness, worthlessness, doubt, failure and fear are devious tormenting agents of the darkness of this world. They make us blame ourselves forever and ever; sentence us to life without parole. I regret dropping out of college. I regretted marrying the person I married. I regretted some of my relationships and it took me years to finally get free.

In John 8:36 Jesus makes a powerful statement of victory that sets us free forever, declaring that whom the son sets free is free indeed. When we have faith in the word, that scripture alone breaks us free from the enemy and ourselves. In one breath it places the responsibility on Jesus' power and the power of his words instead of us. The things we thought, the things others said, the mistakes we made have all been covered under the blood on the cross. Decrees and declarations make it easier to maintain the mind because it counterattacks the negativity with the power of God's word. They replace the word curses, seeds of the enemy, and stinking thinking with the power of our God-given authority and the dominion bestowed on us by God..

Chapter 4

MIND MUSCLE:
"The Gym"

The mind is one of the greatest tools that we possess, and the greatest tool that the Lord has given us to combat against flesh and the enemy. I entitled this chapter Mind Muscle so we can gauge the necessity of building strength in our minds. For the purpose of this approach to the mind, we will take a deeper look into exactly what muscles are and their purpose. Generally, when we think about muscles, it is in association with physical power or strength. Muscle is defined as a bundle of tissue that is stretched or contracted to produce physical strength and power.

Muscles are used to combat things that pose a threat to strength and power. For instance, if I wanted to lift something close to my weight, it would require strength and physical exertion beyond what I have available, causing me to ask someone else for help. Now that we know what a muscle is and what a muscle does, let's discuss how they correlate with one another. If muscle is used to combat the things that pose a threat to strength and power, the mind muscle is significant. A weak mind is a wounded mind. Under the wrong influence, the mind can most be dangerously destructive, causing it to work against the very thing for which it was designed.

It is our God-given responsibility to steward and maintain everything God has given us, especially our minds. Our responsibility goes beyond stewardship. This is illustrated in the parable of the talents. Found in Matthew 25:14-30, it reads,

"Again, it will be like a man going on a journey, who called his servants and entrusted his wealth to them. To one he gave five bags of gold, to another he gave two bags, and to another one bag, each according to his ability. Then he went on his journey. The man that had received five bags went at once and put his money to work and gained five bags more. So also, the one with two bags of gold gained two more. But the man that received one bag went off, dug a hole in the ground and hid his master's money. After a long time the master of those servants returned and settled accounts with them. The man who had received five bags of gold brought the other five. 'Master,' he said 'you entrusted me with five bags of gold. See, I have gained five more.' His master replied, 'Well done, good and faithful servant! You have been faithful with a few things; I will put you in charge of many things. Come and share your master's happiness!' The man with two bags of gold also came. 'Master,' he said, 'you entrusted me with two bags of gold; see, I have gained two more.' His master replied, 'Well done, good and faithful servant! You have been faithful with a few things; I will put you in charge of many things. Come and share your master's happiness!' Then the man who had received one bag of gold came, 'Master,' he said, 'I knew that you are a hard man, harvesting where you have not sown and gathering where you have not scattered seed. So I was afraid and went out and hid your gold in the ground. See, here is what belongs to you.' His master replied, 'You wicked, lazy servant! So you knew that I harvest where I have not sown and gather where I have not scattered seed? Well then, you should have put my money on deposit with the bankers, so that when I returned I would have received it back with interest. So take the bag of gold from him and give it to the one who has ten bags. For whoever has will be given more, and they will have an abundance. Whoever does not have, even what they have will be taken from them."

Many scholars take this passage of scripture and pull different revelations, but can I submit to you something out of the norm? Everything God gives us he gives us with stewardship in mind. What we do with our treasure reveals what we will do with our mind. The mind is a powerful tool but in the hands of idol thoughts, can prove to be deadly. The servant with five bags of gold was wise enough to not only steward what had been placed in his care, but to multiply it. Why? Because that's exactly what we were created to do.

Everything that God has given us has the potential to be greater with his wisdom and direction. Jesus speaks of treasure in this passage and that is exactly what our mind is – a built in treasure and in it lies the image, likeness, power and endless possibilities of God. Pay close attention to the verbiage. Jesus rewards the two servants that multiplied the gold with the same language or verbiage that will be used to those who are received into heaven. Wow! "Well done, my good and faithful servant" is what he says to them. This not only emphasizes his disdain for our lack of stewardship to this life, but also shows how highly he regards fruitfulness. Oftentimes, we do not think about the aspect of stewarding the mind.

Now take a look at how he deals with the servant who refuses to capitalize on his ability to multiply. The servant used excuses to explain why he hid what he had been given to nurture and steward. Jesus uses the subject of laziness to deal with him because of he did not properly steward his blessing. Unpack that in your own story for just a moment. How many opportunities have you had to use the power of your mind to produce increase but allowed the limitations of finite thinking to cause you to miss opportunities to be fruitful?

I'm also reminded of the fig tree that Jesus cursed. It had the leaves and the appearance a tree should have, but it lacked the purpose for which it was created. The fig tree was created to produce fruit. Initially, I thought the Master was a bit harsh in this parable but the more I understand God's way the more I understand the way God operates.

Let's discuss working out our mind and what that looks like for us. Let's look at it from a natural standpoint first. When we desire to gain strength/power we incorporate exercises to make certain that the muscle mass we desire to obtain can be achieved with our workout plan. In order for us to achieve this, we must hit the gym every day. It is necessary to discipline ourselves to be consistent, persistent, and intentional. No one gains muscle accidentally. Building muscle requires determination, commitment, and sacrifice. When a conscious decision is made to follow the regimen, slowly but surely, we will begin to see transformation.

What does it look like when we lack strength of mind? When someone does not have the ability to recover well from mental attacks, they suffer from something called a nervous breakdown. I see people fall into depression, low self-esteem, despair, and hopelessness. Have you ever been in a place where you felt like life had become too much for you? Some people become suicidal.

While they continue to live, mentally they are only existing, unable to see their way out of anything! How does one strengthen their mind? How do you come out of a place of hopelessness and despair and build the necessary strength of mind? BUILD A WALL OF PRAYER!!!

The Bible says in Philippians 4:6-8, "Be anxious for nothing, but in everything by prayer and supplication, with thanksgiving, let your requests be made known to God; and the peace of God, which surpasses all understanding, will guard your hearts and minds through Christ Jesus. Finally, brethren, whatever things are true, whatever things are noble, whatever things are just, whatever things are pure, whatever things are lovely, whatever things are of good report, if there be any virtue and if there be anything praiseworthy – meditate on these things." The mind is the ultimate battlefield in this life. The Lord, our own flesh, and the enemy are all simultaneously warring for control of our minds. In Philippians 4:6 we are cautioned against the dangers of worry and anxiety.

The term anxiety means to be troubled with cares. In essence, what it reveals is a mind that is consumed with the events, circumstances, and traumas of life. There is nothing wrong with having concerns, but when our concerns have us, the problems begin. When we look at the reality of anxiety, we find there is no basis or foundation. It is just a care about something that is out of our control, something that may or may not happen.

Anxiety reveals a lack of trust in God. God promises to replace our worries and anxieties with his peace. We must come before him in a place of prayer, trusting him to show up. The word keep in Philippians 4:7 means to build a fort around or a military guard. It is often associated with the word garrison in the scriptures. The Lord promises to post a guard around the heart and mind of those who trust him with their daily needs. Instead of worrying about things that we cannot change, the word of God instructs us to learn to lean on the Lord. Prayer builds and maintains a wall around the mind that keeps the dangers of life away.

I absolutely love verse 8 of this passage. It talks about the different attributes: true, noble, just, pure, lovely and good report. All of the words used in this verse by Paul describe the word of God. In order to obtain a strong and godly mind, we have to start with the word of God. We have to take initiative and challenge our minds to dwell on the things of God instead of allowing your mind to be filled with evil or gossip or slander or sexuality or immorality or other people and what they are doing or what they are saying.

A mind that is saturated with scripture and fixed on the word of God is a strong mind. No one is ever transformed when the motivation is external. When running a marathon, there are encouragers along the route cheering the runners toward the finish line. Internally, if we are not motivated to finish the race, we will give up and stop short. This life that we live is similar to a marathon. If we are told what to do in order to grow, yet we fail to be motivated to please God in all that we do or if we fail to walk in a manner worthy of being called a child of God, we will always live a mediocre life with a mediocre mind.

Building mind muscle is something we do to ourselves. It is not something done to us or for us. It is important to build a barrier of prayer around ourselves in order to stay strong. When building the mind, intentionality is the key ingredient to hitting the gym every day.

Chapter 5

CORONARY ARTERY DISEASE:
"Blood Clots"

Life can be quite interesting. In fact, in blatant honesty, life can be extremely difficult to navigate sometimes. Things in life have a way of forming, shaping, molding, and making their way into the heart to form opinions and thoughts about life that cause issues with the health of our heart both spiritually and naturally. Proverbs 4:23 says, "Above all else, guard your heart, for everything you do flows from it." This is one of my all-time favorite scriptures. It gives us the principle of why it is so important for the heart to be guarded and protected. If this scripture is true, then everything that I do flows from the heart. In life everything that flows from the heart is not always good. We talked about the mind. Now let's talk about the heart.

Everything that God has given us must be guarded and protected. Those two words are repeated throughout this journey. There must be a prioritization of guarding and protecting ourselves, including our hearts. Now let's discuss the natural for just a moment. Coronary artery disease – what is it and what does it have to do with this? Coronary arteries are blood vessels that carry blood and oxygen to the heart. With coronary artery disease, the arteries become narrow or blocked, preventing blood flow to the heart from being effective. What causes this to happen? Stress – lack of faith or worry and doubt, poor eating habits – mismanagement of food consumption, and failing to exercise regularly – negligence of proper stewardship can cause a thickening of the arteries, which can cause blockages in coronary arteries.

Take a look at some of the different issues listed and contrast them in the spirit versus naturally. Stress in the natural world allows the cares of life to drain us and cause worry. Stress to the natural mind does not allow rest and resolve to lead our thoughts. Spiritually, when we are stressed, we do not have enough faith to believe that God can and will work things out for us. As a result, we carry the burdens of life without trusting in God's word to accomplish what it was set out to do.

The Bible declares to us in Hebrews 11:1, "now faith is the substance of things hoped for, the evidence of things not seen." Faith makes us sure of what we hope for, and it gives us the proof for the conviction of what we cannot see. As we dive a little deeper, we see that faith and stress are on two different sides of the spectrum. Therefore, if we have a stress problem, we have a faith problem. Our lack of faith often causes us to stress about things that God has already resolved. When we don't have the substance or the evidence that faith requires to believe that God is able to do the impossible, it causes us to stress over things, people, places, circumstances and situations.

1 Peter 5:7 says, "casting all your care upon him; for he cares for

you." Stress is an indicator that we have issues with casting. We worry about being able to pay our bills and living paycheck-to-paycheck. We become consumed by materialism and in turn stressed out about maintaining our lifestyles. Sometimes we even become stressed over finances because we do not trust God to provide the basic necessities of life. Jesus says in Matthew 6:25, 27, "Therefore I tell you, do not worry about your life, what you will eat or what you will drink; or about your body, what you will wear. Is not life more than food, and the body more than clothes? Can any one of you by worrying add a single hour to your life?" I mention this passage of scripture because most of us have the greatest struggle with the stresses of life as it pertains to provision and the financial aspects of life.

The aspect of trusting God to be a provider is not our only area of stress. When we face trials and tribulations James 1 :2- 4 says, "Consider it pure joy, my brothers and sisters, whenever you face trials of many kinds, because you know that the testing of your faith produces perseverance." Instead of viewing stress as opposition we should view stress as an opportunity for us to be challenged in our faith in God. There are countless scriptures that give us the ability to keep our hearts sober, and in a posture to believe God beyond what we see.

John 14:1 says, "Let not your heart be troubled: ye believe in God, believe also in me." Belief is the walkway to trusting. Proverbs 3: 5-6 tells us to "trust in the Lord with all your heart and lean not on your own understanding; in all your ways submit to him and he will make your paths straight." Leaning to our own understanding means adopting the fleshly ways of relieving stress. In Psalm 34:4, David encourages us by saying, "I sought the Lord, and he heard me, and delivered me from all my fears." Our fears can also cause stress, and stress causes blockages in the flow of life.

Let's examine the detriment of poor eating habits, or the mismanagement of consumption and intake of food. Although our heart does not eat, it is directly affected by everything we consume. Naturally, when we do not effectively manage what we eat, it can be damaging to our health. It is possible to have too much of a thing. Foods high in salt can cause high blood pressure; foods high in sugar can cause diabetes; foods high in saturated fats can cause high cholesterol. It's not that these foods are horrible for us; however, anything consumed in excess can be dangerous to our health. For example, I am a person that absolutely loves to eat and that can be bad for my health. I like snacks, cakes, and drinking soft drinks and all of those things are very damaging to the body. All of these things get into the bloodline which has to be pumped through the heart. I went through a season when my skin was breaking out a lot and my energy level was low because of the things I was consuming. Eventually I realized that my diet had to change for me to be healthier. I started exercising and doing things differently to promote physical health and longevity of life.

Now let's take a look at this spiritually. We have already determined that stress can become a blood clot. Mismanagement of consumption and intake can also cause spiritual clotting. Whatever it is you put in is what you get out. If you feed your natural man, your natural man will grow. Likewise, if you feed your spirit man, your spirit will grow. Bible declares as in the natural so it's in the spirit. (1 Corinthians 15:46) On this journey we have to be careful to guard what we consume. This takes a great level of discernment. We have to really pay close attention to the things that are deposited in our spirit and be aware of the things that we allow to penetrate our hearts. We must be mindful of our conversations and meditations as they pertain to the words we speak. Everything that we say and do is in direct correlation to what we intake. Once it gets into our spirit, there is a level of meditation that it takes for this thing to travel to the heart.

Some examples of improper intake are unforgiveness or the spirit of offense. When we deal with rejection, the way we are affected may not be visible. Instead, abandonment sneaks into the blood. When monitoring our intake, we choose the things we consume, the things we ponder, the subject matter of our meditation. All of these can become a blood clot if we are not careful. We have to forgive often to protect our peace. Even things that we entertain in conversations can lead to negativity that flow to the blood spiritually.

Let me use unforgiveness as an example really quickly. Unforgiveness hinders our spiritual productivity. We tend to cling to things that cause us to be spiritually ineffective. It stunts our growth and causes breaches in our protection. Matthew 6:12 says, "And forgive us our debts, as we forgive our debtors." Many of us fail to realize that if we are not forgiving then we are not being forgiven. How does that affect us spiritually? If we have positioned ourselves not to forgive those around us for the offenses against us, we have also positioned ourselves to not receive forgiveness from the Lord. This causes spiritual stagnation. It slows the growth process and keeps us, who were formed in his image, from reflecting the image of Christ.

Let's examine how the spirit of rejection will produce a manifestation of pride in our lives. When we are rejected, we try to become our own Savior and our own protector. This behavior always causes us to be paranoid, on the offense, and even on the defense. This is a blood clot because as long as we operate in the place of pride, God cannot get the glory out of our lives. It prohibits us from being able to reach new realms in our relationship with him. It prohibits us from going to deeper depths with God because we have still not resolved in our hearts that he is the Lord over our lives.

Take a moment, if you will, to really assess the blood clots that are in your life. Do you feel abandoned? Do you feel rejected? Are you bitter or angry because of past hurt? Are you offended that you are unable to move beyond where you currently are? Do you deal with the spirit of rejection, or the spirit of Pride? If we are honest, all of us have hidden wounds. We are unwilling to visit these wounds because of the pain there. If not healed, these hidden wounds can form blood clots and stop our spiritual fluidity.

Next, we will deal with the topic of negligence of proper stewardship. What is it that we need to properly steward? First and foremost, we need to properly steward the word of God. That is the remedy to all things. A lot of us share the word of God. We are not ignorant of Satan's devices. We know the things that the enemy desires to do to keep us stunted. Yet, in the moments of warfare when it is time to build our spiritual strength and to really exercise, we neglect those opportunities to gain victory. A moment of opportunity to be the bigger person is also a moment of opportunity to exercise what we know to be true about the power and by the authority of God. Failing to do the work creates blood clots. It is not just enough to know what to do, we have to apply that knowledge.

A lot of us can quote scripture and give good advice to others but fall short when it pertains to ourselves. James 1:22-23 says, "But be doers of the word, and not hearers only, deceiving yourselves. For if anyone is a hearer of the word and not a doer, he is like a man observing his natural face in a mirror; for he observes himself, goes away, and immediately forgets what kind of man he was." Lack of application is one of the biggest blood clots amongst the body of believers. We know a lot. We perceive a lot. We learn a lot. We hear a lot. However, a stumbling block presents itself when it comes to us properly applying God's word.

Now let's return to the natural and look at the process. When doctors catch the blood clots in time, they prescribe a blood thinner. Blood thinners are medicines that prevent blood clots from forming. They do not break up clocks that are already present, but they do stop those clots from getting bigger. It's important to treat blood clots because clots can cause heart attacks, strokes, and blockages. The reality right now in this moment is the doctor did not catch our clots in time. A lot of us are having spiritual heart attacks and have not yet realized it

Chapter 6

CONGESTIVE HEART FAILURE:
"Heart Attacks"

We have discussed in totality how things have a way of getting into the heart. Let's discuss what happens when our attempts to guard and protect our heart fail. Since we are viewing it from the perspective of heart functionality, we have just come across a heart attack. As we examine this naturally versus spiritually my prayer is that we will gain a greater understanding of the dangers in the depths of this.

Congestive Heart Failure is defined as a serious condition where the heart does not pump blood as efficiently as it should. It does not actually mean that the heart has failed or stopped working. It actually means that the heart muscle has become less able to contract over time. This prevents the heart from becoming filled with blood and it is unable to keep up with the body's demands. Blood returns to the heart faster than it can be pumped out, resulting in congestion. To understand the severity of this, we must understand the correlation between blood flow and the heart.

The heart is the muscle at the center of your circulation system. It pumps blood through our bodies as it beats. Oxygen and nutrients are distributed throughout our bodies by this blood, which also carries away unwanted carbon dioxide and waste. Spiritually, we can visualize the blood being the word of God and the heart being the soul. When congestive heart failure occurs spiritually, there are clots that create issues/blockages making it harder to get the blood (word of God) properly filtered through the soul.

When the challenges and impurities of life do not have a place where they can be filtered, the heart will try to compensate so the body will have strength to operate. Ready to go deeper? Okay. The sole purpose of the heart (soul) is to filter the blood flow of impurities so they will not impact the body in a negative way. When clots are present, the blood cannot get to its destination. The heart is forced to overwork in order to accomplish its task and its purpose. This causes stress on the heart, resulting in what we know as a heart attack. In essence, the heart is working overtime to produce the necessary blood flow to keep functioning. When the heart muscle does not function properly, the effects of a heart attack are felt.

When the heart is in distress, the more time that passes without treatment, the greater the damage it sustains. Psalms 119:11-13 declares, "Thy word have I hid in mine heart, that I might not sin against thee. Blessed art thou, O Lord: teach me thy statutes. With my lips have I declared all the judgments of thy mouth." From a spiritual standpoint David is saying that he has hidden the word in his soul (heart) so that in times of trouble, testing, and trial the word in his heart will groom his lips. This is the way God has designed for him.

When we allow the cares of this life to cause clots in our spirit man, it is as if we stop traffic. When there is not a consistent flow, it opens doors and avenues for other entities to get our attention, to consume our time, and to play off feelings of inadequacy and insecurity. This is why the blood flow is indicative and representative of the word of God. Because blood never stops flowing, it shows the importance of us always making certain that the word of God is feeding our soul.

We don't have time to entertain the enemy. When that happens, we allow doors to be opened that lead to places of despair, depression, suicide and various types of warfare that cause error in our lives. The ultimate goal is for us to be victorious. The only way for us to claim victory is to continue to feed our spirit.

When we find ourselves in despair, we can find comfort in the scriptures. Psalms 19:8-14 states, "The precepts of the Lord are right, giving joy to the heart. The commands of the Lord are radiant, giving light to the eyes. The fear of the Lord is pure, enduring forever. The decrees of the Lord are firm, and all of them are righteous. They are more precious than gold, than much pure gold; they are sweeter than honey, than honey from the honeycomb. By them your servant is warned; in keeping them there is great reward. But who can discern their own errors? Forgive my hidden faults. Keep your servant also from willful sins; may they not rule over me. Then I will be blameless, innocent of great transgression. May the words of my mouth and the meditation of my heart be pleasing in your sight, Lord, my Rock and my Redeemer."

What do spiritual heart attacks look like? Proverbs 13:12 declares, "Hope deferred makes the heart sick, but a longing fulfilled is a tree of life. Look at hope as the word of God. Hope deferred is the blood flow (word of God). The issues of life are blood clots, and the heart is the soul. When the blood clots or the issue of life cause a blockage in the flow of the word of God to the soul, the heart becomes sick. It has to work double overtime to accomplish what should be easy. The entire body is affected when this happens. Not only is the heart the central nervous system for the body but it is also the source of oxygen and nutrients for every organ to continue to function. When the heart is sick, everything is sick. When the heart stops, everything stops. A spiritual heart attack is a full-on war against life itself. If the heart is under attack, we must assume the position of battle.

Chapter 7

HEART TRANSPLANT:
"Open Heart Surgery"

Heart attacks, natural or spiritual, can be a very scary time in our lives. Oftentimes we look at life as the canvas to create whatever we desire, but sometimes life just happens. Everything that God does and everything that God allows is absolutely necessary. I have suffered spiritual heart attacks in my life. I have survived several. There are lasting effects. I love cautiously. I trust but only to a certain extent. Even when it came to God, I was still hesitant about the trust because of things that I had experienced. I was damaged, and to be completely honest, the damage was beyond repair. How can I say that? Where is my faith? If you're reading this book it means one of two things, you have either come to the place in your life where your speech hasn't gotten you very far or you're in a season where you need to examine the reasons why you are the way you are, why you respond the way you respond, and why you act and believe the way that you act and believe.

Jeremiah 17:9-10 says, "The heart is deceitful above all things: who can know it?" Nobody wants to give up on their heart. Nobody wants to believe that the things in their heart are wicked. Nobody wants to believe that the things that dwell in the depths of their heart are beyond repair. However, if we haven't yet come to a place in our life when our heart has become our greatest enemy, it's not far from us. Does that mean that we are without hope? Absolutely not. When we find ourselves in cardiac arrest, it is time to do open heart surgery.

Open heart surgery can be a frightening and invasive procedure. Both naturally and spiritually, it requires a level of courage to open up and let something or someone into a place that was once wounded. In the natural we have to lie on the table in an operating room under general anesthesia and be cut open for the surgeon to perform the procedure. Spiritually, we are just as vulnerable, making the spiritual process just as scary as the natural one. We should find relief in knowing this is a process to repair our brokenness and whatever the issue was, it is going to be fixed. That doesn't mean it won't hurt.

Healing hurts and repairs takes work. As human beings we sometimes feel the need or the responsibility to cover up. What do I mean by covering up? Keeping on lock that our hearts are bitter. We hide the fact that we never recovered beyond the age where we were hurt, wounded or traumatized? Some of us deal with post-traumatic stress disorder, but the God that we serve is wise, and so is the spirit that he sent to search us. In 1 Samuel 16:7 the Bible declares, "The Lord said unto Samuel, Look not on his countenance, or on the height of his stature, because I have refused him: for the Lord seeth is not as man seeth; for man looketh on the outward appearance, but the Lord looketh on the heart." This means it doesn't matter what type of poker face we put on for God, he sees our intent and motives and discerns the posture of our hearts.

Sometimes our hearts are beyond repair, but we serve a God that is able to give us a heart transplant. The goal was never for us to become perfected but through Christ. Through our Savior, the sacrifice that God sent to save us that we would be made in the image and in the likeness of him

Chapter 8

MOUTHING OFF:
"Hush Until You Heal"

We've discussed in retrospect the mind and the heart with clear and concise examination of how our language is grossly affected by how we perceive and receive. If they are not closely guarded, examined, and protected, we learned that our lives land in spaces and places that we don't want to be. Let's now look at the concept of hush until you heal. Time and time again we've learned that overwhelming feelings and emotions will always express themselves through our speech. As we journey through scripture, we find several verses that support the notion of this concept. Jesus says in Luke 6:45, "A good man brings good things out of the good stored up in his heart, and an evil man brings evil things out of the evil stored up in his heart. For the mouth speaks what the heart is full of."

The word of God is full of scripture that gives us instruction to heed regarding how reckless and even detrimental our tongue can be. Scripture such as Proverbs 13:3, "He who guards his mouth preserves his life, but he who opens wide his lips shall have destruction." James 3:6 says, "The tongue also is a fire, a world of evil among the parts of the body. It corrupts the whole body, sets the whole course of one's life on fire, and is itself set on fire by hell." Why would scripture talk so harshly concerning the tongue? I believe it's because we don't realize that we speak in direct assault of the good we desire to see. All of the damage can be avoided by one thing: learning to hush when we are uncertain and unsettled. Healing is so important to all aspects of this journey. Damage and hurt may not be our fault but it is, indeed, our responsibility.

Before we deal with the topic of healing, let's first journey through hurt. When we get hurt in the natural world, the body has to go through four distinct stages. These stages have to be completed in order for us to successfully go from hurt to healed. The very first stage is called homeostasis. It is the process by which the body maintains stability while adjusting to the conditions for survival. When we are wounded, we go into something called survival mode. Survival mode is dangerous because some people never make it out of this stage. Oftentimes what happens is instead of us living our intended life and thriving. we live a life in survival mode, not knowing how to function healthily because of trauma that has been sustained. Spiritually, survival mode manifests mistrust, paranoia, and fear. All of these things rebel against God's plan for us, and we live in a state of fear and paranoia since the trauma keeps us from relying on God. We must learn to navigate out of survival mode. Life hurts but God gives us the freedom, power, authority, dominion, and liberty to live in a place of healing. Trauma is so damaging because it often catches us off guard. One moment we're fine and then boom – the next moment we are not. It also sends us into a place of becoming our own protector. Instead of leaning on him, we put God in a box, making it appear as if he doesn't have the ability to protect us.

The next stage we must experience is inflammation. Inflammation is redness, swelling, pain, or the feeling of heat in any area of the body. Inflammation is a defense mechanism. It is the body's way of coming to its own defense and protecting itself. Naturally, this occurs without any prompting. It's like a backup system that automatically activates to protect the body from anything that occurs out of the ordinary. What we see in the process of inflammation is that the body begins to swell. Sometimes we mistake swelling for growth but swelling occurs because of trauma to our muscles. They become inflamed as a response to the pain. When something is inflamed, it becomes sensitive to the touch, causing us to guard and to protect it. The painfulness of inflammation can be distracting. Redness, heat, swelling, and pain are all associated with this second stage. The redness and the heat are caused by increased blood flow. Swelling is the result of the increased movement of fluid and white blood cells to the injured area. It's the releasing of the chemicals and the compression of the nerves in that particular area that causes the pain. In the natural, when things are inflamed, we do our best to avoid any contact with it. The same thing pertains to us as we deal with the realm of the spirit. When things become painful, we tend to situate ourselves in such a way that we avoid them. This is detrimental because healing hurts.

It actually hurts more to revisit the pain than when the initial trauma happened. As we go throughout life, we learn that it takes courage to go back and heal our wounds. It takes intentionality to revisit a place that was very painful. It's not only extremely dangerous to stay in a place of inflammation spiritually but also naturally, prolonged inflammation can lead to a lack of strength in the muscle to recover and repair from the damage. So, spiritually, how do we address swelling? The number one objective is to protect ourselves from further damage. We accomplish this goal by not allowing ourselves to cycle back into the situations that injured us. The next thing we want to do is rest both naturally and spiritually. This can be helpful because going into battle wounded only causes more damage. Rest allows us time to recover from our injuries.

During the resting period we need to ice it. Icing controls the pain. Spiritually, in our lives we sometimes have the opportunity to control the levels of pain that we will go through. How do we do that? By not allowing ourselves in certain places, we take back the dominion, authority and power that God has given us. The next step in the process is compression. Compression is used for support and controlling the swelling. At some point in our lives, we have to take control over the things that happen to us. Just because it happened, does not mean that it becomes our identity. Sometimes we allow ourselves to become what happened to us and cannot move forward into our calling.

Last but not least, healing requires elevation. Elevation naturally is for decreasing bleeding and edema, which is the buildup of tissue. However, when we elevate spiritually, we call the thing that once caused the trauma to be beneath us. We learn from the things that have happened and cause ourselves to operate from a place of wisdom. We rise beyond what once tried to keep us low.

We have talked about hurt now let's deal with the topic of healing. In the first chapter of the book of Luke verses eleven through twenty, we read the story of a man by the name of Zechariah. He encounters an angel named Gabriel, who tells him not to fear because his prayers have been heard by God and that his wife, Elizabeth, is going to bear a son. They are to call his name

John. Gabriel goes on to tell Zechariah how John will be a great joy and a delight to him. Zechariah is told that John will do many things to lead people to the Lord in his lifetime. Because of Zechariah's trauma of being childless, he opens his mouth in uncertainty towards the angel. He asks how in the world is this going to be? Zechariah spoke from a wounded place. Zechariah, standing before Gabriel, one of the angels of the Lord who sits in the very presence of God, questions the authority and the word spoken out of heaven over the direction of his life and his son's life. All he can think about is how long he had been praying without an answer. As a result of Zechariah speaking out of turn, the angel Gabriel sentenced him to silence. Zechariah's tongue was to cleave to the roof of his mouth until God had manifested the very thing that he spoke into existence before the foundations of the world. We must take a serious look at what is taking place in this story and not fall victim to the mindset and mentality of Zechariah. It is so important for us to heal from the things that have disappointed us in past seasons. We will forfeit something that God has destined and designed for us if we don't allow our mouths to line up with God's will.

In the next few passages, we will walk you through the process by breaking down the word heal in a simple acronym. Starting with the letter H, H is for honesty. Many times, we neglect being honest with ourselves about the pain that we have experienced and the fact that the majority of our pain is self-inflicted. How can we be so indifferent to the fact that we are wounded? When we hurt, we are the victim, but at some point, we have to choose to be the victor. At some point we have to take responsibility for the part we played in our pain. Most of us have no desire to be held accountable or to even acknowledge this truth. For others, this may not be the case. Sometimes, indeed, life just happens. However, if there is responsibility that needs to be assumed in our pain, we have to be honest with ourselves. We should evaluate every situation to make certain we are not the problem, and our wounds are not self-inflicted. We tend to create narratives and stories that are simply not the truth because of the hurt we have endured in our lives. We create new storylines and make excuses for people because we have adapted to some type of God complex. We are not honest about our situations. Honesty is sobering and honesty also takes courage.

Let's move on to the E, why don't we? The E in heal is simply for exposure. When we have been wounded and we have been in places in life that hurt, our first response is to hide, to cover up our wounds. We do not want others to see our vulnerability. We hide. We lie about the things that have happened to us. We created a façade. If we hide the truth long enough, we eventually begin to believe our façade. It is always the enemy's plot and plan to keep things in the dark. The Bible declares that everything in the dark must come to the light. Exposure is necessary and needs to take place so that the damage can be accurately assessed. When we have a natural wound and cover it with a bandage, it keeps the wound moist, preventing it from being able to properly heal. When the Band-Aid is pulled off, it opens up and exposes the wound to the air. This is necessary for the wound to dry out enough to start the healing process. Most of us don't give things time to air out because we are so embarrassed by what happened to us or because we are so traumatized about other individuals knowing, but things must be exposed in order to be healed.

Next, we'll move to the letter A. The A is for acceptance. A lot of our issues with healing come from not wanting to accept the reality of what has happened. Sometimes we have a tough time accepting the realities of life. We cannot deal with the raw truth that life has to offer or with the hand that life has dealt us, and so we have a difficult time accepting what God allows. Acceptance is a major part of the healing process. Truthfully, God cannot heal anything that we pretend is not there. We have to first acknowledge the wounds, the pain, the mistrust, and the things that actually happened so that we can move into a place of healing. If we break an arm but walk around as if that arm is not broken, we won't go to the doctor. We won't have it checked out or placed in a cast. That arm may heal, but it won't heal properly. We must accept the fact that we are wounded in order to heal. Many of us like to walk around pretending everything is okay. Accepting what happened does not mean becoming what happened. It simply means that we acknowledge that this happened, and we believe that God is going to give us the strength to heal from it.

Last but not least, the L stands for love. Love is the final stage of healing. The L in heal does not stand for just any love. It is the love of God. It is what we consider to be agape. Love is the only thing that the Bible declares does not and will never fail. The word of God teaches us that God is love. It is the binding agent to everything that we ever feel, do, go through, or experience. It is what causes people to be intentional. It causes change. It causes salvation. Let's take this naturally for just a moment. When we are in love, everything feels good. Our bodies feel great. Emotionally, we feel unstoppable. Even our regular, day-to-day stressors don't get us down. It is almost as though love gives us superpowers. Whether it's romantic love, the love we have for our children, the love we have for friends, or even the love we have for a stranger, love makes us feel alive!

Love is multi-faceted. It generates appreciation, kindness, empathy, and care. Just to share a bit of my testimony – I was a child that didn't really feel much love. My mother was addicted to drugs and my father was addicted to alcohol and women. So, love for me in my mind was always second-hand. It was never first, but always a back-burner type of love. I grew up oftentimes feeling like I wasn't good enough to be loved or to be a priority. I felt that my mother loved the drugs more than me and my father loved the women and the alcohol more than me. So, I settled. I settled for second-hand love. I settled for my version of love, the version I had created in my mind.

When I first encountered God, I was in such a low place. Everything that I thought was love had betrayed me. I had a skewed and perverted perspective of what love was. It wasn't until I was so hurt by the very thing that I called love that I was able to run into the arms of a Father who was perfect. Everything about him healed my inner depths. He was everything I had been trying to find in everything and everyone else. I begin to spend hours in the presence of God, in the word of God, and laying in his presence. As I began to tell him who he was in a place of worship, he began to tell me who I was. In those moments that was all that mattered. The love that I displayed in his presence was healing me internally. The attention that I was seeking, the love that I desired, and every area where I had lack, his love filled. All of a sudden, nothing else mattered, his love was enough to heal the wounds of rejection that I felt from my mother, to heal the wounds of abandonment that I felt for my father, to heal the abuse that I subjected myself to for years in a loveless marriage. I was able to look at my wounds and a bury them in a place in God's arms called love. It was a place that I never wanted to leave.

God's love is the greatest healing force in the universe and outside of it. 1 Corinthians 13:4-5 declares, "Love is patient, love is kind. It does not envy, it does not boast, it is not proud. It does not dishonor others, it is not self-seeking, it is not easily angered, it keeps no record of wrongs."

Chapter 9

MOUTH MANAGEMENT:
"Coals from the Altar"

We've dealt with the topic of healing, now let's deal with burning coals from the altar and exactly what that means for us moving forward. God is often referred to as a consuming fire, a dual-natured fire. In order to make this make more sense, let's discuss what the fire is normally used to do. A dual-natured fire from God in correlation to the scriptures often leads to the belief that God has the power to consume and destroy everything that is not like him while simultaneously cleansing and purifying everything that he desires to use. Hebrews 12:29 reveals to us, "Our God is a consuming fire."

We continually see throughout scripture that God consistently represents himself in the form of fire. God appeared to Moses at the burning bush in Exodus 3:2, "And the angel of the Lord appeared unto him in a flame of fire out of the midst of a bush: and he looked, and behold, the bush burned with fire, and the bush was not consumed." In this passage, we see him as a revealer. We also see in Exodus 13:21 where God leads the people through the wilderness with a fire by night and a cloud by day, revealing him as a guide and protector. In the book of Acts chapter 2, God is also seen as cloven tongues of fire representing the power of the Holy Spirit and the power of God falling up on a people. In Daniel 3:16-28, we find a powerful depiction of the three Hebrew boys, Shadrach, Meshach, and Abednego, being cast into the fiery furnace. While the King's intention was to use it as a fear tactic, God used it to show an entire backslidden nation that he is the refiner. If we read the story. it teaches us that instead of God using the fire to harm us, many times he uses it to consume the things intended to harm us whether we are aware of it or not. In the process of these boys being cast Into the fire, the men that threw them into the fire were consumed. The fire proved to be protection of both their faith and their ability to trust and believe that God was there to keep them safe.

In Zechariah 2:5 God also extends grace and mercy to the children of Israel. It states, "I will be a wall of fire around Jerusalem." This scripture once again shows God's protection and presence. Malachi 3:3 declares, "He will sit as a refiner and purifier of silver; he will purify and refine them like gold and silver." God's plan for us is so fail-proof that he literally leaves no room for error. Everything that we picked up along this way of life that we allowed to interfere with destiny and purpose, to hinder us from our calling has been absolutely annihilated by the works of God's wisdom and his omniscience to the world. His promise to us is to be the refiner even though things in life that cause us to become callous, worn, hurt, sick, hopeless, and even in despair. His promise is to show up and allow us to triumph. What does God intend to do with the things that we willingly surrender? God's promise is to produce something powerful and amazing through the trials that are far more valuable than even gold.

Job 23:10 declares, "But he knows the way that I take; when he has tested me, I will come forth as gold." The word of God repeatedly explains how God desires to operate as a heavenly refiner in our lives; he mirrors the process of the earthly refiners as a symbolism of purifying an ore. An ore is a solid material made up of metal. It is what we now call coal. This is meant to help us understand the purpose behind our pain and our issues. Specifically, to conform us into an image of Christ, replicating his integrity and his character. Psalm 66:10 says, "For you, God, tested us; refined us like silver." The refiner in Biblical times broke up the ore (coal) so that precious metals could be exposed to the heat. If we correlate this to the natural, we are all a rough rock in our brokenness in need of God and his refining fire to purify the things in us that he desires to use. In Jeremiah 23:29 we find these words: "Is not my word like fire, declares the Lord, and like a hammer that breaks a rock into pieces?" The refiner, who would be God in this situation, puts the broken coal into a fireproof melting pot that is able to withstand extreme heat before placing the coal into the furnace. Our refiner puts us into the fiery furnace of life sometimes to purify our mind, heart, and mouth. The process continues as the refiner watches the coal melt in the melting pot to see the layers of impurity form on the surface. He then removes the dross if we're thinking from a natural perspective. The dross spiritually represents anything that prohibits us from being everything that God has created us to be.

Proverbs 25:4 says, "Remove the dross from the silver, and a silversmith can produce a vessel." What happens next is very necessary but does not feel good. The refiner raises the temperature to higher degrees and the heat extracts the dross. These impurities are things that keep us from purpose, hindrances sent by the enemy to stagnate our process, or the self-sabotage that we operate in. After the refiner removes these impurities, he increases the heat even more and places the melting pot back into the even hotter furnace. As we move through the steps of a natural refiner and compare to God, we see that this process continues over and over with patience. The refiner continues to remove layer after layer of dross and the silver and the gold becomes more precious and purer than it was before.

The love of God is shown so profoundly in this process because the refiner continues the process until all impurities have been removed. Spiritually, this is the process that most of us abandon. It is necessary for us to continue the process to reach the level of purification required for us to be formed in the image and likeness of our God. The amazing part comes next. In order to gauge his process, the refiner looks for his own reflection on the surface of the melted silver or gold in the melting pot. The more dross that is removed, the less distorted the image of the Father is. If we're looking at it spiritually, only when the refiner sees a clear reflection of himself is the process complete. Most of us will live our lives in the fire. Most of us will live our lives in subsequent places where we are continually being put into the melting pot. The heat of life will continually be turned up so that we can be purified.

There will always be things that result in dross in our lives, hindering us from moving forward into God's destiny and purpose but God is a faithful refiner. He will always be there to remove every impurification as long as we are willing to submit to the process that he has started in us and through us. We must be faithful to the process of the refiner allowing him to remove the

impurities of life so that we can live in the place that was predestined for us before the foundations of the world. Romans 8:29
tells us that we are predestined to be conformed to the image of
Christ. Not only is the image of Christ our destiny in our purpose
but it is our inheritance. Isaiah 6:1 that declares, "In the year that
King Uzziah died, I saw the Lord sitting on a throne, high and lifted
up, and the train of His robe filled the temple. Above it stood
seraphim; each one had six wings: with two he covered his face,
with two he covered his feet, and with two he flew. And one cried
to another said: 'Holy, holy, holy is the Lord of hosts; the whole
earth is full of his glory!' And the post of the door were shaken by
the voice of him who cried out, and the house was filled with
smoke. So I said: 'Woe is me, for I am undone! Because I am a man
of unclean lips, and I dwell in the midst of a people of unclean lips;
for my eyes have seen the King, the Lord of hosts.' Then one of
the seraphim flew to me, having in his hand a live coal, which he
had taken with the tongs from the altar. And he touched my mouth
with it, and said: 'Behold, this has touched your lips; your iniquity
is taken away, and your sin purged.'"

Sometimes God has to remove things from our lives in order for
us to see clearly. Here in this vision of the prophet Isaiah we see
that King Uzziah had to die in order for him to see the Lord. The
Lord's powerful presence comes into this vision where Isaiah is and
the first thing Isaiah notices beyond God's splendor is that there
are things within him that need to be deconstructed and purified.
What things in our lives need to die in order for us to see the Lord?
What things do we still have that are restricting and distracting our
focus, causing us to be off guard to keep us from seeing the Lord?
The presence of God will always cause us to reflect internally. When
we have truly been before the Father, we will see how far away we are

from the precepts and responsibilities that God has given us.

Throughout this book we have seen the ways that God has prioritized speech and how he has given us authority and power through the things that we speak. The Lord has prioritized dealing with the way that we use our mouths. In this passage Isaiah the prophet encounters the Holiness of God and of all the things that God could have dealt with in Isaiah's life he chose to deal with his mouth. God was not ignorant to the fact that Isaiah had a problem with his mouth. God needed Isaiah to see that he had a problem with his mouth. It was a revelation for Isaiah himself to understand and to realize the way that we use our mouth can either destroy us or usher us into the center of God's will. We live in a culture now where the world pays no attention to how destructive words can be. Even the church treats the way we use our mouths as a minuscule or trivial matter. We find ourselves in a situation where the world is in a complete state of chaos because of the things that we profess and confess. Every day we have the choice to either speak words from our flesh, from the enemy, or from our spirit. When the angel pressed the hot coal against the prophet's lips, it represented destruction accompanied by purification. God wants to burn up our old ways of speaking and the old ways of using our mouth. He wants us to speak life and liberty in every circumstance, especially when we do not feel it. If we always speak from the way we feel, rather than God's will, it will cause chaos to erupt into our life on a continual basis.

Chapter 10

MASTERING THE MOUTH:
"Sweet Water"

In James 3:2-12 the Bible says, "We all stumble in many ways. Anyone who is never at fault in what they say is perfect, able to keep their whole body in check.

When we put bits into the mouths of horses to make them obey us, we can turn the whole animal. Or take ships as an example. Although they are so large and are driven by strong winds, they are steered by a very small rudder wherever the pilot wants to go.

Likewise, the tongue is a small part of the body, but it makes great boasts. Consider what a great forest is set on fire by a small spark. The tongue also is a fire, a world of evil among the parts of the body. It corrupts the whole body, sets the whole course of one's life on fire, and is itself set on fire by hell. All kinds of animals, birds, reptiles and sea creatures are being tamed and have been tamed by mankind, but no human being can tame the tongue. It is a restless evil, full of deadly poison. With the tongue we praise our

Lord and Father, and with it we curse human beings, who have been made in God's likeness. Out of the same mouth come praise and cursing. My brothers and sisters, this should not be. Can both fresh water [SWEET WATER] and salt water flow from the same spring? My brothers and sisters, can a fig tree bear olives, or a grapevine bear figs? Neither can a salt spring produce fresh water." The fact of the matter is what you put in, is what you should get out! GOD IS LOOKING FOR A ROI – A return on his investment. Are you willing to fight for it?

I pulled the title of this book from a familiar passage in scriptures that I feel we often overlook. In Matthew 26:73 it says, "And a little later those who stood by came up and said to Peter, 'Surely you also are one of them, for your speech betrays you.'" If we follow this story in context, we're in the heat of the moment of Jesus' betrayal and Peter's denial. Some bystanders profess a simple, yet powerful phrase. They tell Peter, "YOUR SPEECH BETRAYS YOU." Let me submit that our doesn't have to betray us. Most theologians argue that Peter's Galilean accent gave him away during his denial of Jesus, that the dialect of the Galileans gave him away, but let's dig a bit deeper. What does the word accent actually mean? According to Webster, it means a distinctive mode of pronunciation of a language associated with a place of origin. To put it into lay terms, an accent is a language categorized by a distinct tone that helps identify and distinguish places of origin.

If we can look at this spiritually for a moment, let's unpack where Peters' accent originated. We were created by God in the image of God. Before we ever had a natural origin, we had a spiritual one. We know this because God tells Jeremiah that before he was ever formed in his mother's womb, he knew him. Our DNA is engrafted with the laws, rules, and regulations of heaven. We carry a power, dominion, and authority that we've been given through inheritance to speak as God speaks. Peter was not only formed in God's likeness and image, but he was being groomed by God made flesh – Jesus Christ. Peter, who studied, taught, fasted and prayed with the Messiah himself, denies, refuses to admit knowing, Jesus. In an attempt to further convince his audience of his deceit, Peter curses and denies Jesus again. The accent (origin) will always reveal our identity. It will give us away. I'm going to help you start reversing this process by giving you things to decree and declare.

Decree & Declare

- I decree & declare according to Ephesians 1:3 that I am blessed with every spiritual blessing and Heavenly places in Christ.

- I decree and I declare according to Ephesians 1:4 that I am chosen in Christ before the foundations of the world, that I may be holy and blameless before the father.

- I decree and declare Deuteronomy 28:13 that the Lord makes me the head and not the tail, above and not beneath.

- I decree and declare Nehemiah 8:10 that I will not be sad or depressed because the joy of the Lord is my strength.

- I decree and declare Deuteronomy 28:6 that I am blessed coming in and blessed going out.

- I decree and declare Philippians 4:13 that I can do all things through Christ who gives me strength.

- I decree and declare 2 Timothy 1:7 God is not giving me a spirit of fear but of power of love and of a sound mind.

- I decree and declare Isaiah 41:10 I will not fear because God is with me.

- I decree and declare 1 Peter 2:24 that by his stripes I am healed.

- I decree and declare Matthew 5:14 that I am the light of the world.

- I decree and declare 2 Corinthians 5:17 I am a new creature in Christ Jesus.

- I decree and declare Colossians 1:12-13 I am delivered from the powers of darkness.

- I decree and declare 1 John 4:4 that greater is he who is in me than he who is in the world.

- I decree and declare 1 Corinthians 3:16 that the spirit of God dwells in me.

- I decree and declare 2 Corinthians 57 that I will walk by faith and not by sight.

- I decree and declare Isaiah 54:17 that no weapon that is formed against me will be able to prosper and every tongue that rises up against me in judgment shall be condemned.

- I decree and declare Philippians 4:19 that all of my riches will be supplied according to his riches and glory in Christ Jesus.

- I decree and declare Psalms 91:1-2 that I live under the supernatural protection of God.

- I decree and declare Jeremiah 29:11 that God has great plans for me and I am filled with the hope of a great future.

- I decree and declare 1 John 3:1-2 that I am a child of God.

- I decree and declare Romans 8:31 that if God be for me then who can be against me?

- I decree and declare Psalms 23:1 that the Lord is my shepherd and I shall not want.

- I decree and declare 1 Peter 5:7 that I cast all my cares upon the Lord because he cares for me.

- I decree and declare Philippians 1:6 that I know that he who has begun a good work in me shall complete it until the day of Jesus Christ.

- I decree and declare Philippians 4:6 that I am anxious for nothing but in everything by prayer and supplication with thanksgiving I will let my request be made known unto God and that the peace of God which surpasses all understanding will guard my heart and my mind in Christ Jesus.

- I decree and declare Psalms 103:3 that my God forgives all of my sins.

- I decree and declare Galatians 3:13 that I have been redeemed from the curse of the law.

- I decree and declare Romans 8:28 that all things work together for my good because I love the Lord and I'm called according to his purpose.

- I decree and declare Galatians 2:20 that it is no longer I who lives but Christ who lives in me.

- I decree and declare Romans 8:37 that in all things I am more than a conqueror through him that loves me.

- I decree and declare 1 Corinthians 1:30 that I am redeemed, made holy and righteous in Christ.

- I decree and declare 2 Timothy 1:7 that I am released from a spirit of fear.

- I decree and declare Ephesians 5:20 that I will give thanks always for everything to God in the name of the father my Lord Jesus Christ.

- I decree and declare Romans 8:6 that I set my mind on the spirit while I find life in peace.

- I decree and declare 2 Corinthians 10:4 that the weapons of my warfare are not carnal but mighty through God to the pulling down of strongholds.

- I decree and declare that according to Philippians 4:8 I will meditate on things that are true, noble, just, pure, lovely, of a good report, virtuous, and praiseworthy.

- Live in and by the authority that God has given you!

𝔇ecree & 𝔇eclare

ABOUT THE AUTHOR

Prophetess Special Scales was born in Houston, Texas to Phillisa Adams and Mervyn Scales on August 1, 1984.

She was ordained as an Evangelist in November 2018 for her passion and love for sin-sick souls. In June of 2021, she was ordained into the office of the Prophet where she serves faithfully at Rebirth Apostolic Ministries.

She is a loving mother of three children – two sons, Antonio Wilson and JohnPaul Minnex, and a daughter, Trinity Minnex.

Special is a humble and highly respected Prophetess, Intercessor, Psalmist, and Worship Leader with a teaching anointing that Heaven responds to.

She is also a Texas Board Certified Christian Counselor.

Having the heart and mind of God, she demonstrates every attribute of the Lord. She loves the word of God and is blessed with the gift of knowledge and wisdom, often with a zeal and excitement in sharing the breakdown and revelation of the word.

She's an honest and trustworthy woman of God that loves and has a passion for doing the will of God.

Made in the USA
Columbia, SC
13 February 2024

31466329R00046

Publishing rights belong to Poe Boy Publishing

ISBN: 979-8-9863099-4-1

DEAD SOCIALS

A Novel

by Jeff Hill

For the Larrys.
This book is dedicated to my grandpa and my first friend.

ADVANCE PRAISE FOR DEAD SOCIALS

Fasten your seatbelts for this macabre rollercoaster ride on Jeff Hill's supernatural thriller *Dead Socials*. Hill grabs the reader by the throat from the first page and never lets go. The story is masterfully plotted with crisp pacing and tension that escalates throughout the story, culminating in a gripping climax.

Gregory Lee Renz, author of *Beneath the Flames*

What breaks a human? What turns them into a monster? What keeps them grieving, haunting the rest of us? Jed Hollingsworth, the protagonist of this gripping story, is going out to find out. Not because he wants to, but because he's the only one who can.

There's a terrible mystery at the heart of the book and it keeps the reader riveted with a twisted timeline that turns on itself until the puzzle is solved. In this book, everyone is haunted by the past, the living and the dead, and only Jed has the means to untie the knots and allow life and death to move forward. It's a terrifying ride. By the time you're done, you'll be seeing ghosts around every corner.

Jeff Hill has given us the horror book we earned. He wakes the dead and allows them to confront us. In addition to being a thrilling read,*Dead Socials* reaches down deep, digs up the ghosts of our culture and lets them out to haunt us. The intertwining narratives of violence are compelling and poignant – and feel all too real. An exceptional and timely read.

Julie Carpenter, author of *Things Get Weird in Whistlestop*

It takes a lot of nerve to write a book like *Dead Socials*. Despite its cascade of voices from beyond the grave, this is a book about the difficulties of living... about the demons we haul around with us every earthbound day. Irreverent, brazen, and told at a thriller's pace, Jeff Hill's debut is about as audacious as they come.

David Hollander, author *Anthropica* and *L. I. E.*

One part classic ghost story, one part shrewd exposé on youth gun violence, with a garnish of online dating relatability, *Dead Socials* is funny, weird, scary and impossible to forget. As if *Fear and Loathing in Las Vegas*, *The Shining*, *Ghost Hunters*, and *The New York Times* had a baby to save the digital generation, Jeff Hill's debut novel just might be the fever dream we need to wake the nation up.

Claudia Lux, author of *Sign Here*

CHAPTER ONE

Now

I've learned throughout the years that it's best to keep life uniform.

I always start my interviews the exact same way. This makes people uncomfortable, but that accomplishes two things for me: It helps me remain objective and not get attached to the person I'm talking to, no matter how horrific or sad or compelling their story. And it helps me take control of the situation and gain the upper hand, no matter how terrible or disturbed or threatening the person may be.

As a child, I used to see things. But I wrote them off as dreams or hallucinations or an overactive imagination, just like my parents always did. I was so involved once school started, that I just ignored the things I used to see and avoided alone time. This was a challenge because my parents had me later in their lives, choosing careers over children and then fertility drugs over nature, resulting in little Jed, their only child. Me.

I knew that what I was seeing wasn't normal, so I did everything in my power to avoid detection. And everything in my power to avoid the alone times… sports, clubs, activities, school, friends, girls, girlfriends, you name it. All for the sake not of fitness, or social standing, or friendship. But rather for the sake of avoidance.

I got through high school with no trouble at all. Into my dream school, the University of Kansas, just up the highway to Lawrence, with even less trouble than that. I was smart, I tried hard, I was involved, and mom and dad had a lot of money because of mom being a divorce lawyer and dad a cardiovascular surgeon, their ages, and having only one child to support. My first semester of college was great. I had everything that I had in high school and then some. Sleep became something I did because I had to, but I was never alone again.

Then my parents died in a car accident, and things changed.

I started drinking. I started using recreational drugs. And I had a seemingly endless cash flow. I was rushed by a fraternity that "felt bad" for me, but in all honesty, knew I wouldn't say no. I bankrolled parties. I paid kids to go to classes for me. I bought exams, professors, friends, girls, girlfriends, and I stopped seeing things. When graduation happened, I had a job lined up at the *New York Times*, but I blew it. The *Times* likes sources, and they thought mine were made up, so they moved me to the Op Ed section because I had a following, but then that started to be a bigger problem than my paycheck was worth to them, so I was sort of in limbo when the story broke. The one that only I could tell. And when the one woman I ever loved gave me an ultimatum, I knew I had to take a chance.

But I was too late. Because I was on the bus back home when it happened. Social media let me know first, because *of course* it did. No phone calls. No texts. Not at first.

No. The way I found out what happened at Sarah Falls High School was through Twitter. The nation was simultaneously "shook" and "woke," whatever the fuck that even means. Hopes and prayers were in no short supply. The President cried on national television. Other nations made it political right off the bat, while celebrities pledged their support through fundraisers and videos and links to said fundraisers and videos posted only slightly higher than links to movie trailers and fan pages. What would cause two kids to kill their classmates and their teachers?

It was reminiscent of the way I found out what happened on the east coast a year ago, through Snapchat, an app I rarely checked but for some reason that day, decided to look through. Back then the world was glued to their TVs and the best minds from the FBI, CIA, Homeland Security, and just about every other organization that would require a black tie, suit, and sunglasses showed up. They all had their theories. What would cause a guy with the world at his fingertips to kill all his friends and family members?

But that story is another one for another time. Time is meaningless. A school shooting, a mass murder. Years apart. Yet happening, to me at least, somehow simultaneously. Let's just say that it refocused me. Put me back on track. But it was too late, because by the time I got back home to fix my own life, my own life was over. And I had questions that needed answers. Because this time was different from last year. Because a year ago, I didn't care. I chose not to get on a bus to upstate New York, even though Drake was the closest thing I ever had to a best friend.

But that was college. And this was… family.

Sarah Falls, Kansas is my hometown. It is where my parents are buried. And unfortunately, after what happened one autumn in the heart of America, no one will ever claim this town as theirs again. And the graveyard will be expanding to the other side of the highway at the edge of town.

Sarah Falls isn't a ghost town by definition, but there are definitely ghosts in Sarah Falls. And I should know, because not only have I stopped drinking and moved away from the hard drugs, but for the first time since I was a little kid, no one's here to tell me that what I'm seeing isn't real.

Then again, why should you trust me at all? I'm an alcoholic. An addict. I'm not well. And I'm standing in front of a burning mansion that I set on fire after I got what I came for.

CHAPTER TWO

Monday, September 26
8:00 AM
Sarah Falls, Kansas
7 days after the shooting

A child stops being a child when he takes a life. A person stops being a person when he enjoys it. And a spirit cannot rest until such lights are extinguished once and for all.

The classroom is bright, with the blinds of all five windows open to reveal an unusually warm fall morning. The sun is shining down on Sarah Falls, giving the high school a glow that one might suggest is almost supernatural. But one wouldn't actually say such a thing. No, that would be heartless. Not after what happened here.

The off-white color of the newly painted classroom complements the grayish spackled linoleum on the floors, fluorescent lights illuminating the portions of the room not quite penetrated by the outside world's natural light.

The room is empty. Like many rooms, it might remain empty. Best case scenario, it might someday become a meeting room. A place where only adults go, when absolutely necessary, to plan and complain and watch the clock as their students might do during their lectures or note-taking sessions. No, this isn't a classroom. Not anymore. And it won't be a room for children. Not after what happened here.

As is a requirement in all rooms in Sarah Falls High School, the stars and stripes and red, white, and blue of the American flag are prominently placed at the front of the room, serving as a constant reminder of the freedoms the rest of the country's schools enjoy. But as the metal detectors are being installed at every entrance, every exit, and the new bullet-proof glass windows are being sealed shut from the inside, freedom is the last word that comes to mind when you ask the student body how they feel about the school. Armed security guards escort the nearly silent staff and visitors such as me to and from the parking lot in the morning. Patrol cars circle the block, pulling over anyone who looks suspicious, which, after the incident, is everyone.

Except for me. My press badge and my hometown hero status get me past the yellow tape, past the police, and set up in my own special room. A room that used to be my fifth period American literature class.

Which brings us here. Now. My first interview.

And… Start recording…

"I'm Jed Hollingsworth. But because of the nature of this interview, you can just call me Jed. Sound good? I'm a journalist and I'm going to tell the story of what the papers are calling The Sarah Falls High School Massacre. Alrighty. Let's begin. So, for the record, can I ask your name?"

"Anne Marie. Anne Marie DeLucco. Annie to my friends. I guess you can call me Annie, even though we're not really friends."

"Okay. Thanks, Annie. I will. Is it okay with you if I ask a few questions about, well, *you,* before we get started and dig deeper into the incident that happened last…"

"Shooting, Jed. You can call it what it was. It was a shooting, where two kids no one even knew came into our classrooms and killed a bunch of our friends and made Sarah Falls High School a terrifying place to return to."

She stops and rubs her throat with her freckled arm. Her long red hair falls in front of her face as she begins a coughing spell.

I hand her a box of tissues, which she refuses.

"I'm all right. I just can't seem to shake this cough. And my throat constantly hurts. You know? Anyway, what did you want to know about me, Jed? There's not a lot special about me. Why don't you talk to the other survivors? I'm sure they're all much more interesting people to talk to and get to know. After all, I'm just plain old Anne Marie DeLucco…"

"Annie to your friends."

"Yeah. All, like, *three* of them."

"Oh, come on, Annie. I'm sure you've got more people who care about you than you think. I'm sure your parents and your family and your teachers…"

"Don't count. They're adults. It's their job to care about kids. No matter how boring or uninteresting or just plain, well, *normal* they are."

Another coughing spell. This time I offer her a cough drop. And she again refuses, pushing her hair out of her face.

10

"No, I'm good, Jed. Just, you know, haven't been able to shake this cough since…"

"The incident."

"Shooting."

And another spell. I try to reach across the table, try to touch her hand. She pulls away.

She knows. I know she knows, deep down, but it is still, hard for her to understand. To accept. Which is what makes my next line of questioning so hard. And why I have to start from the beginning.

"So, Annie. The inci… shooting. Before. Who were you? What was your story? What did you do for fun, you know, before and after the halls of Sarah Falls High School?"

"I guess you could say I'm a bookworm. I go to school, I pay attention, I try to ignore the cute boys who don't even notice me, and I go through the motions. They always say that girls like me find guys who *like* girls like me in college, so I guess that's my main focus. When I get home from school, I study. Or research colleges."

"You were a sophomore, is that right?"

"Yeah. I'm a sophomore. But still, it never hurts to work on the grade point average and look into schools early, you know?"

I know. I was a little bit like her when I was her age. I wanted so desperately to leave Sarah Falls, never knowing just how much I needed it until I left. Never knowing how much it needed me until I returned.

"Makes sense. So, other than school-related stuff, what else did you do in your free time? You know, for fun? Friends? Clubs? Sports?"

"Yeah. *Right.*"

The coughing spells are becoming more and more violent each time they rear their ugly heads. This time I offer her the box of tissues again, and I know she knows. She has to. She's coughing up blood.

It's days like this that really make me hate my job. But it is also stories like Annie DeLucco's that make this job so important. I do what everyone wants to do but isn't brave enough to do themselves. I get the stories. The hard ones. The ones that change everything. Forever.

"I don't have any friends. My family barely even knows I exist. The only club that would have me would be the clubs full of girls who hate themselves as much as I do and I've always figured, what

11

the heck's the point, you know? Just sit still, be quiet, get good grades, and get out of Sarah Falls. Get to somewhere, you know, *normal*. Like me."

And that's when I try again to reach for her hand, and this time, I swear, she almost lets me reach out to her. She almost lets me make contact. But, of course, she isn't ready yet. Her story isn't told, so she isn't going to let me in. Not yet. Not completely.

"Sorry, Jed. Can we just get on with the rest of the interview? Just skip over the boring stuff… I'm not trying to be a spas. I just, you know, don't really want to talk about myself. If I can help you with your Sarah Falls High School shooting story, I can do that. But enough is enough when it comes to the *me* stuff., okay?"

"Sure thing."

Coughing. Blood. Hiding. And I don't even try to touch her. I know better. I know she knows.

"The series of events are all honestly still a little blurry… So bear with me."

"That I can do, Annie. That I can do. Whenever you're ready."

She tells me her story. She talks about how Rick Smith and Jameson Allan came into her classroom with semi-automatic weapons and told the students to get down on the floor, away from the windows. They said if anyone yelled out or even made so much as a peep, they were going to get it like Mr. Jacobson did. That's when a student asked, "What do you mean? Mr. Jacobson's right there."

Rick Smith shot Mr. Jacobson point blank in the face, grabbed the student by the shirt collar and threw him against the white board, shooting him a dozen times in front of the whole class. That student's name was Gavin Armstrong. Annie had had a crush on him since they were in ninth grade.

That part of her story is very vivid, full of details only someone who was as attentive and good at staying safe and silent as Annie would have been able to deliver. The rest of her story is a bit less lucid. More dream-like. But her nightmare is about to end.

Several minutes passed as the gunmen split up and started distributing papers with names of students on them. They were telling the students that if anyone knew where these kids were or could be hiding at this point in the day, they'd better let them know as soon as it came to them, or they'd be sorry.

That's when Annie did something that struck me as odd.

She confronted the gunmen.

"Or we'll be sorry? What does that even *mean*?"

Of course, she knew what it meant. She knew exactly what it meant.

"And they… And they…"

"It's okay, Annie. You don't have to go on."

"But, Jed… They… They…"

Coughing. Blood everywhere. The hole in her throat where Rick Smith shoved his father's hunting knife has completely come open. She can't even talk anymore. But it doesn't matter. Annie DeLucco doesn't need to talk anymore. And she knows that. I am going to talk for her. I am going to tell her story.

But for some reason, that really isn't enough. Because when I turn off the electromagnetic camera equipment, the seismographic pulse recorder, and shut my notebook, this interview is not over. Far from it. This poor girl knows she is not done on this earth. She is not done at all. Because it isn't fair. She isn't going anywhere. Because the one thing she ever really wanted, the one thing all fifteen-year-old girls ever really want, is to be noticed. And touched. And when I reach across the table, and she finally allows me to embrace her hand, mine goes right through hers.

She cries until there is nothing left of her. And as much as it pains me to tell her in this way, part of me rests easy in knowing she accepts it. But there will always be a huge part of me that stays up late at night and wonders where she went when she passed on.

And if she was still alone when she got there.

And… Stop recording…

So there it is. There you have it. My first interview is in the books and though I know my work here is important, it still leaves me feeling a little uneasy. But I never waver. Not once. I know I need to do this. For girls like Annie. For the kids who can't speak up and tell their stories. For the teachers who need to teach one last lesson.

For myself.

After all, I grew up here. That's right, I was a Sarah Falls Wildcat.

My parents were born and raised here, and it feels like I just put them both into the ground. My very first tee ball game was here when I was seven. My dad was my third-grade soccer coach. My mom was my seventh-grade English teacher after she retired. My first kiss was at the movie theater here when I was fourteen. Amy Henderson. I lost my virginity to Kristy DeGraw parked outside one of Sarah Falls' countless cornfields when I was seventeen. I graduated, left, had what seemed like another lifetime flash by in just five short years, and came back here. And because of what just happened last week, I feel like I'm never going to leave Sarah Falls again.

My facts aren't all in yet, but soon they will be. After all, I'm a journalist. And a really good one at that. You can Google my articles in *The New York Times* about gun control, cyberbullying, and education reform. And you can also look at all my nationally syndicated Op Eds about my thoughts on who is to blame, what is the cause, and the role we all play in this crazy world full of guns and ghosts. One has facts. One, not so much. And the facts are a journalist's Achilles' Heel when it comes to telling a story that's worth a damn. And God help me, I wish it weren't, but this one is. It's the one everyone's going to want to tell.

Two gunmen walked into Sarah Falls High School last Monday at 11:19, two minutes before first lunch, and opened fire. After less than forty-five minutes, the two gunmen were done. They had killed thirty-one students and fifteen teachers, before finally turning the guns on themselves rather than face the local police. They were both seniors at Sarah Falls High School, they left no note, and their parents saw no warning signs.

I was standing outside the schoolyard five minutes after the news hit all the local channels, and it looked like a movie star or the President had just arrived. There was media everywhere. There were National Guardsmen everywhere. The police were flustered. The mayor looked tired. The parents and students and concerned citizens all looked like they'd been through hell that day. And they had.

But the reason I'm still here is simple. I have a job to do. Like I said, I'm a journalist, and if the people of the world aren't told the tale of what the papers will undoubtedly label something as unfeeling and heartless as "The Sarah Falls High School Massacre," who's to tell the world that it even happened? If it's not in print, it doesn't count. If it didn't happen to you, or near you, or even in your peripherals, you don't care. It's sick. It's sad. But it's true.

And that's why I'm here. Because it did happen. To me. To my family. To my friends. To the family and friends of Amy Henderson. To the family and friends of Kristy DeGraw. And to the residents of Sarah Falls, who will never forgive, will never leave, and you can rest assured, never forget.

CHAPTER THREE

Sunday, October 2
3:30 AM
Kansas City, Missouri
183 days after the book deal

So here I am, drunk again, trying my best to fall asleep in this swanky hotel in KC. My agent says I need to put down roots and buy a house or something, but he's also the asshole who made me publish my book on Sarah Falls as fiction. That's right. As in, *not real*. He said that it would work better if it was "based on true events." You know. For the movie tie-in. Because these days, you've got to think about the movie tie-in.

I have no control over the screenplay, but it's being written by someone who is "edgy" but not quite young enough that she's going to stand her ground with producers. The movie is a planned trilogy and there are even rumors that I might get a substantial cut if they make above a certain profit margin. I'm listed as an executive producer. I have no idea what that means, but it pays enough for me to live in a hotel room and buy every food, drink, drug, and person I would ever want.

That's exactly what I'm doing. That, and, you know, continuing to record all this. There are over one hundred people who have died within the walls of this hotel, most of whom died quietly and quickly, none of whom have a story to tell. No murders. No accidents. All suicides and heart attacks and alcohol poisoning. All intentional, in the eyes of the afterlife air traffic controllers.

I feel like a sell-out. My agent is brokering this multi-book deal and a TV series and a movie trilogy and even for some fucking reason, merchandising, but somewhere along the way he decided to just write off the stories of the victims of Sarah Falls. "Based on actual events," though? This phrase haunts me, literally, because some of the ghosts are back. Hence the being drunk part. If I'm drunk, my second abilities don't work.

I pick up my phone. My agent has downloaded a bunch of dating apps for me, even some for men seeking men because he doesn't know what I like, and I've been swiping right, swiping left, and even messaging, all while drinking and doing drugs for months. Tinder, Bumble, Grindr, Clover, Happn, and even something douchey called The League, which apparently I'm also in because of my looks and money and fame. And my whiteness.

But on a particularly dark night in a moment of temporary sanity, I decided that I needed to do the right thing and come clean. Then, in a second moment of temporary sanity, I decided that that was just too hard. So here I am. I have decided to just overdose. If I kill myself, the story goes on without me and it's someone else's problem.

I swallow a bottle of what I was told is Oxy. I chug what's left in the minibar. I even smoke a little something that shouldn't probably be smoked. Then I wait for the light.

And it comes. But not from where I want it to come.

My phone vibrates and lights up. I look at it because why the fuck not.

It's an email notification linked with my Twitter account, the one that my agent set up for me for promotional reasons.

"Jed," it says, "It's Drake. I fucked up. I need your help... bad. I remember back in college you saying something about you having a weird connection to another world or something and well here we are. Please come. Like I said, it's bad."

And that's all it said. Things are starting to shake, lights are starting to turn on all over the place, and my entire body starts to hurt. So I get up and run to the bathroom and vomit about five times in less than a minute.

I call my agent. The world stops spinning, and as I look into the mirror at myself and the ghosts of those strong enough to follow me from Sarah Falls, I hate what I see.

"Jed?" he answers.

"I have a sequel idea."

The squeal he lets out is almost otherworldly. I can hear the cash register sounds go off inside his head. But before he can tell me that he wants me on a red eye flight to New York City for a meeting and a train to upstate New York for said story, I cut him off.

"Dude. Stop. Just, shut up."

My head spins. It splits. The ghosts start yelling.

"Everyone. Just... stop."

They all do. Except for him. He's still asking if I'm okay. As if there's ever going to be a yes when he asks.

"I'm renting a car. I'm driving upstate. I'll email you when I have Wi-Fi. I'll text you when I have service. And I'll call you if I need anything."

He's silent for the first time since I've met him.

"Two words," I tell him. "Best seller."

I hang up. And vomit again for good measure.

My first book is a best seller. I'm on *The Los Angeles Times* best-selling authors list. But the pressure is too much. The returned ghosts are too much. The lawsuits, the press, the constant noise is just...

Then Drake contacted me. On Twitter, of all things.

So here I am. Booking a car and planning out a route. If I drove straight through, it'd take me at least twenty hours. I'm going to split it up over the course of a couple of weeks. After all, there's no rush. It's not like Drake's going anywhere.

Along the way, I'll stop, I'll fill up on gas and food and sleep and booze and maybe do a little swiping on some of the apps my agent installed. I'll tell some stories. I'll write. I'll talk to you all.

And when I get to upstate New York and finally see Drake's place, this reportedly haunted mansion, I'll get to work. And get my mind off and as far away as I can get it from Sarah Falls and my failures that refuse to stay dead and buried there.

Everyone who's ever lived in Drake's place has died there under mysterious circumstances. You've read all about it. The papers called it Suicide Mansion. And when Drake realized he was in over his head and tried to sell the place, the mansion got him, too.

Drake tweeted me less than ten minutes ago. But Drake killed almost everyone we went to college with at his house, then himself, five months after we graduated. That was three years ago.

CHAPTER FOUR

Monday, September 26
8:30 AM
Sarah Falls, Kansas
7 days after the shooting

And… Start recording…

"I'm Jed Hollingsworth. But because of the nature of this interview, you can just call me Jed. Sound good? I'm a journalist and I'm going to tell the story of what the papers are calling The Sarah Falls High School Massacre. Alrighty. Let's begin. So, for the record, can I ask your name?"

"Dan Scott."

"Okay, Dan. Is there anything I should know about you before we dive right into the interview?"

"Nah, man. It's all cool."

"Can you please tell me a little bit about yourself? Such as your hobbies, interests, what type of student you were, and anything else that might be relevant or important for the rest of the world to know about you?"

"The rest of the world?"

"It's a figure of speech, Dan. What I meant was…"

"Dude, just chill, okay. Not a biggie. You really are new to this, aren't you?"

"Not new to interviewing. Just new to telling stories about…"

"Stiffs."

"Excuse me?"

He laughs. A total stoner laugh. You know the type.

"What do you mean by stiffs, Dan?"

"Dead kids. The ones who didn't survive. All that crapola. I get it, dude. No pressure here. I'm just kinda going with the flow, you feel me? Not entirely sure why I didn't pass on or pass over or pass out or whatever those eggheads call it these days, but whatevs. I'm pretty, you know, okay with it. My life was kinda boring before all the blood and the guts and the terror, so, you know, in a way, I guess I owe that ass face something."

"And that, umm…"

"Ass face."

"Yeah. Him. By him you are referring to…"

"The kid who shot me in the heart. Rick. Rick Smith."

"I see…"

An awkward pause, as he looks out the window at a group of kids cutting class downstairs smoking pot.

"Sucks, dude."

I know what he means but ask anyway.

"What sucks, Dan?"

"Not being able to, you know, enjoy weed anymore. That's probably the worst thing about my current state of being."

"You mean, after all that happened, *that's* the one thing you miss?"

He starts laughing again.

"No, fucker. Of course that's not it. God, what are you, a tard or something? There's lots of shit I miss. I miss my friends. I miss my family. I miss my dog. I miss, well, God, this is dumb as shit, but I sorta miss school. Well, not school as a whole, but I miss looking at all the hotties in fifth period. I guess I could still do that, but, well, you know… It'd just be sorta creepy and pathetic. I mean, it's not like they can talk to me. Or do it with me."

I laugh uncomfortably.

"Not that they would have even if I wasn't a stiff."

"And how does that make you feel, Dan?"

"Eff, dudeski. Are you a psychoanalyst or an interviewer? Make up your Goddamned mind already. Geeze."

He laughs. And it hits me. He's a kid. They're all kids. And they're always going to be kids. They're never going to grow up. They're never going to get any better. They're never going to fix their problems or live their lives or even, in Dan's case, see just how much they are missing out on by living on the fringes of society, just passing the moments until the next great big high.

"Wanna hear a joke?" he asks, pulling a one-eighty.

"Umm… Sure."

"It's more of, like, a philosophical question that I think is funny. All things considered."

I nod. He continues.

"Are farts just like food ghosts with unfinished business?"

I want to laugh, but I'm not sure if it's because I find it funny or because I just don't know what to do. He laughs. I smile. Kids, man.

"We used to sit around in my mom's basement before all the shit went down and things got heavy and I became a stiff, you know? It was crazy, the stuff we'd talk about when we were high. We were like poets and shit."

"How so?" I'm genuinely interested.

"Like have you heard about the Peter Pan theory?"

I have, but I pretend like it's new so he'll open up a little more.

"Here's the theory. Stay with me. Peter Pan is like a guardian angel of sorts. Neverland is actually Heaven and that's why no one ages. It's sort of a sad but easy way to explain death to little kids. Or, you know, justify it to the adults they leave behind."

He starts to trail off and I ask him what he's thinking about.

"Nothin'. Just my parents, I guess." He shrugs. "Anyway, the Peter Pan thing is just a bunch of stoners talking about life and death. There's a ton of theories out there for what's basically just a dumb book that was made into several dumb movies. The shadow is the bad guy. Peter Pan is the bad guy. If you leave the Lost Boys, he kills you. If you leave the Lost Boys, you become a pirate. Whatever, dude. There's a difference between philosophy and stoner philosophy, but man was it fun to talk about stuff like that when I was alive."

I feel like college would have been a great place for Dan. He would have focused on what mattered in life: the big questions. And maybe he would have gotten his act together enough to pass a few classes and find direction.

He laughs again. "Hey. Here's another one. And maybe I can answer this one when I'm done here. The light at the end of the tunnel debate. You feelin' me, Jed?"

He's almost ready to tell his story.

"Yeah, I'm feeling you, Dan. What do you think it is?"

"Well, to be honest, I think the reason you see it is because you're being born. You leave the world crying because you died, you enter the world crying because you died, and every time you cry but don't know why, it's because you remember you died. Dying sucks. Light or no light, déjà vu, or no déjà vu. It takes a lot out of a guy."

He stops. I can tell he wants to ask my opinion, but I don't let him get us off track. I think we're onto the right line of questioning.

"Let's talk about the incident, Dan."

"Not much to say. I was lighting a joint in the boy's bathroom during algebra class and ass face came in with a bunch of gym bags full of stuff that was clinking around. I told him to fuck off and let a brother smoke in peace and he flipped shit. He opened the bathroom stall door and shot me in the heart. It was weird."

The laughter from the kids outside gets louder and louder as Dan starts crying. School is back in session and in the ninth-grade wing, it's almost as if the shooting never even happened.

"It's been a week," Dan says, looking down. "And it's like no one even really fucking cares. Or misses me."

"I do," I offer, but it sounds disingenuous, so I start writing down the name of my next subject.

He starts to cry as he sees the light.

Dan fades. "Fuck you, man."

I don't think he's talking to me. I think he's talking to God.

And I turn off the tape.

And... Stop recording...

Dan's gone, but I still have a story to tell, and we're just getting started. My name is Jed Hollingsworth, and Sarah Falls is my home. It may not be yours, you may not have even heard of it before last week, but believe me, it's not that different from every single small town in the good old U. S. of A. I could waste your time and tell you all about the history and the geography and the socioeconomic bullshit that every other amateur journalist would do, but that's not important.

That's a lie. It is important. But it's also already out there. Look it up. Read a newspaper. Get on the web and Google us if it makes you feel better. And after you've done so, come back. I'll still be here.

Always have been. Always will be.

CHAPTER FIVE

Sunday, October 2
5:30 PM
Lincoln, Nebraska and Lawrence, Kansas
184 days after the book deal

I'm on a road trip. By myself. My first stop was supposed to be Lawrence, Kansas. But my car breaks down in the middle of nowhere, of course. I grab some things from home and have a friend from Sarah Falls drive me to Lincoln, Nebraska in exchange for an impromptu exorcism for his little brother and his little brother's roommate.

Enter Greg the Grand Manse ghost. Greg was former military, disgruntled, and very, very on-edge all the time when he was alive. His passive aggressiveness was only matched by his full-on aggressiveness. He would do little things like put his foot in the door of the property manager's office as she'd try to shut the door on him, leave notes saying "I know what you are and I'm going to tell the world" on the front door of the owner's apartment, throw away things that were legally supposed to be recycled on purpose, run the sink in the gym and other commons areas at all hours, leave all lights on all day every day, and make fake accounts on all forms of social media to blast the company.

Then he "disappeared" and turned up dead in his apartment, an apparent suicide by hanging. But even now, he refuses to leave.

When I confronted him after he showed up, my friend's brother's roommate insisted we use a Ouija board to "summon" him, he just told me what I had assumed. The property manager had him killed, staged it like a suicide, and he refuses to move on until everyone moves out of the Manse and the guy loses his cash cow or, better yet, someone proves it.

I told my friend's brother and his roommate the story. One of them is pre-law at the University and the other wants to be a cop, so it's fitting. And as I leave the creepy old historical building, I see Greg flicking on the lights to a hallway that is now empty because he's scared off the last three years' worth of tenants permanently.

"You're going to fuck with them until they go to prison, aren't you?" I ask.

He smiles, nods, and heads toward the public restroom.

Weirdly enough, there are very few ghosts in Lincoln, Nebraska. It's a happy place. No one really leaves, and when they do, they go back. But when they die, they move on. All in all, a pretty happy place. The property manager is a rare exception in terms of assholes. Upon further inspection on my phone, heading to the car dealership, I find out why: He's not from Lincoln.

When all this is done, I could see myself living here. There's something appealing about a relatively ghost-free zone.

I get my new car and drive to Lawrence, Kansas. Right past Sarah Falls and head straight for the university.

I went to school at KU, so it's nice to reconnect at the usual haunts and get the usual amount of hammered with old college buddies. We talk about life. We talk about death. We talk about Drake.

I crash on one of the couches at my old fraternity house. I take a look at my various dating apps. The profiles are fun, but nothing promising.

A few that make me laugh include, but are certainly not limited to:

"I'm a carefully written, fact-checked essay in the streets and an unmoderated comments section in the sheets."

"5'10" searching for a deep tissue massage therapist."

"I love BYOB sushi spots and running in the park. Allergic to cats and douchebags."

"Just a cupcake looking for her stud muffin."

"I was once told I looked like a fat female Chris Pratt. Twice. Twice I've been told I looked like a fat female Chris Pratt. I should probably just change my name to Kris Fatt."

"I put the HOT in psychotic."

"Ask me about the fruit scoot."

"One time DMX called me Drew Barrymore."

"Stay in drugs; eat your school; don't do vegetables."

I match with a girl named Mallori, a second-year senior at KU. Her "about me" section on her profile simply says "Victory lap. DTF."

"Hey," she sends. It's currently three AM.

"Hey," I respond. Some writer I turned out to be.

We talk about nothing for about four messages and then she

invites me to her apartment near campus. I leave my old fraternity house where I'm crashing, get a few high fives as I walk to "smash," whatever the fuck that means, and I'm messaging her for directions when it dawns on me: this is the first time I've ever done this. Is this smart? Is this how stupid people get killed?

I'm at her place. I'm drinking. She's on top of me. Then it's over.

"So," she says. "You're a writer?"

"Yeah."

"What do you write?"

Nonfiction. "Fiction," I say.

"Like, books and stuff?"

"Something like that."

I start putting on my clothes and she slides over and takes up as much of the bed as she can, half yawning and half talking. "Cool cool."

"Right." What the hell is wrong with me?

I head toward the door as she stops me. "What's your book about?"

As I glimpse my face in the mirror, I don't recognize myself anymore and I decide this is horrible and I have to make myself feel better by any means necessary.

"My first book, *Guns and Ghosts*, was released and instantly became a best-seller. But on top of the pressures of my mental illness, my overnight success, and the fact that my agent was insistent on me maintaining that it was a work of fiction, I'm being sued by a survivor of the Sarah Falls High School Massacre and recruited by the producers of a reality TV paranormal investigation program. So a few nights ago, I was planning on killing myself, but when a deceased college buddy of mine sent me a late night tweet, I dropped everything and now I'm heading to the reportedly haunted mansion in upstate New York where he allegedly killed all my friends and then committed suicide."

She isn't moving. She's not sure if I'm kidding or high or what.

So I keep talking.

"What's most likely going to happen next will be part road trip, part social commentary, and, as per usual, part book. And even if it may be presented as fiction, you will now know that my stories are as real as death itself. I was hoping people would have learned something from my last book, but that didn't work out so well because I'm a piece of shit."

I walk to the front of her apartment. She follows me with the bedsheet wrapped around her body.

As I walk into the hallway, she slowly shuts the door behind me. I stand there for a while, not hearing her back away from the door. I hear the lock, then the deadbolt.

It's five in the morning now and as I plug my phone into my car and check the app, I notice that she has sent me a message.

"You're a fucking psycho."

"Yeah." I respond. "You're probably right."

She unmatches me. I recline the driver's seat and try to get a couple of hours of rest. I sleep like shit. And I'm on the road again in the morning.

CHAPTER SIX

Monday, September 26
9:00 AM
Sarah Falls, Kansas
7 days after the shooting

And… Start recording…

"I'm Jed Hollingsworth. But because of the nature of this interview, you can just call me Jed. Sound good? I'm a journalist and I'm going to tell the story of what the papers are calling The Sarah Falls High School Massacre. Alrighty. Let's begin. So, for the record, can I ask your name?"

"Aidan Montgomery Stockwell III, son of Aidan Montgomery Stockwell Jr. and Martha Catherine Stockwell of Stockwell Pharmaceuticals and Stockwell Electric of Sarah Falls."

"Uh… Yeah. Okay. So, Aidan…"

"For the sake of this interview, I would prefer you called me Mr. Stockwell, Mr. Hollingsworth. I do not know you, nor do I wish to know you. I am doing this for one reason and one reason alone. As far as I can tell, you are the only person who can see or hear me. This interests me, but do not mistake my willingness to answer a few of your questions as some sort of token of appreciation for your talents. I know your work. I am quite aware of Sarah Falls' own golden boy reporter and his exploits. And other, shall we say, characteristics. No, I am doing this as a simple business transaction. Nothing more, nothing less. Do you understand me, Mr. Hollingsworth?"

"It's Jed, I insist. And yes, Mr. Stockwell, I think I do understand."

The boy stops being a boy and starts being a man just then. He changes. I can't describe it completely or even fully understand it, but he changes. I swear, right before my eyes, he becomes something else.

"Pleasantries do not suit you, nor do they strengthen my resolve."

He doesn't even know what he was saying, but my God, he sure acts like he does. This little elitist prick just might be the breaking point in my story. His side of things just might make this the story I had been waiting for since I started this investigation.

"Okay, Mr. Stockwell. Enlighten me. What do you want?"

"Tit for tat, you say?"

Who does he think he is, Hannibal Lecter? Ridiculously, I go on. I should end it all right here and now, but the intrigue of the story gets the best of me.

"Sure."

"You want my side of the story? You want me to retell my final moments? You want me to help you change the world and remember Sarah Falls and its people and how good and great and wonderful they were and are and will always be? Great. Splendid. I can do that. But I want something in return. I want you to do something no other person can do for me. I want you to do this thing, and I want you to do it now. Or as fast as you can. And if you cannot, let's just say things will turn from professional to, well, less professional."

A threat? I have an inclination it's a bluff, so I go on. I listen. I press him for more. And I do the worst possible thing I could do to the late, as it turned out to be not-so-great Aidan Montgomery Stockwell III. I taunt him.

"You'll what? Hurt me? I've been through this a few times, kid. I know you think you're tough shit because your mommy and daddy own the whole city and can push people around and have bent over backwards and given you every single thing your heart has ever desired, that you can threaten me. But I have news for you, kiddo. You're dead. Not alive. Not physical. You're astral, and I'm not. So no matter how much you want to scare me, that's all you can do. Scare. You can't touch me."

"Hmm..."

"Hmm...? Is that all you have to say? How dare you threaten me. I'm doing this for you. For all of you!"

"Two things, Mr. Hollingsworth..."

"Jed! If we're to the point where you're threatening me, I think we can skip the formalities, as you would put it. I'm Jed, the guy who's trying to give you a break and a chance of a lifetime here. I'm trying to tell your story, you turd."

"Mr. Hollingsworth... Jed... There are two things you have made a colossal error in assuming. First and foremost, is the fact you think I am stupid enough to actually believe this whole ordeal wasn't set in motion because of your own greed and desire for fame and fortune. And the second, and in your case, significantly more important of the two, is this..."

He does it again. But it's different this time. The boy stopped being a boy and started being a man earlier, but this was scary. He changes again. I can't describe it completely or even fully understand it, but I swear, right before my eyes, he becomes something else entirely. He was a boy, then a man. And now he is a monster. A force to be reckoned with. A threat.

He reaches across the table and grabs my shirt, pulling me in toward him, his eyes as black as night and his breath smelling of a rotting carcass and a decaying soul.

"I'm not like the other ghosts. I'm not a weakling. If you don't do what I want you to do, I will not haunt you. I will not scare you. I will do exactly what I've been doing my whole life. I will fuck you."

His grip gets tighter and he pulls me halfway across the table, looking directly into my eyes and analyzing my sweat and tears and reading my every thought and fear.

"I will wait until you are sleeping, when you are finally drifting off, and I will rape you to death. And when you cross over, I will spend the rest of eternity ripping what's left of you to shreds. And do you know why I'll do this? Not for revenge, but for something much more primal. Something much easier to grasp, for a feeble-minded individual like yourself." But he doesn't even have to say it. I know why. It was the same reason all sociopaths do what they do. "Because I can."

He lets me go. I readjust my collar and his eyes return to normal. He isn't even breathing heavily. He doesn't even break a sweat.

Then he gets up.

"Where are you going?"

"Oh, really, Jed. Come on. I have things to do. And it's not like you are getting anywhere with your stupid story anyway. You want my side of the tale? Fine. Here it is. Write this nugget down. Sometimes fucked up shit happens to people who are just at the wrong place at the wrong time. And sometimes, just sometimes, the losers and the wastes and the underlings rise up, steal their daddy's guns, and kill the people who actually mean something. Why do they do it? Fuck if I know. I don't really give two shits. Those assholes killed us because they were jealous probably. Kids like that think life is overrated. But life isn't overrated… Life is everything. It doesn't matter in the end, and you know why?" He pauses. Looks at me as he starts to fade away. And winks. "Because you're going to find a way to bring me back."

"But... That's impossible! How the hell am I supposed to do that?"

"Impossible? As opposed to, you know, what you're doing right now? Talking to a dead kid? Come on, Jed. Get real." He fades, whispering, "And get to work."

This is a matter of life and death. But Stockwell gets me thinking. I have to do something different. I have to figure out why they did what they did. I know why they killed him. He was a monster. But why did they kill everyone else? Why did they do it so quickly, so methodically, and so ruthlessly? I have to find out. And the only way to do that is to go back and start doing things the old-fashioned way. I have to talk to someone else.

Someone living. While I still can.

And... Stop recording...

I'm not going to tell you all the facts. I'm going to tell you about the people. And to best do that, I have to give you a little of the background on the main character of this story. AKA me. Sorry for taking the center stage, but that's all there is to it. It's my interviews. It's my story. And who best to tell it than the guy who's lived here his whole life?

I've been doing research and going through legal hoops for what seems like days now, and I just can't seem to get anywhere. You've all heard the stories by now, I'm sure. And you're all just waiting, or dreading, the impending barrage of endless documentaries and made-for-TV movies about The Sarah Falls High School Massacre. Great. You do that.

But I'm trying to tell a story. And not just for me. Or my career. But for my friends. And their families. And the good people of Sarah Falls who were silenced before they had a chance to tell their story.

You see, everyone has a story, whether they know it or not. And everyone's story is worth telling, whether they admit it or not. I had a professor in college who told us all that we had at least one great story to tell. All of us. I of course dismissed him as a quack at first, because, after all, it was a fiction writing class, so he kind of got paid to say stuff like that, but after I graduated and realized he wasn't talking about fiction, it got me thinking. What if everyone *does* have a story to tell? And what if everyone's story was equally or maybe even more important than the ones we read and hear about every day of our lives?

And thoughts like that really started to scare me. Thoughts like that are dangerous. Thoughts like that just might be truths, and truths cannot be ignored. Or clouded. I stopped taking my meds. And I stopped clouding my judgment. And I opened my eyes, not just to the world around me, but the world inside me. And the voices.

Now I'll stop you right there. I get it. You think I'm a schizophrenic who hears voices. Good. Great. That's neat for you. But you know what? Whether I'm crazy or not, what I do is different and what I give to others is important. I tell stories. And I get the quotes no one else can get… Or maybe I should say I get the quotes that no one else is willing or able to get.

I don't want them. Believe me. I would give this up in a heartbeat if I could. But I simply can't do that. They won't leave me alone until I give them the peace they need. And the whole "ghosts have unfinished business and can't move on to the afterlife until all unfinished business is completed or, you know, no longer unfinished" is bull to a certain extent. People are greedy and selfish in nature. I'm guilty. You're guilty. And if you think I'm lying, you're an idiot. So why should the dead be any different?

And why should they have to be? I mean, people are still people. Even if they're no longer living, they still have wants and hopes and dreams. And desires.

What I'm saying is this isn't the normal story about a group of people mourning the loss of innocence and a wonderful town's fall from grace. No. This is a very different story. A story that will keep you up at night. A story that will, if I do this right, change you.

But Aidan's wrong. I am not writing this for profit. I am not writing this for fame. Hell, I'm not even writing this for the ghosts that follow me and torment me and won't let me live my life. No, I'm doing this for Sarah Falls. And I'm doing this for you. All of you. Because some day, if you've read this and you understand what kind of living and walking hell every single day of my life is, maybe, just maybe, you'll take it easy on me.

After all, I'm just one man. And they, soon to be you, are many. So don't go anywhere. Because I'm not. They're not. And this story is going to twist and turn and make you laugh, cry, and question everything.

It's only been a little over a week and the world is over it. As predicted, they all moved on. But also as predicted, we didn't. How could we? I mean, the news crews came in, told their story, made their buck, made their point, and moved out as quick as they came in. Swooped and scooped, as one of the survivors called it. And now they're done. With all of it. With us.

But that's where I come into play.

You can search the police records. I did. You can read the articles, like you already most likely have done. It really isn't that hard nowadays with all the modern advancements in technology and the internet to search something as supposedly classified as the emergency calls that were made both to and from the police station the day of the shooting and a few days after when people were walking on eggshells and trying not to get killed or have any sort of repeat of the incident. It's kind of ridiculous. They all acted like it was a nuclear fallout or something. Yes, there is going to be a scar. And yes there is going to be a huge gap and a gigantic change in the rest of everyone's lives forever and ever and all that, but seriously. There's not going to be another shooting. Hell, there's not even going to be another incident or probably even murder or crime that leads to death for years. If we're lucky, ever again. But still, it didn't stop the crazies. Or the easily manipulated. Or the scared.

And who can blame them, really?

So go ahead. Do your research and come back to me. I'll be here. Doing the real work. Telling the rest of the story. You know, the one you can't just read about in *Newsweek* or watch on *Dateline*. The one about the ones who didn't survive. The ones who "left people behind" in their absence. The "lucky ones" as one idiotic Presidential candidate so infamously remarked.

Lucky? Bull. And the ones who were left behind just don't have the same argument they used to with me. They don't. Not after what I've seen. What I've been through.

But this isn't about me. I don't want your sympathy. I just want you to understand. And I guess that's enough for now.

Not everything happens for a reason. Good doesn't always triumph over evil. And sometimes, unfortunately, bad shit just happens to decent people. If there's a God, which I'm not entirely sure there even can be after what I've seen, I can tell you one thing about Him: He's a child. A vicious, bitter, angry child. Why else would He let things like this happen to me? Happen to us? Happen to Sarah Falls?

Overloading you a bit there, am I? Good. Because these aren't just statistics. These aren't just names and dates. They're people. Honest, hardworking, good people. And I knew them all. Some before the incident, some after. All are important. Got it? All of them.

All right. Enough complaining. You've put up with enough of me for one day. Just sit back and listen to the stories of others. I'll try to keep it simple. I'll try to keep it unbiased. And I'll do my best to honor the living. And the dead... That is, if I don't join them.

CHAPTER SEVEN

Monday, October 3
3:00 PM
Chicago, Illinois
184 days after the book deal

My next stop is Chicago, Illinois.

I stay at this Bed and Breakfast in the Wicker Park neighborhood. It's walking distance from anywhere and everywhere I'd ever want to go if I ever decided to visit Chicago again and it's run by an artist couple who understand my need for privacy. They also recognize me immediately from my "novel" and their daughter has already binged the entire first season of the Netflix series adaptation of said book.

They feed me. They give me their best room. I sign a copy of my book for them and I head upstairs to sleep. When I wake up, I'm not sure what time it is, but I know that it is night.

I check my phone to see the time but get distracted by all the notifications on the front screen. I open a few apps, do some swiping, and a message grabs my attention.

"Not sure how this all works," I see, a guy who looks like a writer, is a writer, possibly was a writer.

"Me neither, pal." I respond.

"Drinks?" he asks.

And, rather than go into detail about what this app is for and why I even have it, I say, "Sure."

We meet up at his place, a few blocks away.

Four beers later, and he's telling me that he is a writer. He knows exactly who I am. He didn't know I was "you know," and then he makes a move.

I'm not into it, so it gets awkward for a few minutes and I walk over to his kitchen. I open his fridge and grab two more beers.

"Tell me a story," I say, handing him one of his own beers.

So he does.

"Her name was Chloe."

And from that sentence forward, he tells a story to a fellow writer that only he could tell. I'd tell you the specifics, word for word, but

I feel like this is already bordering on plagiarism, so I'll just give you the Sparknotes version.

Chicago Chloe was the witch that got away.

This dude, Sam, first came to Chicago on a writer's residency fellowship. He fell in love with the city and never left.

"I was trying to avoid writer's block one night by partying hard with friends new and old alike when I met her. A real-life, honest-to-God practicing witch."

As he told it, his friends tried to talk him out of it, saying she was bat shit crazy and may or may not have killed people, but the opportunity for a story outweighed the danger.

"You can relate," he suggests.

And boy, could I ever.

The story goes that she lived alone, or maybe had roommates, but her apartment was weird and in a nice part of town full of weird but rich, or as I like to call them, "eccentric" people. There were warning signs, literally, plastered all over the streets and buildings and poles as they drunkenly walked to her place.

Sam had turned his phone to silent because his friends were giving him a hard time for trying to bang the witch.

"I'm normally not even, like, into girls. You know?"

He chugs his beer and picks up mine, winks, and starts drinking it while he tells the rest of his story.

The warning signs were literal. Missing neighborhood pets.

"Her apartment was... different." I look around his apartment. Also different. "She just tried to get me drunk." I start to realize I am drunk. "And then she told me to wait while she 'changed into something more comfortable.'"

He gets up and starts to head back toward what I assume is his bedroom.

"You listening?" he asks, almost yelling from his room.

And then nature over nurture or God knows what takes ahold of me and I realize that something is terribly wrong. Sam didn't say anything about having a pet, but his entire living room is covered with newspapers. Nor did he say anything about roommates, but he clearly cannot afford to live somewhere like this by himself.

I say, "Yeah," and he continues his story, yelling but also pausing every now and then as if to hint that I should come join him on what I'm assuming is his bed. I'm looking around the apartment and realizing that it's very sparsely decorated. The rooms are all shut. I open one and get all the information I need to make the decision to run back to the B & B without saying goodbye or even asking for the rest of Chicago Chloe's story.

I arrive at the bed and breakfast around two AM and the daughter of its owners is sneaking into her part of the house.

"Rough night?" she jokes, a little drunk.

I run up the stairs and I hear her saying, "Shh!!!" I'm not sure if she's talking to me, the cat, or herself, but her parents' light comes on as I shut and lock the door to my room for the night. I look out the window and I see Sam standing in the street. He holds up his phone.

I check mine.

Another notification.

"You didn't let me finish my story," it says.

I block him.

He may or may not have killed his roommates. He may or may not have something to do with the disappearances of numerous neighborhood pets and may or may not have been Chloe.

The panic starts to set in and I honestly don't know what to do, but everything goes black very quickly and the next thing I know, it's daylight and there's a knock on the door announcing breakfast will be served in thirty minutes.

He drugged me.

I pack my things. I make my bed. And as I walk toward the door, something catches the corner of my eye. A faint line, drawn in what appears to be white chalk, coming out from underneath my bed. Upon moving my bed, I see a giant pentagram.

As I eat my breakfast, I see the icon of the app on my phone and decide I'll check it again when I'm not in Chicago anymore. And I don't think I'll ever go back. Because something leads me to believe that Sam wasn't who I was speaking with last night. And I don't think he's going to let me get away again if our paths cross.

CHAPTER EIGHT

Monday, September 26
10:00 AM
Sarah Falls, Kansas
7 days after the shooting

And... Start recording...

"I'm Jed Hollingsworth. But because of the nature of this interview, you can just call me Jed. Sound good? I'm a journalist and I'm going to tell the story of what the papers are calling The Sarah Falls High School Massacre. Alrighty. Let's begin. So, for the record, can I ask your name?"

"Thad. Thad Jensen."

"Okay, Thad. And you were, umm, how do I put this, friends with Jameson Allan?"

"Yeah. I mean, I guess you could say he was my best friend. I mean, I was his best friend, and he was my only friend, so yeah. Best friends. I guess."

He moves his glasses up to scratch his eyes. He's going to cry, but not yet. I can always tell when people are going to cry. Living people, that is. They have tells. And the glasses raise is probably the most common of the lot. But not yet. Thad isn't going to break down. Not yet.

"So, as his best friend, you had to have known he was planning something. I mean, not to this extent exactly, but, you know. Didn't you?"

"No."

Short. Simple. To the point. But it closes my line of questioning. So I decide to try it again later. Time to go back further. Start from the beginning. Of their friendship, I mean. I know he's lying, and I kind of understand why, being his best friend, possibly his only friend and all, but I know nonetheless. And he is going to tell me what I need to hear.

"When did you two begin your friendship, would you say?"

"We met in middle school. Then we met, like *really* met, in high school."

"I see. So, you and Jameson knew each other for quite a while before…"

"Before he killed a bunch of jerks who probably deserved it?"

"Excuse me?"

"Yeah, I know. Boohoo. Popular kids and jocks and cheerleaders died. And teachers who had tenure and didn't care anymore got whacked. Sad deal. But you know what? They all had it coming. They were dead the instant they started messing with Jameson Allan."

"Okay, so, tell me what they did. And who they were. Let's start there, I guess."

"The popular kids."

"What about the popular kids?"

"You know what, Jed? Screw you. This story that you're trying to tell is bull shit. You're trying to paint my friend in a bad light? Trying to glorify the kids who made his life a living hell day in and day out ever since we were back in seventh grade? Well, you're a bigger idiot than I thought. I agreed to do this for one reason and one alone, so stop with the condescending questions and, you know what, stop with the questions altogether. I'll tell you your damn story. But it's not going to be yours. And you aren't going to like what you hear. Believe it or not, Jameson wasn't a monster. He was a kid. A scared, lonely, brilliant, angry, beautiful kid."

And that last sentence says it all.

"Yeah. The papers leave that out. They leave out the fact he was scared. I had to walk to school two hours early and stay two hours late every day in seventh, and eighth grade. I thought I'd have to wait until I got my driver's license before I could go to school on time."

"Because they would tease you before and after school?"

"Tease? What are you, from 1951? No, they beat the shit out of us. Every single Goddamn day. And that wasn't even the worst part. The stuff they did every day before and after school just made me tougher. Bitter, but tougher. It was what they did during school that hurt the worst. And before you ask, yes, the teachers saw it. They just looked the other way."

Another glasses raise. Another eye rub. No tears. Not yet.

"You said you thought you'd have to wait until you got your license. What did you mean by that?" I ask.

"I met Jameson."

"Again," I echo.

"Yeah. On Grindr, actually."

I write it down and he corrects me, taking out the "e" in my note. He kind of laughs and explains that it's "like Tinder, but, you know, gay." Which answers another set of questions.

"You're saying that bullying caused the shooting?"

He sighs, smirks, and goes on.

"There you go again with those outdated terms. Did you know the jocks used to tie us up in the same locker in middle school? Oh, but they didn't just do it because they thought it was funny and they could get a rise out of us or their other friends. They did it for another reason entirely. They did it because they thought they were justified."

The glasses come off. And the crying begins.

"They did it because they thought we were gay."

I hand him the box of tissues. He takes about five and just looks at them, starting to place them on top of one another, folding them perfectly into smaller square after smaller square until they are just neatly-folded wads of unused tissues.

The crying stops.

"What else happened?"

"We told the principal. But he didn't do anything. So we just waited them out. *Waiting until high school is part of life,* my mom used to tell me. *Boys will be boys,* my dad used to tell me. But neither of them knew. How could they? I wasn't going to break their hearts twice. So I just let them go on believing that Jameson and I were nerds and things would get better when we got away from the jocks and went to high school. Or at least there would be enough other nerds to form a nerd club."

Hesitantly, I ask another question.

"These boys. These, *jocks*, as you put it. Who *were* they exactly? Could you give me their names?"

"Of course I can. But they're not going to surprise you one bit."

And he gives me the names of not two or three boys, but over a dozen of them. All athletes. All privileged. All smart. All old enough to know better.

And mostly all dead.

"I see."

"You know why I wear glasses, Jed?"

This seems a little off topic, but I let it slide. And I'm glad I do, because it leads directly into the most important line of questioning I'm going to go through today after I decided to start interviewing not only the victims, but the survivors. The ones left behind.

"I just started this year. I can't see out of my left eye at all because it pushed too hard against my brain. Before this year, I had perfect vision. 20/20. Not anymore, though. Not after the 'last straw,' as Jameson put it."

And he tells me the reason. The *real* reason. The meaning behind the massacre.

"Jameson and I decided to go to the Homecoming dance for some strange reason. He thought it would be an okay thing for us to do, but you know what? I knew. Right then and there, it wasn't safe. It wasn't ever going to be safe for us in Sarah Falls. Part of me still thinks it will never be safe for us, or people like us, anywhere."

"What happened the night of the Homecoming dance?"

He goes on, bravely, without tears.

"We didn't dance. Hell, we didn't even have time to dance. We just stood there, talking to each other. People-watching was one of our favorite pastimes, you know. I can still see him now, walking toward us with his crew."

"Who?"

But I know who. I know exactly who was going to alter the series of events forever. Not just for Jameson Allan. Not just for Thad Jensen. But for all forty-six victims of the Sarah Falls High School Massacre. For all their friends and family. And for the rest of the town.

"Their leader. Aidan Montgomery Stockwell III."

I knew it.

"Him and his goons came up to us and forced us outside, past the teachers and chaperones, past the parking lot, and into the football shower house."

"And what did they do to you then?"

"Oh, you mean after they humiliated us by making us strip all our clothes off and take pictures together? They tied Jameson up, grabbed baseball bats from the supply closet, and beat me within an inch of my life. I'm blind in one eye and will probably walk with a limp for the rest of my life."

Boys will be boys.

"But that's not why, Jed. Not all of it. I got off easy. What they did to me was strictly physical. What they did to him…"

He trails off a bit, and I'm starting to understand, sympathize even, but I still have one question.

"But what about all the innocent people who died? You know… The other thirty-six victims of the shooting?"

"No."

"No? *No* what? I don't understand."

"No. As in, *no one* was innocent. As in no, don't you dare use that word. Every single person who died that day was dead the day I lost my sight in my right eye."

"But, if what you just told me was true, that list should have been only sixteen people long. And it was. I saw it. There were many other deaths that day, not to mention injuries. And I don't even…"

"No, Jed. Every person who didn't die just got off lucky. The plan wasn't just for those sixteen meatheads. It was for everyone. Everyone in the whole damn school. They all knew. They all ignored it. As far as Jameson was concerned, they all might as well have watched what those assholes did to us."

"I see. So everyone who didn't die…?"

The tears are back, but he isn't wiping them away now. He's continuing his story. He still has more to tell.

"The video that went viral. You've seen it, right?"

I have. Everyone has.

While I nod, he continues. "You know what they did to him. How messed up is that? You know he couldn't walk for almost a week afterward?"

Violent sobs, then… nothing.

"I misspoke earlier. They didn't deserve it. No one deserves that. Not even the sixteen of them. Not even Stockwell." He pauses. "Well, *maybe* Stockwell."

I can't help but somewhat agree after our encounter.

"But you know what I mean, Jed. They kind of had it coming. Make sense?"

"In a weird way. Yeah. It does make sense."

"But you've still got two more things to learn, Jed. And I've got both of the answers for the questions you have remaining on your little checklist in that notebook of yours. Why didn't I tell anyone this before you? And how did Jameson Allan meet Rick Smith?"

"One at a time. And Thad, like I said before, take your time."

"No, I'm just going to tell it like it is. That's what Jameson liked best about me. And that's the way I'm going to stay."

"Okay. Go ahead."

"Well, I hate these kids because they were all ignorant, stuck up, rich little snobs who got everything they ever wanted and they didn't ever understand what it meant to learn anything. A lesson, of any kind, ever. And even in death, they're not done. Rumor has it you're telling their stories. Making them into these larger-than-life, over-the-top heroes. Well, they weren't. They were all assholes. Each and every one of them."

"Now, Thad. That's not fair."

"Fuck fair!"

He cools down.

"Did you know they still make fun of Jameson Allan on Facebook? Why can't they just leave him alone? I told his mom to write Mark Zuckerberg personally or at least try to get it taken down. But she doesn't want to. She says that even though she loves her son dearly, what he did was wrong. And if the town needs to do that type of thing to make themselves feel better and move on? Then they deserve it. God! There's that word again. Deserve."

"Entitlement. If I could define the town of Sarah Falls with one word and only one word, it would be, and always probably will be that. For better or worse. Probably not going to change. Entitlement."

"Yeah. Well, it's weird, you know. A dead friend. A dead Facebook friend. But I think the main reason I want it taken down is the fact that it's stuck in limbo, you know? Like this whole stupid town. No one ever really moves on. No one ever probably will. But I want to. I want it to be over with. I'm tired of logging in every day and seeing people spout hatred and jokes at a dead kid's expense. I'm tired of seeing little advertisements and friend suggestions based upon my friendship with a dead kid. I'm tired of seeing that relationship request from a kid I should have kissed, a kid I loved so much it hurt sometimes, and a kid that if I would have dated, could have possibly talked some sense into and prevented this whole damn thing."

He pauses.

"Before you get all blubbery-eyed and tell me you're so sorry and go on and on with all that other bull shit, I'll finish my story and answer your last unasked question. Rick Smith. How he met Jameson Allan. And more importantly, how he got involved in the worst death toll this town has ever seen in its long and proud history."

"Yes. How did they meet?"

"He came out of nowhere and just, well, wanted in."

"Wanted in? What do you mean by that, Thad?"

"Jameson started talking about this *idea* of his. It started after I got out of the hospital and my parents wanted to keep it hush-hush, because of the whole gay thing. You see, everyone knew what happened, but no one knew why it happened. And they wanted it kept that way. And Jameson's parents? They're just... They didn't understand. And now that he's dead, they probably won't even think about it ever again."

Oh, how *wrong* youthful spite can be sometimes.

"Anyway, Rick Smith saw his plan. The list, the strategies, the whole thing, one day when Jameson dropped his notebook in the bathroom. He picked it up and read it. Cover to cover. And one day, out of the blue, he returned it. With a request."

"He wanted in."

"He wanted in."

"But why? It wasn't his battle. Why kill so many people for no reason?"

"That's just the thing. It all goes back to Facebook again. Jameson Allan had forty-three Facebook friends, including nineteen family members who *had* to be his friend. But Rick Smith? The creep didn't even have a Facebook. He had just started school at Sarah Falls like three days before the plan took shape. He was a nobody, and boy oh boy did that piss him off. Dude had seen one too many movies, I guess. Thought it would be, you know, *cool*."

"To be famous."

We both sigh.

"Yeah," he says. "Fucked up."

"You can say that again."

And, either because he didn't understand me or because his story has finally been told and his sense of humor has returned, he repeats, "Yeah. Fucked up."

And... Stop recording...

There were dead bodies. There was chaos. Then there were funerals, and stories, and newscasts, and articles, and they all left. Everyone but us. Everyone came into Sarah Falls when the tragedy happened. They labeled it a massacre, they made their buck, they made their careers, and they made off with their spoils. But we stayed. We have to. We live here.

So far, I've learned one thing from these interviews. The living matter. I know that sounds strange to someone who is actually one of the living, but hear me out. Everyone talks about the living. How many times do you sit at home with your family or at work with your colleagues or at wherever the hell you go with your friends and talk the talk and shoot the shit about yourselves and other people? Right. Now, think about this, and answer honestly. How much of that time is spent talking about the dead? Exactly.

It's morbid. It's sad. It's wrong. They're dead. You did your best while they were alive and you honored them the best you could when they died. But you moved on. You had to. You still have to. Because they're dead and buried and gone. And though that's morbid, and sad, and sometimes, more often than not, wrong, it is what it is. You can't do anything about it and the best way to honor the dead is by living. Right?

Wrong. You have to tell their story. But I understand. You can't. It's just too hard for you. And I get it, believe me, I of all people get it, but when the ghosts started talking to me while I was a kid, I knew nothing was ever going to be the same again. Not for me, not for my readers, and hopefully, if I wanted them to go away, not for those who weren't quite ready to move on yet.

And that's what this is all about, when you get right down to it. Moving on. The ghosts can't leave yet because they have unfinished business. I get it. And I honestly don't even really mind that they come to me. After all, who else are they going to go to? As far as I can tell, I'm the only one alive who can see the dead, let alone talk to them, reason with them, and help them in any way I can. Those people who have the shows, whether they're televised, radio programs, movies, or just plain psychics, doesn't matter. They're fakes. Phonies. I'm sure they have been doing it so long that they either know they're frauds but have to pay the bills, know their frauds but don't really give a crap one way or the other, or they're actually insane and believe they are talking to ghosts.

Me? I'm no fraud. I wish I was sometimes, but sadly, I'm not. I'm the genuine article. The real deal. The Jennifer Love Hewitt of Sarah Falls. But enough about me. And more about Sarah Falls. And the incident.

The living matter. Because they hold the key to the dead. And why they haven't moved on yet. Every single ghost I have talked to has moved on relatively soon after their story was told or at least they came to some sort of terms with their situation. But I've been running into a bit of a snag here recently. And that's why I have to talk to the living, even though it seems almost new to me, as weird as it may sound to you. You see, I'm so used to operating on the periphery of life that I don't really know how to talk to living people without immense and an almost petrifyingly ridiculous sense of uncomfortable feelings rushing through me. It's weird, but it is sort of true. That's why this is so difficult for me.

But with people like Aidan Montgomery Stockwell III quite literally threatening my very life if I don't give him what he wants, I don't really have a choice. Not to mention my obligation to the people and the town of Sarah Falls. And my duty as a journalist to tell the story. The whole thing, not just the shock value stuff and not just the morality tales. But the whole thing, as it happened, to whom it happened, and about the people who survived as well as those who didn't. And that's why I'm no longer a journalist. Not in the classic newspaper or nightly news sense. I'm going to write a book. And I'm going to get it published. And maybe, just maybe, I'll convince America this was more than just a one and done thing.

It's not just a tragedy in small town America. It is America. I have to do some more research and clear my head a bit. Stay tuned.

CHAPTER NINE

Tuesday, October 4
1:30 PM
Indianapolis, Indiana
185 days after the book deal

This one made the news. It happened in the early nineties. You've probably heard it. But I'll let Ned tell you the story. After all, it's his. He tells me at the cabin his parents used to take him to for family reunions. I drove by the location of his story. There are at least fifty ghosts down there, at that state park and campground site. According to Ned, most of them are "his people."

"So I'm a kid," he starts. "The whole family is together for grandma and grandpa's wedding anniversary. They are renewing their wedding vows, or something like that. I'm not entirely sure why that's a big deal at the time, but it's an excuse to get the whole group together and have a party. My mom and dad are calling it the biggest family reunion in history. There are literally more people here right now than go to school with me. They're saying that middle school is going to be full of lots of new and exciting people to be friends with, but I don't really care. All my friends that I need to know are at this party right now.

"'Ned,' I hear my mom call, no doubt wanting some sort of photo with me and my friends. 'Honey, we need to get a picture of you with all your little friends for grandma and grandpa's fridge.'

"I get all my friends together and we pose in some ridiculous picture for my mom to give her mom and dad. Then, as promised, we take a series of fun pictures after that, making weird faces and generally looking stupid. I let her drag me to this thing for two reasons. One, it makes her happy, and this close to my birthday, a happy mom guarantees a good birthday present. And two, she let me bring my entire group of friends.

"The park is right off the interstate, and we have the whole thing to ourselves. Mom rented out this place like a year ago or something crazy like that. There are a bunch of big tents, tables everywhere, and of course, most importantly, the giant playground. It's the biggest thing I've ever seen and, to be honest, the coolest thing, too. We've been playing on it all morning and afternoon, pausing for a few photos every now and then for mom and everyone else who asks. Like I said, birthday soon.

"After the impromptu photo shoot, we all run over to the giant fortress area with the bridges and all the tunnels and start a new game of freeze tag. Jake is 'it' this time, because he lost to me in a game of paper, scissors, rock. Naturally, since I'm the best there is at that game.

"I've found this awesome hiding place (I know what you're thinking, hide and seek is for hiding, freeze tag is for running, but what do you know? I'm the one who always won.) and I can not only see everyone running around, but, more importantly, they can't see me and even if they do, I have two exits, not just one. A good hiding place should also be functional, that's something dad told me when I was just a kid. He's in the marines. I suppose they do a lot of hiding on their secret missions, but mom says I'm not supposed to ask about stuff like that.

"Jake tags Mikey, Mikey tags Dillon, Dillon tags Jake again, and it goes on and on like this for what seems like forever. Finally, I get bored with my hiding place and decide to make myself known. But as I'm walking out of the perfect hiding place, I see that the game has stopped and everyone is looking up by the edge of the park, right next to the interstate.

"There are state troopers speeding by, their lights flashing and their sirens about as loud as can be. Everyone is just watching, even the adults. The music has stopped, and my friends are just pointing and wondering what is going on. I'll admit it, even I'm a bit curious as to who they're chasing. I count four cars go by, but I know that even more than that have gone by, because I wasn't paying attention until long after everyone else started looking. Before I can even ask what my friends think is going on, another set of three cop cars go by, lights and sirens just as loud and just as bright as before. They must be going like a hundred miles an hour at least.

"'Must be something really bad,' I say.

"'Cool,' Mikey responds. 'Do you think they're chasing a killer or something? Like a mass murderer or an escaped lunatic?'

"He does have a point. What if it's something serious? What if the person's a crazed bad guy from all those movies that mom and dad watch and I'm not supposed to but I do anyway from the top of the steps every Friday night?

"But those thoughts are immediately put out of my mind when Mikey pushes Jake and the game starts again. So I go back into my hiding spot, deciding that it's better to wait it out by myself and think about who or what those cops were after while my friends get tired. Besides, if they're running around this whole time, I'll conserve my energy and when I decide to actually make my location known, I'll be able to run laps around them for the rest of the game.

"So I sit here, and I think to myself: Obviously not everyone is as concerned with the strange moment that just happened as I am. Most of the adults are back to doing what they were doing. Eating, dancing, listening to stories about when grandma and grandpa were young.

"But just as I find out that my hiding spot is not nearly as perfect as I thought it was and Jake tags me, catching me completely off guard, I look up to the side of the interstate again, at the top of the hill above the park. My dad and three of my mom's brothers are talking to a group of people who are pulled up on the side of the interstate.

"'I'm going to go see what's up,' I tell my friends.

"'Sure,' Jake says. 'Right after you get tagged, you want the game to be over. Typical Ned move right there.'

"I tag Mikey and say, 'There, just keep going and I'll be back in a few minutes.'

"I walk up past my ginormous family and see what's going on. There is a van with not one, but what looks like two flat tires. The group consists of four big guys, one little guy, and a woman with a bunch of tattoos on her neck. I'm not going to lie, they're all pretty scary looking.

"'What's the deal, dad?'

"'These folks just needed a hand with their van. They must have run something over that didn't agree with their tires. Your uncles and I replaced one with the spare they had, but I just sent your mom to bring our van up so we can give them our spare.'

"'Oh.'

"They all look at me. I think they know I'm scared, but how? And more importantly, why am I scared of them? Something just isn't quite right.

"Mom pulls the van up right next to theirs and pops the trunk.

Dad is whistling while he picks up the tire, as if it weighs nothing, and plops it down on the ground next to the strangers' van. My uncles are all talking about something else while Dad does all this on his own. He makes changing a tire look like it's the easiest thing in the world.

"'That'll do it, friends,' he says, brushing the gravel off his pants.

"'Thanks,'" one of the big guys says.

"My dad reaches out to shake his hand, and the big guy reluctantly offers his. There is blood on it. Dad doesn't see it. Neither do my uncles, or my mom. But the tattoo lady sees it. And she sees that I see it, too.

"'Let me grab you some cash for the tire,' the guy says.

"'Oh, that's no big…' my mom starts to say, but my dad cuts her off.

"The guy reaches into the van and pulls out a giant duffle bag from beneath the legs of a person I didn't see at first. A boy. Probably about my age. He looks terrified, or maybe not terrified, but really sad. Like the kind of sad where something so terrible has happened that you know you're never going to be the same afterwards. Or something is about to happen. We lock eyes and he starts muttering what I think is another language, then I realize is numbers. He's counting. This weird, sad little kid is frantically counting as he fidgets with a watch in his gloved hands.

"What I'm assuming is the kid's dad pulls out what looks to be a wad of bills. He hands my dad a hundred-dollar bill. 'Hope this'll cover it. We're kind of in a hurry and need to get back on the road.'

"'This is too much,' my dad says. 'Have anything smaller?'

"'Look, man,' the tattoo lady says, 'We're in a hurry. Just take the money and we'll be on our way.'

"Then one of my uncles looks at the bill and makes a comment. A comment that I know, right then and there, will change everything. The kind of comment that…"

The kind of comment that gets people killed, I think to myself.

"'What'd you guys do to get that money, rob a bank or something?'

"He laughs. No one else does.

"My dad puts the bill in his pocket and grabs me, pushing me quickly over to my mom. She grabs me and we start walking, almost instinctively back to the party. There are a lot of people watching us, but not like they are concerned, just like they are interested. Mom is concerned. Dad is concerned. I am scared.

"As we walk down, I look back and see two of the big guys hit my uncle. I also see that there are bullet holes on the side of the van.

"Then the next five minutes are kind of a blur. There's a lot of running, a lot of screaming, and a lot of shooting. It's kind of like a moving blackout. The next thing I know, we are all lined up on our knees, what's left of us. I look around the field and see that almost all my family has been killed, shot in the head.

"We are lined up, and there is nothing we can do. No one is coming. We are out in the middle of nowhere. Old people music is playing, I think it's polka. A gunshot is heard, and I now have no grandparents. Another is heard and I've lost my favorite aunt. And so on and so forth.

"Then it comes to my mom. She grabs my hand and tells me that everything is going to be okay.

"'Ned, don't you worry,' she says. 'Daddy's going to...'

"A gunshot, and her blood covers my face. I can taste it in my mouth.

"The tattoo lady points the gun at my mom and shoots again. 'Daddy was the first one we took out, bitch.'

"There are more sirens in the distance, and I just know that this is the end. They're not going to get to me in time. I look around and see that I'm the only one left. They've executed all of us. My friends. My family. Everyone I've ever known. And she doesn't have to say what she's thinking. I know. I'm next.

"She puts the gun up to my head and her friends are running back to their van, laughing, and taking drinks from the wine that my mom so carefully picked out for what was supposed to be one of the happiest days of our family's lives.

"I close my eyes, the sirens getting louder, the bank robbers starting their van, and prepare for the end. But something happens.

"Click.

"'Hmm,' the tattoo lady says. 'Out of bullets.'

"She grabs her shotgun and turns it around, hitting me in the head.

"When I wake up, there are cop cars all around, and a young policeman is puking his guts out. I get up and walk over to my mom. She is covered by a white sheet. The sheriff runs over to me and puts a blanket on me. He talks to me for an hour, but I don't hear any of it. The only thing I hear is that damn polka music."

I pay for Ned's breakfast, even though he insists I don't have to.

"You gonna go to the park where it happened?" he asks.

"Yeah," I tell him.

"Good. Write about it. And when you do," he says as he gets up and walks toward the door of the bar and grille, "make sure you're honest this time."

I drive there. I talk to a few of the ghosts. Ned's story checks out. But there's unfortunately nothing more to it than that. It's a terrible thing that happened to a group of good people.

I apologize to them, hear their stories, help them cross over. Then the other ten-to-fifteen ghosts who died there at another time for another reason want their turn. I stopped feeling heartless years ago when I started pretending I couldn't see them. I'd never get anything done if I did this full time.

I'm back on the road and they run after me as far as their limits will let them. When I get past the spot where they died, they simply fade into the dust their bodies became long, long ago.

CHAPTER TEN

Monday, September 26
10:30 AM
Sarah Falls, Kansas
7 days after the shooting

And... Start recording...

"I'm Jed Hollingsworth. But because of the nature of this interview, you can just call me Jed. Sound good? I'm a journalist and I'm going to tell the story of what the papers are calling The Sarah Falls High School Massacre. Alrighty. Let's begin. So, for the record, can I ask your name?"

"David Lester. I'm the Social Studies teacher here at Sarah Falls High School as well as the baseball coach and Student Council faculty advisor. My students call me Mr. Lester, my athletes call me Coach, and any and all former students like yourself can call me Dave."

"Thank you, sir. But I'm more comfortable still calling you Coach, if that's all right with you...?"

"Sure thing, Jed my boy."

A smile, and a flood of memories comes back to me in an instant. High school was good to me. I had a lot of friends. I had my parents. I had good coaches, good teachers, and a good outlook on life. And because of people like Coach Dave Lester and the rest of the Wildcats staff, I had a future.

"All right. Let's get started, shall we?"

A series of nods and he's down to business. Back to school with Mr. Lester.

"For the record, and I understand I already know all this stuff, but for the record, can you tell me a little bit about yourself?"

"As I said before, I'm Coach David Lester. And I've been teaching and coaching and helping out in any way I can at this high school for, damn, I'd say around a hundred or so years now."

He laughs. I laugh. He continues.

"No, all kidding aside, it will be nineteen years come this next August. And I'll tell you, Jed. As one rational adult to another, I never once considered retiring. Not a single day."

"Until the incident, that is... Right?"

"No sir. Not a one. In fact, I think the shooting gave me a little extra boost. A little more willpower to come into work each and every day. I know it sounds terrible, but it made me reevaluate the job I do. Does that make sense, Jed?"

"I think I see where you're going with this, Coach. But for the sake of an actual quote that I can use in my book… Could you continue a little further with that thought?"

"Of course I can. A book, you say? So I was right. I was talking with Vicky, you remember my wife, don't you? Of course you do. Anyway, I was chatting with her just the other night when you called me up out of the blue to ask me if you could stop by the school and do a little interview with me, and I said to her, 'I'll bet he's gonna write a book on this.' And boy, was I right. Ha! Good old Jed Hollingsworth. You know, you always were one of my favorite students."

"Thanks, Coach. I just thought back to that journalism class you taught as a senior elective. You remember what you used to say at the end of every class period?"

"Like the back of my hand."

And we both say it, verbatim, at the exact same time.

"Always remember, kiddos: The best journalists don't shut up. The best journalists don't give up. And the best journalists don't write stories, they tell truths."

"Exactly! And I knew I couldn't do this story justice with just one article. Or even two or three or hell, a dozen. It had to be a book."

"Yes it does, Jed. Yes, it does."

"So, back on track here, what else do you do with your days here at Sarah Falls High School? I mean, I saw the journalism class is no longer offered, which sort of bummed me out, to be honest, but I'm assuming there are still plenty of things to keep a great teacher like yourself busy all year long."

"Ha. Flattery, from a past student, is literally the best reward a teacher can ever get. I'm going to let you in on a little secret, Jed my boy. We get paid crap."

We both laugh again at this.

"No, seriously. I'm sure you're analyzing the school system and the whole infrastructure of public education as part of your research for this book of yours, so I'll stay out of your way and just offer any advice you may want from an old timer like myself, but I'll just say this one thing: Compliments are few and far between. And that's why they're worth so damn much to people like me. Sure, I could give every single kid an A if I wanted to. And sure, I could cheat and push my kids farther than reasonable to win state championship after state championship if I really wanted to. And when it comes to Student Council, I could really just put whoever the hell I wanted in charge and run the whole school. If I really wanted to. But I don't. Because that would be wrong. And because, well…"

"You actually care."

"Yep. You got it. Always were bright, Jed my boy."

"So you care. You're still teaching, you're still coaching, and not doing so bad yourself as the newspapers and the statistics come pouring in after every home and away game, and you're still the best advisor here and making Stu Co a fun place to be and a worthwhile organization to be part of. What else?"

"What else what? I come to school at six o'clock every morning and I leave school at eight o'clock every night. I spend my time with Vicky. And I do it all over again. Five days a week. Every week."

"What about your free time?"

"Summer? That's none of your business, son."

We both laugh again and I am immediately reminded of the shirt he used to wear every single year on the last day of school. On the front it said, "Three reasons to become an educator." And on the back it said, in bold, in all caps, "1. JUNE, 2. JULY, 3. AUGUST." It made me crack up every single year. And I'm willing to bet he still has it and proudly wears it. Tenure is a great thing in a small town, but a sense of humor, a good attitude, and the teaching chops to back those up are unparalleled in Sarah Falls.

Needless to say, and you can quote me on this: Coach was, is, and always will be, the man. No joke.

"Okay, enough preliminary stuff. So, I hate to do this to you, Coach, but…"

"I understand. The nitty gritty. The important stuff. We'll have to catch a game over a few beers some time and talk about everything else. But for the sake of your book and the interview, not to mention the fact I only have a little bit left of my plan period, we really should move onto the recount of the day of the shooting. That is why you're here, isn't it?"

I nod. He nods. And I begin one of the most important interviews on Sarah Falls.

"The day of the incident, can you tell me your side of the story?"

"I was in the room I've been in for the last fifteen years. Right next to the east entrance to the building. And that was where they tried to leave. And by the time they got to my end of the building, I had done what any self-respecting educator, parent, and human being would have done. I had bypassed the main office on the school phone and called the police on my cell. I grabbed any and all students in the hallways or immediately outside of the door and pulled them into my room. I locked the doors. I put the kids all up against the one wall that has no visibility from the door or any of the windows, told them to be quiet, stay down, and that everything was going to be okay."

I start to ask another question, but Coach waves me off and continues.

"It was the longest forty minutes of my entire life." He stops briefly, clears his throat, and continues again. "Then Rick Smith came. By then, Jameson Allan had already killed himself. And when he came walking, no, he was *strutting*, down the hallway, I made a decision."

He slowly opened up the door, grabbed a trash can from the hallway, and hit him over the head with it. The next thirty seconds were told in complete order. No stops. No blackouts. No fuzziness. Just as Coach always told us when we got into trouble and went to his office after practice or before school. *Complete clarity, boys. Never hurt anyone.*

"It caught him off guard at first, but I knew I was in over my head the instant he got up. He grabbed a pistol, the only weapon he had left at this point in his spree. He shot me in the knee and smiled. I swear, Jed, that kid wasn't a kid anymore. He was something else. In all my years, I had never seen anything look like that. Anything laugh like that. Nothing human."

I think immediately of Aidan Montgomery Stockwell III. And I'm back to reality. Back to the Coach's story. And he finishes it with clarity. Like always.

"I saw the door was opening and Suzy Appleton was peeking her head out, asking if I was okay. Then she screamed, and I went primal. I grabbed the gun and tried to wrestle it away from what used to be one of my senior government and politics kids, and it went off. Into his throat. He died in my arms and had nothing clever or witty to say."

"What did that feel like, Coach? If you don't mind me asking…"

"Well, as your former teacher and baseball coach, I'll tell you… It was unnerving, to say the least. Here I am, sworn to teach as well as protect each and every single kid who walks into my building. And I did just that. So yes, this loss of human life is terrible. And I felt like a killer. And a failure. And then the reports came in. And kept coming. And kept coming." Boy, did they ever. "And then I changed my mind."

"How so?"

"I thought about it a little differently after the numbers came in. After the nightmares started. After I was given a medal and offered early retirement."

"What changed?"

"Everything. Nothing. I don't know, Jed. But I'll tell you one thing. As your former teacher and coach, I gave you that answer, but to be completely honest with you, I have another one to give you as an adult and your friend."

"Yes, Coach?

"You see, after I thought about it real hard, I changed my mind. When that kid died in my arms, I thought I was supposed to feel all those things. So I did. Not really, but I convinced myself that it was the right thing to feel. But when it comes right down to it, I didn't feel a thing." He pauses, interrupts his own train of thought. "No, that's not right, either. I felt something all right. It was just something I didn't understand. Honestly, it's something I don't think I'll ever truly understand. But it gave me a new reason to come here every single day. You see, I was toying with the idea of early retirement. As are most of the teachers here. But seeing you here, telling the story of everyone who can't bear to relive it one more day… It made me realize something."

"What is it, Coach?"

"We're not just educators. Anyone can educate. It's not that hard. But the teachers? The real ones, I mean. That's a tough job. And I think you don't really know what that truly means until you're put into an impossible situation. And let me tell you, Jed my boy… This incident that we're going to be talking about forever in Sarah Falls at this here high school, it was an impossible situation, any and every single way you look at it."

And I am reminded of another thing he used to say out on the baseball diamond every single day of practice. And as I recall those words, he repeats them.

"There are two types of people in this world. Those who think. And those who act."

"I remember, Coach."

"But I'm going to let you in on another little secret. I'm full of it. I honestly didn't know until that day that I had been lying to all of you all along. There aren't two types of people. There are actually three. There are those who think. And those who act. I was right about that, but I found out I'm one of the third group. Those who do both."

He pauses, takes a breath, and the bell rings. Plan period is over for the day, and I have to leave. But he walks over to the door and shuts it, finishing up the interview uninterrupted and giving it his utmost attention.

"It is our responsibility to teach as well as protect these kids. Anyone else who disagrees or feels differently is just plain wrong and should retire immediately or seek another line of work. And that's why I'm still here. I saved countless lives. And even though I had to take a bullet to do it, I'd do it again and again if I had to. It's not my job. It's my career. It's not my life. It's my purpose. And I don't teach. I change lives. Literally. Even if I have to fight for them. Even if I have to save them. And even, sadly, if I have to take them."

Then I ask the question I don't want to ask. "Should we arm our teachers? Is that the next logical step?"

He starts to answer, then shakes his head and pauses.

The kids open the door and start pouring into the room and I am greeted by the new student body and remember just how much I loved high school here. Things have changed for sure, but it is going to be up to teachers like David Lester to make sure that even though the halls are going to be eerie, the church on Sunday is going to be quiet, and the homes and parks and clubs are going to be a little different, social studies class is always going to be the same. And now, now that he truly knows why he's here, it will always be safe.

"Thanks, Coach. Before I forget, one last question: Do you have a Facebook?"

"Me? Hell no. I don't have time for that crap. Too many issues involved. If you ask me, Facebook is just a way for bullies to become more creative. Facebook, Twitter, Snapchat, and all those other socials turn loners into psychos."

"Fair enough. I'll let you get to your class. Thanks again, Coach."

"Any time, Jed my boy. Any time."

And… Stop recording…

So where was I? Oh, yeah. "It's not just a tragedy in small town America. It is America." Let me explain, as I download Tinder and create a new account. For research purposes.

The bullying never ended. Not really. It still goes on, according to Thad. It doesn't matter that there are still good teachers. For every good one, there's a burnout who looks the other way. It doesn't matter that there has been bloodshed. For every one person who remembers, there are a handful of others who want to simply forget and move on. Bullying will always exist. It will always be a problem. And in this digital day and age, it's not getting any better. It's getting worse. It's getting easier. And it's getting out of control.

Facebook. Bullying. The education system. Entitlement. Wealth. Poverty. Small town America. Overcrowded school systems. Underpaid teachers. Security. Easy access to weapons. Parenting, or lack thereof. All of these are enough to write book after book after book, but I know that isn't reasonable. I can't overdo it. The readers will just shut me out and tell me to shut up. So I'm going to make this quick. These are my philosophies, but bear with me. They're important. And I think I'm right.

Who doesn't? Every writer thinks he is right, otherwise he wouldn't have bothered to write it, you know what I mean? Of course you do. You've probably written a few versions of your own manifesto more than a couple of times at this point in your life. But me? Hell, I may be wrong. I may be right. I may be insane. But I'm sharing it with you. And the world. So listen. Because at the end of the day, at least I was brave enough to get it published. So hear me out. I promise. You won't regret your decision.

CHAPTER ELEVEN

Wednesday, October 5
9:00 PM
Samson, Ohio
186 days after the book deal

Have you ever read "A Christmas Carol" by Charles Dickens? Of course you have. It's only the most widely-adapted story of all time. *It's a Wonderful Life*, *Collateral Beauty*, *Scrooged*, *The Family Man*. Every show that's lasted more than one season has done the Dickensian tale for an episode. Crime shows. Superhero shows. Dramas. Comedies. Dramedies, whatever the fuck those even are. Hell, even the Muppets have had a crack.

I suppose it was only a matter of time before I had my own "Christmas Carol" about a town destroyed by tragedy and exploited by a reporter. And yes, the irony is not lost on the parallels to my own experience with the Sarah Falls High School Massacre and the Sarah Falls Reaper stories.

But I digress. And I'm super tired. Here's another question for you: Have you ever been to Samson, Ohio? Let me tell you... when people use the term "ghost town" they aren't talking about places like this, but they should be. Samson, Ohio has a population of zero people. Literally. No one lives there. There are about twentyish houses, a K-12 school, a post office, a gas station which is also a motel which is also a diner which is also a general store, a strip mall with a theater, and that's about it. No kids. No adults. Not a single soul.

Well, that's not true. There are plenty of souls. And dogs. Hungry pets left by their owners. But the big question is why? Where is everyone? What happened here? I'm determined to find out. It only seems fair, since I'm filling up my gas, checking in at the motel, and eating from the vending machines essentially for free.

I park my car in a street of an obviously uninhabited house that looks as harmless as an abandoned house in the middle of a ghost town can look. Then I walk up the driveway and open the door, which just takes a quick nudge.

I check my surroundings, do a little snooping, and pull out my stuff. I set up camp in what looks like it used to be the master bedroom. And, much to I'm assuming would be your surprise, I actually fall asleep.

"Hey," I hear, waking up from what turns out to be more of a nap. I frantically grab my phone and turn on the flashlight app, seeing a little girl who appears to be no older than six-or-so tugging on the edge of my sleeping bag. It's times like these I'm glad I almost always seem to fall asleep fully clothed.

There's no electricity, so I can't plug in my equipment or see very well, but I know she's a ghost.

"Who are you? And what are you doing in my mom and dad's bed?" the little girl asks.

"Sorry," I say, getting up and dusting off the spot where I had been these last, apparently, four hours. "I'm Jed."

I put out my hand and she looks at it, debates, and decides not to shake. I'm not sure if that's because she knows it's not possible or because she thinks it might not be possible or if, and I hope this isn't the case, she's shy and doesn't shake strangers' hands because she's afraid of stranger danger. I hope it's not that. Because the only reason to ever be afraid of a stranger is that they might do something horrible to you. And what's more horrible than death?

She hops up on the bed next to me and gets under the covers.

"You gonna read me a story or what?" she asks, nodding toward the nightstand at my right. A stack of classics, nothing from my childhood. All older. When did Samson, Ohio disappear off the map? How long has this town been a ghost town?

"Not enough light to read, sweetheart," I tell her.

She laughs. An innocent laugh. Not threatening in the least. Then the lights turn on.

"How did…"

And she cuts me off. "Duh, silly. I'm a ghost. I can do whatever I want as long as I stay in this house."

So there it is. The answer to my first question.

"Can I ask you a question?" I begin.

She looks irritated as she starts to fade in and out of focus. She sighs and shrugs, which I take as nonverbal permission to continue.

"What happened here?"

She looks down at the stack of books. She says nothing. So I keep at it.

"I mean, where are your parents?"

"I dunno," she says. "I woke up. They didn't. And now I'm here and they're... not. Can you read me a story now?"

So I do. *The Little Engine That Could* put her fast asleep. I know she's asleep not because of her tiny snoring or her peaceful little smile on her face, but because the lights turn off and do not come back on. I get up slowly from the bed and walk toward the door of the bedroom, making sure not to wake her.

As I reach the bottom of the stairs and head toward the front door, the lights begin to flicker again.

"You're going?" she asks, suddenly appearing at my side with the saddest look I've ever seen on a ghost's face before.

"I have to," I tell her. "I need to figure out what happened here."

"Go do adult stuff?" she asks, slightly judgmental in her tone.

"Right." I tell her. I open the door and I feel her grip tighten on my leg.

"You know," she says, "I could make you stay if I really wanted to."

And as I feel circulation begin to cut off and her eyeballs roll into the back of her head and her teeth all fall out of her mouth, believe me, I know.

"But that would be mean," I tell her.

She releases me. I walk outside and shut the door. As I walk down the street to the post office, I hear the faint sound of a little girl crying.

My own little "Ghost of Christmases Past" is a chilling reminder of the innocence lost on every single one of my stops not only on this road trip, but in my entire life so far.

Then I head to the post office. Un-mailed letters and a room full of Christmas presents. All ready to go. Forever stuck in limbo. Sort of like me.

My own little "Ghost of Christmases Present" is a chilling reminder of the decisions that I should be making, could be making, but most likely, won't be making because life is hard, and death is hard, and I live my life walking the line between the both of them so fuck if I know what to do.

Then I head to the strip mall and the movie theater. And it all comes back to me. I've been to this town before.

My own little "Ghost of Christmases Yet to Come" is not a warning, not a moral, but rather, a flat-out threat: It's only a matter of time before this is me.

Someone came in and shot everyone during a screening of the newest Disney movie at the time. I reported on this story when I was with the paper. Before the ghosts came back. Before my return to Sarah Falls. Before I became the Jed I am today.

So before I know it, I'm leaving the town behind. It was strange to see it up close and personal. It was even stranger to experience the feelings still remaining not from a newsfeed or a second-hand interview or a scholarly journal. I didn't ruin this town. But I certainly didn't help it. Maybe when I'm done I'll come back and do right by that little girl in the house. Maybe when I'm done I'll come back and make sure all those packages get delivered to their rightful destinations. Maybe when I'm done I'll push play on whatever movie was being screened and put a bullet in my own brain.

Just when I'm starting to feel sorry for myself, my car breaks down. This seems to be a thing with me. People die, so why shouldn't cars, right?

I call AAA. They say they're about an hour out.

I use my unlimited data plan to look on the web. I can't help but search Samson. The first hit is my story, most likely because of my name and Sarah Falls. This is the story that first made me somewhat famous. I wrote it as a short story, linked it to an article, then rewrote it as an article and an interview. I know what you're thinking: "He's done this before. First Samson, then Sarah Falls, and now he's going to do it to his friend, Drake." And, well… You're right.

Then I use my unlimited data plan to open Grindr, an app I haven't used since the whole Chicago Chloe incident. I see a cluster of guys and talk to the nearest one out of curiosity. He's horny and lonely. It turns out he's also dead. He was taken out to the country and beaten to death when he professed his love to one of his hookups. Now he's stuck in this app-and-find cycle.

I see my windows are all fogged over from my heavy breathing inside. The ghost is 2,000 feet away. Then 800 feet away. Then 70 feet away. Then I hear a knock on my car door.

It's the AAA guy with a spare tire.

While he puts it on, I delete Grindr. And while I drive away, I see the bloody boy, can't be a day over eighteen, shrug and pull out his phone to search for his next shot at true love.

CHAPTER TWELVE

Monday, September 26
11:00 AM
Sarah Falls, Kansas
7 days after the shooting

And… Start recording…

"I'm Jed Hollingsworth. But because of the nature of this interview, you can just call me Jed. Sound good? I'm a journalist and I'm going to tell the story of what the papers are calling The Sarah Falls High School Massacre. Alrighty. Let's begin. So, for the record, can I ask your name?"

"Jenny Armstrong. English teacher. I teach composition, creative writing, and tenth grade English. And I'm the yearbook advisor."

"Thank you, Miss Armstrong. And this is your first year at Sarah Falls High School. Is that correct?"

"Yes. It's actually my first year teaching."

"I see."

"I think we're actually the same age, Jed."

"I can't even imagine being in a high school every day at my age. You must be something special, Jenny."

She blushes. I blush. Blah blah blah.

"Moving on. Can you tell me anything about yourself?"

"What do you mean?"

"Do you have anything that might be relevant to my book you would like me to enter alongside your interview transcript and the basic stuff I put into all my pre-interview notes?"

"Well, I'm pretty basic. I grew up in a small town down the road from Sarah Falls. Went to college up state. Got my degree in education. Got my teaching license. And moved here as soon as there was a job opening."

And I know she wanted to say something like "If only I had known how much of a mistake that had been." But she didn't say it. And I greatly appreciate her not doing so.

"What made you want to move here?"

"The job."

"That's it?"

"Yeah. Like I said. Pretty basic stuff."

"Okay. So… Tell me about the day of the incident."

I reach out for her hand and she does not pull away. She embraces it and looks deep into my eyes. I know what is happening before she does, but I also know that what is happening is totally wrong and can't ever be.

"I can't even hate them. They were just scared kids. You know?"

"No, I don't know. Do you know what Coach Lester said to me just last period when I interviewed him? He said those kids stopped being kids the instant they took a life."

"Hmm… Well, I guess that's going to be just another thing on the long list of teaching and life philosophies on which the Coach and I are never going to be on the same page. And I guess we can just leave it at that."

"Yeah."

"Hmm…"

"So, what happened after the incident?"

"What do you mean? I'm still here. A bunch of people aren't. That's all there is to it."

"And how does that make you feel, Jenny?"

The tears come quick and are gone just as swiftly. I offer her the Kleenex from the box next to us. She takes a few and answers.

"How am I *supposed* to feel? Or how do I *really* feel?"

"Whichever. Both. I don't know, honestly. Just tell me what you think is right."

And I regret it as soon as the words leave my mouth.

"Right and wrong serve no place in these halls anymore. Not after what Rick and Jameson did here. Not after all the death. Not after everything changed."

"I misspoke. I apologize."

But it's too late. The spark is gone. If it was ever there to begin with. And along with the spark, the troubled life of Miss Jenny Armstrong is no longer an open book. The spark and the story are gone. And the interview goes right out the window with them.

"I'm sorry, Jed. I'm sure you're a great guy and I know this story means a lot to you, but to be honest, I don't really have anything to contribute. I didn't see anything. It was during my plan period. I was hiding under my desk and looking through my cell phone contact list the whole time. Just sitting there. Crying and shaking and searching."

"Searching? For what, Jenny?"

"Someone to text. To call. Someone who cared. Someone. Anyone."

And this is where our interview stops. I could do the right thing. I could say the right thing. But I am on a mission. And I am running out of time. Maybe another time. Maybe another place. Maybe another life. But not this one. This much is crystal clear.

There will be no second interview. There will most likely be no second contact. And that is for the best. Because when I look around the room at all the students who died just right outside of Miss Jenny Armstrong's English classroom as she hid underneath her desk and felt sorry for herself, door locked, pretending not to hear their screams and their cries and their knocks, I no longer have anything left to say to her. My attraction is replaced by pity.

As the Coach would say, *it is time for her to find a new line of employment.* And I know there will be no second contact between us. Not because of how the interview went. Not because, deep down, I think she knows I know what she'd done and not done and just how much of a coward she was in a time when the school needed leaders and heroes. No, I know she's leaving.

On my way out, I notice a folder with the words "next quarter" on them. I notice the folder is empty. And I also notice the walls are bare. Miss Jenny Armstrong isn't coming back in October. Her teaching career, as well as her spirit, died with all the kids she was too afraid to let into her locked English classroom the day of the Sarah Falls High School Massacre a week ago.

And... Stop recording...

I need lunch. And a nap. And a change of scenery.

CHAPTER THIRTEEN

Thursday, October 6
11:00 AM
Berlin, Maryland
187 days after the book deal

I'm on my way to the funeral of a college professor of mine, natural causes, when I get a notification on my phone. I pull over to a gas station in rural Maryland, admire the beauty of it all, and strike up a conversation on Tinder with a girl named Cali.

"Is Cali short for California?" I ask.

She sends an eye-roll emoji and responds with "No. It's short for Callin."

She's cute and I'm feeling it, so I go for it and tease her a bit about how that's not a real name and her parents must be either hippies or uneducated. It's much nicer than I'm letting on. I swear.

She hits back with me having no room to talk. She then calls me a hick.

"I'll have you know that I'm actually named after the fictional President of the United States of America in the beloved TV drama, *The West Wing*," I proclaim proudly.

She sends a laugh-cry emoji. "That might be worse."

I notice she's only about twenty miles away and suggest a meetup. She says she can't because she has an early flight. I check the time, noticing that it's nearing midnight.

"Pilot?" I ask.

"Flight attendant," she corrects.

"World traveler," I complement.

"Runaway," she downplays.

"Heart-breaker," I flirt.

"Sleep-needer," she ends.

I close the app, get gas, and head to the motel, knowing that I'll skip the funeral in the morning but will make an appearance at the house of my dead professor's wife sometime after I wake up.

When I wake up the next afternoon, I check Tinder and see that Cali is over a thousand miles away. But that's the beauty of road trips and flights: You never know when you'll meet again. The odds are against us. But the odds are always against me, so I'm not calling this a loss… yet.

Maybe next time we'll be closer.

I drive a few more miles and before I know it, I'm at the graveyard. I can't bring myself to step in and pay my respects at the grave. I can't help but keep the tradition of holding my breath as I pass the graveyard alive. And I can't imagine what it would be like to be buried alive… something that I have instructed in my last will and testament to be addressed. I'm going out in an old-fashioned style: with a string attached to my right pointer finger, out through a tiny slit in the coffin, run all the way six feet up and attached to a tiny little bell. You know. Just in case.

I park. I go inside the house, or rather, estate of my late professor and former colleague. He did well for himself. He was admired. And in death, mourned. Or so it appears on the outside.

Somehow, miraculously, no one here knows me. And no one here is worrying about this random young-ish guy walking around and enjoying the spread of good food and wine. I overhear some crazy shit.

It turns out my former professor's widow belonged to a group of elite grievers. These Maryland matriarchs are quite a sight. One lost a lover in a car accident. This makes me think of my own parents' tragic car accident that resulted in their deaths, and my inheritance, and I have no desire to tell that tale again. The only interesting thing about her is that she is practically bragging about cutting the brake line and getting away with it. Another lost her husband the way she lost all her previous husbands: a heart attack. I'd think she was a black widow if she didn't appear to be so sad. But looks are always deceiving, as I see the looks she gives my late professor's painted portrait on the mantle. They're all awful.

Discussions primarily led by one member of the group, an elderly gay man whom they've all looked the other way on for years, ending with secrets now public, calling them out on their antics once and for all with a comment, before decking their leader. As if this isn't enough of a movie scene already, I sneak past them and into the hallway, overhearing him yell "I don't hit women, but you're not a woman. You're a cunt."

But they're not all bad.

One of the women is called by her nickname "F. C.," short for "fortune cookie," because she is constantly talking in clichés and giving out unsolicited life advice. She used to work at a Hallmark just to read the cards. She's so cheesy but comes off as genuine. Her favorite was "While you're holding a grudge, others are dancing." She reminds me of my own mother.

She makes me smile for the first time in what seems like years.

"I know you," I hear a whispered voice come from behind me, derailing my conversation with F. C.

A man in his early fifties, a man I do in fact know, approaches with a plate overflowing with just about every food item you can imagine.

He looks at me, looks at his plate, and says "Nervous eater."

He's the principal of Sarah Falls High School.

"Before I turned fifty," he blurts out, not even remotely interested in addressing the awkwardness of us both being in the middle of nowhere in Maryland and having shared such a horrific past, "I had only ever been to eight funerals in my life."

Nervous eater. Nervous chatter. It's all the same to me.

"My great grandmother, Bettie," he goes on. Why the *fuck* is he still talking to me? "My childhood friend, Sam. And my dad's boss, Steven. All three of those occurred before high school and taught me various lessons about the importance of time, the value of life, and the reality of death."

He eats about a fourth of his plate quickly and awkwardly.

"In college, I had a professor die in a plane crash, a roommate overdose on heroin, and an uncle lose his battle with cancer. All of these affected me a great deal more than the first three funerals I attended as a kid. Aaron, Kyle, and Jake left me shaken but focused and made me who I am today."

He finishes eating the food on his plate and then looks in envy at the scraps on mine until I pour my leftovers onto his.

"Then no one died until I was forty-five. A former student of mine lost both of his parents in a car accident. This saddened the entire town, but as my wife pointed out, 'things happen' and we were at the age where they seemed to happen more and more frequently. The average middle-aged American reads the front page of the newspaper to be informed, the local section to join the breakroom conversations, the sports section to change the subject, and the obituaries to see who they lost last night."

He pauses awkwardly. Principal Eric Ellison was my eleventh-grade chemistry teacher. He was a nice guy. He cried at my parents' funeral. More than I did, actually.

"You know who Carl Reiner is?" I ask him.

He gives me a strange look. "Yeah. What does that have to do with..."

"He has a funny joke about obituaries," I cut him off. "He says he wakes up every morning, has a cup of coffee, and checks the obituaries section of the newspaper. If he's not in them, he starts his day."

He doesn't laugh. No one ever does.

"Jump forward to age fifty," he resumes. "I turned the big 5-0, received many accolades on a career well-done, and took the big boy job as the principal of Sarah Falls High School. Death was the last thing on my mind."

Then it happened.

"As of today, I've now attended more funerals than years I've lived."

I start to talk and he literally, honest-to-God, shushes me. Puts his finger up to my lips and stops me right in my tracks.

"Let that sink in, Jed. Let that sink in. This is the world we live in now. You know, I used to like you. A lot. I used to feel bad for you. But whatever you're doing here, just... don't. It's not worth it. Pay your respects. Move on. And don't ruin Berlin like you did Sarah Falls."

He has raised his voice. People are looking. People are recognizing me. People are... Are people actually Tweeting?

I see a couple of camera flashes.

"Everywhere you go, people's lives have already been ruined. I defended you while you were writing your book. I defended you while you were on tour. But this? What did this man do that could possibly warrant you being here?"

My old professor's wife walks over. I look at her, then down at my feet.

"He taught me how to lie."

It is just now that I realize that I have a tail. I suspected it back in Chicago, but it's obvious now. The producers of the paranormal investigation reality TV show. I'd be pissed if I didn't know exactly what they were doing. They're filming the pilot. And they're doing it as sneakily as possible.

So I pay my respects. I say my goodbyes. And as I hit the road, I remember that not all the ghosts of Sarah Falls are dead.

CHAPTER FOURTEEN

And... Start recording...

"I'm Jed Hollingsworth. But because of the nature of this interview, you can just call me Jed. Sound good? I'm a journalist and I'm going to tell the story of what the papers are calling The Sarah Falls High School Massacre. Alrighty. Let's begin. So, for the record, can I ask your name?"

"Julia Rothstein. And this is my husband, Albert."

"Al."

"Okay, I don't usually interview more than one person at a time, so I guess you'll have to forgive me if I seem a little off my game today."

"No problem, honey. As my husband would most likely tell you, behind my back that is, I do most of the talking in the family anyway."

He nods. I nod. She nods. And away we go.

"Alrighty. So, Mr. and Mrs. Rothstein. Julia. Al. Can you tell me a little bit about yourselves? How long have you lived in Sarah Falls? What do you both do for a living? What is your connection to the incident?"

"We've been here forever, Jed. You know that. Born and raised, the both of us. And that's the way both of our kids grew up, too. And hopefully, God forbid another tragedy, they come back to us after they make the leap and go to college. Irene is a junior at Sarah Falls High School and Arthur is a senior there this year. Art's on the football team, speech and debate team, and has straight A's for his grades. Irene is a cheerleader, has decent grades, and stays out way too late on weekends. But you know what? I love them both. Equally. To death."

"We both love them."

"To death, no doubt. What do you both do for a living? For the record..."

"Al's the head CPA over at First National Bank on Main Street and I'm Dr. Goldman's secretary, as you know."

I nod. I've known Julia pretty well ever since I started seeing Marty Goldman after my parents died. She's like a second mother to me, which is probably the only reason she's allowing me to interview her whole family. She's always believed in me.

"Okay, thanks. So is there anything else you want to let me or the readers know about your family before we get down to the day of the incident?"

"Just that, like you know, we are good people. And stuff like this happens for a reason. I know that's unpopular to say, Jed, but there is a reason both of our kids made it out of this unscathed."

"I see. Can you elaborate on that?"

"Of course. We go to Temple as often as we can. We live the way the good people of Sarah Falls are supposed to live. We help out when we can. We don't shop above our means. And we care about our neighborhood, our town, and our schools. That's why we value this place so much. And I know it's wrong or even tacky to speak ill of the dearly departed, but you know what? Rumor has it, a lot of those kids got what they deserved…"

"Honey!"

"It's true, Al. And you know it. Why, just the other day, they said one of the shooters was a homosexual. Now, I don't know what floats your boat and forgive me if I'm stepping on anyone's toes here, but there's a reason and a rhyme for everything. And just because you choose to live an unnatural lifestyle, doesn't mean you can go around spewing your words and your disease and your hatred at a small town that might not be as progressive as you want it to be. It certainly doesn't give you the excuse to kill people."

Even if they deserve it, are going to be the next words out of her mouth, but I think she realizes my jaw has almost completely dropped. So she spares me and her husband.

"Moving on, can you tell me exactly what happened the day of the incident?"

"Yes. Of course. Al had the day off because his stomach problems were acting up and I was home on an early morning break from the office when I first got a text message from Irene. It was short and simple. All it said was 'Mom, I love you very much and I am sorry.' I just assumed she wanted money or something for her impending weekend social calendar."

"But that wasn't it, was it?"

Al and Julia Rothstein both nod simultaneously and hold hands, showing their matching wedding bands and a tenderness not often seen in the aftermath of the Sarah Falls High School Massacre.

"No, it wasn't. The shooters had already arrived and were killing everyone. It was chaos by the time I got that text from my daughter. And before I could even show it to Al, who was just getting out of the bathroom for the sixth time that morning, his cell phone rang. It was Art."

She begins to cry and her husband comforts her.

"I'll tell the rest, hon. Don't worry your little head. I can let Jed know."

So he does. And I listen. And it is powerful beyond words.

"My son called me, whispering the same things that my daughter had told my wife via text message just a few minutes prior. But before I could say anything else or ask him why the blazes he had his cell phone out during the middle of class, he told me to be quiet and listen. I was on speaker phone."

They both continue to tell me the story of their son's classroom, one of the rooms that had been taken over by Rick Smith and Jameson Allan near the beginning of their killing spree. They recount the death of the teacher, Mr. Tyler Jacobson. The shooting of Gavin Armstrong was next. And finally the murder of poor Annie DeLucco. All the time, on speaker. Not knowing what to do. Not knowing how to help. Being completely helpless.

"No, not helpless. It was over before we knew it and we were in the SUV headed straight to the high school. By the time we got there, there were cops everywhere. There were firemen and emergency personnel and even the media was starting to show up. And then it happened."

"What happened, Julia?"

"I said to my husband, I said, 'I will do anything to protect my kids. Anything.' He nodded, distracted the chief of police and his men, and I ran for the doors of the high school."

"You did not!"

"You bet your buns I did. I didn't get very far, but let me tell you, if I had, I would have killed those two boys before anyone would have been able to even know what was going on. Don't mess with a

Momma Bear, son. Never mess with a Momma Bear."

The story seems to be over. Like any other proud parent of Sarah Falls, they both go on for about three more hours. Their son and their daughter even came into the kitchen and seemed to enjoy hearing their praises being spoken to a "bigshot journalist," as their dad kept calling me. I interviewed them. It wasn't anything new. They were affected, yes, but not in a profound sense. They were a good old-fashioned proud family that valued morals and hard work. And they were set in their ways. In some ways, they're more grown up than I am.

Long story short, I just want you to know that the kids ended up being okay. And they will go on with their lives. They will graduate. They will go to college and move onto bigger and better things. But because of the way they were raised and the type of parents they have, they will inevitably return to Sarah Falls.

Because. After all, according to their parents, they survived. *For a reason.* And that really said it all. But whatever it really meant is up to you to decide.

And… Stop recording…

Does bullying lead to these incidents? There are a hell of a lot of people who would place the blame almost entirely on the media, but let's give them a rest. It's a tired argument. Now, social media. That's a kicker. And it's a constantly-changing, always-evolving beast. America Online Instant Messenger went out of style. Then Facebook appeared, and made Myspace seem outdated. Facebook chat absorbed the lack of AIM. Twitter made it easier to stalk people. And all the while Facebook still held strong. Then Google Plus showed up. Kicked a little. Died. Which led everyone back to Facebook, where privacy is nonexistent. Then dating apps, Snapchat, and about a hundred others joined the battle for screen time dominance. Instagram has taken the lead. But they're owned by Facebook.

All aimed at kids, but sometimes the teachers are worse than the students. Don't believe me? There are some examples of student posts, teacher posts, friend posts, and parent posts, just from the last few weeks here in Sarah Falls. These are actual examples. Look them up if you don't believe me. Cyberbullying is the new regular bullying. It's powerful. It's present. And if we don't do something quickly, it's only going to get worse.

CHAPTER FIFTEEN

Friday, October 3
7:30 PM
Philadelphia, Pennsylvania
188 days after the book deal

That's right. I'm in Philly, the City of Brotherly Love. Or, more aptly, the city of longing lovers and dangerous weirdos. I half expect every other person I see to be straight out of an episode of *It's Always Sunny in Philadelphia*, to be honest. I need some sleep, so I park, go to my hotel, take a shower, and pass out.

I wake up around ten and decide to do some swiping.

And I reconnect with Cali. She's the flight attendant I've been talking with sporadically throughout the entire road trip. And, as luck would have it, we're in the same city. Actually, we're in the same hotel. I suggest we meet in the bar downstairs for a drink and talk in person.

She says yes, but she needs about an hour to get ready.

We message back and forth as she gets ready and I have drinks in my room.

"I heard the other day," she messages me, "that when a person dies and no one will miss them, like, they're all alone in the world, that their mourning is assigned to a random human."

"I hadn't heard that one," I say, wondering where this is going.

"I guess this is probably why you just sometimes feel sad. For no reason."

"Are you sad?" I find myself asking.

"Not right now," she says.

"So why are you thinking of it?"

"Just how my brain works."

"So why bring it up?"

A few minutes pass with no response. Did I blow it? Did it get weird just when it was starting to get real?

"Anyway, just thought it was something you'd find interesting."

"Yeah," I say.

"From now on, if anyone asks me why I'm randomly sad, instead of saying 'I don't know,' I'm going to look them straight in the eyes and say 'I've been assigned to mourn the death of a stranger.'"

A pause.

"You are such a weirdo," I say.

I'm falling in love with you, I want to say.

She sends a cute emoji and continues to get ready. It's now eleven. Then She gets cold feet. She says she has an early flight tomorrow. She says it's too weird. She says it's just too soon after a bad breakup and she doesn't want me to be a rebound because she's afraid she's falling for me and before I know it, it's two-thirty in the morning and we've covered just about everything that we would have covered over drinks downstairs.

All on Tinder.

We talk about our ideal "dream date," which is just the two of us on a beach near Long Island, drinking cold beers, reading throwaway trashy paperbacks, holding hands, and just listening to the waves crash.

She says she knows who I am and has all along. And doesn't care. She makes fun of me by talking about my book and subsequent adaptations. She mentions films and TV shows and even other books that exploited such tragedies. Documentaries like *Bowling for Columbine*. Episodes of *Glee*, *American Horror Story*, and *Buffy the Vampire Slayer*. Movies like *Unfriended*, *Megan is Missing*, *Friend Request*, *V/H/S*, The *Fallout*, *Beautiful Boy*, and *Rudderless*. Books like *Nineteen Minutes* by Jodi Picoult, *Men, Women, and Children* by Chad Kultgen, *Hashtag Good Guy with a Gun* by Jeff Chon, *Rage* by Stephen King as Richard Bachman, now out of print as per the author's own wishes and *Apt Pupil* also by Stephen King but oddly not out of print even though it's the same book but featuring a Nazi war criminal grooming and competing with someone equally nasty.

And our love story ends before it can even really begin as I decide to delete all the apps. Except for Tinder. I can't help but keep that one. Just in case she changes her mind before her flight. Just in case we cross paths again. Just in case…

Some more memorable profiles:

"I purposely get caught taking pictures of strangers doing stupid shit in public. I guess you can say I'm a bit of a thrill-seeker."

"I have a laugh track app that I've been dying to use at your expense."

"No butt stuff, guys. Exit only."

"Is it racist that I have a white noise machine in my bedroom to drown out all the Black Lives Matter protests that happen outside my apartment?"

"I'm a six pretending to be an eight. Looking for a ten."

"If you're pretty, you're pretty. To be beautiful, you have to be good. Otherwise, it's just 'Congratulations about your face.'"

"Be real: a solid friendship is much more valuable than a one-time fuck."

"Dating apps are like having a bar in your pocket."

"I give 365% 100 days a year."

"Hope you like bad girls. 'Cuz I'm bad at everything."

"6'1" if it matters. Still 6'1" if it doesn't."

I match with someone who is staying in the same hotel as I am. It is a bizarre story, to say the least.

I go to her room, she's wearing only a robe, and she hands me a bottle of water. She is Russian and her accent is thick, her English limited. Before I know it, we're in the bathroom and she's in the bathtub and she's asking me to pee on her.

"I've never really done anything like this before," I admit. "What are, umm, the rules, I guess?"

"As long as some gets in my mouth."

I think this is called water sports.

Long story short, I receive the best blowjob I've ever received and am not sure if I need to give her money or apologize or just leave. She starts the shower. I leave a hundred bucks on the bedroom table, then pick it up and put it back into my wallet. She's singing something in Russian and I think about writing a note, but instead just put my shoes on and head back to my own hotel room and try not to think about Cali and how fucked up this world really is if you look hard enough.

I immediately unmatch the Russian. I seriously contemplate deleting the app, but for some idiotic reason, I just can't bring myself to go through with such a simple act. And I make the drive toward New York.

On the road, I see the same car I saw in Maryland following me. These "real life ghost hunters" have no idea what they're in for when we get to Drake's place. To be fair, neither do I.

CHAPTER SIXTEEN

Monday, September 26
7:30 PM
Sarah Falls, Kansas
7 days after the shooting

And… Start recording…

"I'm Jed Hollingsworth. But because of the nature of this interview, you can just call me Jed. Sound good? I'm a journalist and I'm going to tell the story of what the papers are calling The Sarah Falls High School Massacre. Alrighty. Let's begin. So, for the record, can I ask your name?"

"You know who I am, Jed."

"Yes. Yes, I suppose I do, Mr. Stockwell. So. Shall we begin?"

"Of course."

"Where were you when you first heard what was going on at Sarah Falls High School the day of the incident?"

"Work. As per usual. Unfortunately, I think that's not my second home. It is my first home. All family matters took priority after the work was done. And unfortunately, the work, as you may imagine, is never done. Not for people like me. Not for our family."

"Yes. Of course. I understand, sir."

"My son sent me a text and I ignored it at first. I was in one of my late morning meetings at the time. Then he called. And I had to see. So I looked at the phone number, saw it was him, and dismissed myself early from the meeting. And what my son, my *only* son, told me that day… It changed me."

"I see."

"No, you cannot possibly see, Jed. Do you have children? No. Do you have wacked priorities that you don't know about until it is too late? No. Have you ever lost anyone you've cared for so much you lose sight of your goals, your money, your own wellbeing, and your future after you realize they are gone and you will never be able to see them again?"

I start to tell him that yes, I *could* understand. But I pause, and he looks almost embarrassed, as if he didn't know but suddenly remembered.

"Oh, God. I'm so sorry, Jed. I didn't even *think*."

"It's okay, sir."

"Your parents. No, it's not okay. Please forgive me."

"It really is okay. I just want you to understand that how I lost my parents, though under very different circumstances, can really help me understand what you and the whole town of Sarah Falls is going through right now. Or at least try."

"Yes. A tragedy is a tragedy. You're right."

"But again, Mr. Stockwell. I'm not dumb enough to think that a school shooting is comparable to a car accident."

"No, I suppose it's not. But still, they left a big hole in your heart. I can tell."

"They left me pretty well off. Mom and Dad both had substantial life insurance policies. And everything was paid off. And left to me. But you know all that, so let's get back on topic. Let's get back to you. And the phone call you had with your son before... Before the incident."

"Before that bastard Rick Smith killed him? Yes. Let's."

He tells me all about how his son was killed. How he was on the car phone and how his son, a strong boy and a strong leader, cried and begged for his mother in front of the whole class. And how Rick Smith didn't just shoot him and get it over with. Nothing quick for this boy. No, that would have been too good in his eyes. Too fair.

"He... Did things to him."

"What kind of things, sir?"

He coughs, turns red, and mutters, "Sexual things."

I set down my notepad and look him in the eyes. We meet, for just one instant, as equals. And then he tells me. And that information is for he and I alone. I'm sorry, but some things even I can't divulge. Some things are just too evil.

"I was so scared I didn't even know that I had refused a driver. I was driving myself, breaking every single traffic law there was on my way to the high school. And hoping, and praying, and my God, I was crying and screaming, that my son would be all right."

He pauses, looks at a framed photo of his son on the edge of his desk.

"But I knew. Deep down, I knew. You know me, Jed. I was in the service. I am, shall we say, a realist when it comes to everything in my life. That's how I built my empire in Sarah Falls. That's how I have kept it up and running and prospering so long. All this time, I have been a realist. And that's why when I found out Rick Smith not only knew I was on the other line but he had in fact dialed the number personally, I looked at the speedometer and realized I was driving eighty-six miles per hour in a school zone. And I knew no matter how fast I drove, no matter how much I begged and pleaded and hoped and fought, my son was gone."

And he was. Rick Smith did those things to his son in front of his classmates and finally shot him, execution style, in the back of the head.

"I'm going to sue, as you no doubt know. Not for the money, but to make an example out of everyone involved."

"For the record, how are you going about this?"

"I'm suing everyone. The school. The district. The principal. The teachers. The parents of the shooters. And by God, I'll have my day in court. And when I'm done, I'll take everything they have."

He says he is going to take the jobs away from the parents. He is going to take them for every cent they're worth. He is going to blackball them. Ruin their lives. Make them pay. Make them lose everything, just like he did when he lost his only son. His legacy. He is going to make them move. The parents of Rick Smith and Jameson Allan are going to have to leave the town of Sarah Falls forever and never return.

So he says.

But it isn't about the money. He makes that much clear.

"But if it's not for the money, do you mind me asking, what is it for?"

"I'm going to take every single penny I get and ensure this and anything that could ever be considered even remotely similar to this, never happens again."

Part of me hopes he will win. But part of me, the self-preservation side of me, hopes he doesn't. After all, his son is after me.

"Thank you for your time, Mr. Stockwell."

"Jed, please. Call me Aidan."

His son is there. I can't see him, but I can feel him. And more importantly, I can smell him. That earthy, just-recently-buried smell. That *death* smell.

"Yes. Thank you, Aidan. And again, I'm sorry for your loss."

"Not as sorry as the town of Sarah Falls is going to be."

He shakes my hand and escorts me out of his office. He never smiles. He never threatens. He doesn't have to.

And... Stop recording...

Have you spoken to your kids recently about their role models? There is no such thing as an American movie star anymore, because it's just not profitable or even ideal to be an American in the rest of the world's eyes. James Blunt famously wrote a song lyric that said "It's times like these I don't want to be a superstar, because reality TV killed them all in America." This is sad but true.

You know how America doesn't really have a royal family? But yet we're obsessed with other country's "royalty." Jenny Armstrong's English class once had a prize-winning student essay contest entry called: "The Royal Family We Deserve," in which the brilliant-yet-jaded student argues that the Kardashians are in fact the closest thing we have or will ever have to a royal family of our own. It's sick. It's disgusting. And if it wasn't so funny, it would disturb me.

American society is a beast all its own. Violence in the media. Violence in video games. Violence among our role models. If you can't look to the teachers and you can't even go on the internet, where are you supposed to find a good person to look up to? How are you supposed to know what the hell is right and wrong when no one in the entire country seems to give a damn about anyone or anything beyond themselves? Why is it so fucking hard?

I need some sleep, so I head back to my parents' house. It's my house, but I'll never actually own it. So I live here sometimes, pay someone to watch over it other times, never rent it out, never change a thing. It's not right to do so. After all, it's mine, but not really.

The winds are strong against the two closed windows in the lime green bedroom, as if the rest of the world is trying to see how I'm doing. For the first time since my early childhood, I notice the color scheme of the room and feel so much smaller than I ever remember feeling when I would sneak in early on Sunday mornings and push my way into the middle of my parents' bed. The once-springy baby blue carpet now flat and hard to the touch, my perfectly-shined black dress shoes almost tapping the original flooring beneath as I walk to make sure both windows are properly shut.

I glimpse the flash of a camera down the street and immediately pull the blinds shut, falling back onto the bed, sinking into the

Tempur-Pedic mattress that I bought them when they wouldn't let me buy them a new car after I got a scholarship. I fall onto my back and look up at the ceiling fan my grandpa installed almost twenty summers ago, back when I was still young, back when there was still time, back when this room was brighter, back before it was part of a house that I now owned. Back before the people of Sarah Falls came to expect death and funerals and mourning to be a never-ending cycle.

Back before I came back to tell that story.

And back before reporters were trying to get in and get the real scoop, the real story about Sarah Falls and the return of the prodigal son. Into the house, into the story, into the room itself. These fucking reporters and their need to know. The Precious Moments figurines that clutter up all three custom-made shelving units on the main walls of the room all look back at me as I will myself enough energy to get up and leave the room.

The smell is even the same, I think to myself, catching a glimpse of my tired-looking face in the vanity mirror stacked three-feet high with both *In-Fisherman* magazines and *Entertainment Weekly* issues from several years' worth of door-to-door back-to-school fundraisers neither of my parents could ever refuse around this time of year.

The dust on the magazines serves as a reminder of a different life. A simpler one. One that I can never have again. I sleep through the night, but only because I finish a bottle of *Jameson*.

CHAPTER SEVENTEEN

Saturday, October 4
6:00 PM
New York, New York
189 days after the book deal

My next stop is New York, New York.

Because I can't just go to upstate New York without stopping in my favorite city on the planet. To be fair, I only ever frequent Manhattan. There's something alluring about the city that really does never sleep. And the fact that you can just disappear in a crowd and be whoever you want to be is something that obviously appeals to me. Especially nowadays.

I check into a nice hotel near Times Square, spending three to four times more than I should but billing it to my agent.

Pop up the ol' Tinder and head to a dive bar. After getting sufficiently lit, I browse and begin "the hunt" as my bartender calls it.

"My tits are real, but my smile is not."

"Make me scream so loud my boyfriend moves out."

"Name's Chloe, but the C and L are silent."

"I'm economically illiterate and will make you wanna cunta punta."

"How about you do you and I'll do me... and maybe, if you're lucky... you."

"Tell me your file format preferences."

"Follow me on Insta or I'll murder your family."

"Lazy eye, hard worker."

"Smart girl looking for smart guy to make stupid decisions with."

"Beauty fades, but stupid is forever."

"I recently bought a houseplant and it needs a positive male role model."

"Dad bods and dad jokes are a surefire way to my heart."

"Sam I am. Unless you are also a Sam, in which case Sam we are."

"If you don't look like your profile, you're buying me drinks until you do."

"Are those sunglasses in your pocket or is your penis just shaped like a pair of sunglasses?"

"Funny, but not funny enough to make you look bad."

"25% of my life is just waving at someone who is actually waving at someone else behind me."

"When security guards tell me I can't bring in outside food, I just tell them it's a service burrito."

"I could be the best catfish you ever tasted."

"Pretty down to earth, but mostly because I'm only 5'1."

"Fuck the police. Then fuck me."

"Kanye attitude with Drake feelings."

I slam a few beers. I have a few shots. And once the bartender realizes that I tip well, he opens up about the party in the bathroom, which I don't refuse.

A couple of Brooklyn Brobags and Bridge and Tunnel assholes try their best to fit in, so I join them and try to retain my virtual anonymity as long as I can. Before I know it, it's college all over again. Friends, stories, and bar after bar after bar and I'm loving every second of my old life while the ghosts from my new life start to scream and fade.

I could get used to this, I'm thinking to myself, when the next thing I know, I'm in a bar I don't recognize on the Lower East Side. There's hardly anyone in here. And the guy sitting next to me sends me a signal that should scream *run*, but those are always good stories, so I sit, I introduce myself, and shake his hand.

And that, friends, was the night that I met the Devil.

CHAPTER EIGHTEEN

Tuesday, September 27
8:00 AM
Sarah Falls, Kansas
8 days after the shooting

And… Start recording…

"I'm Jed Hollingsworth. But because of the nature of this interview, you can just call me Jed. Sound good? I'm a journalist and I'm going to tell the story of what the papers are calling The Sarah Falls High School Massacre. Alrighty. Let's begin. So, for the record, can I ask your name?"

I'm hungover. I hope she can't tell.

"Rain Devereaux."

"Okay, and Rain, what year in school are you?"

"I'm a senior."

"All right. Thanks. Can you tell me a little bit about yourself?"

"Like what, exactly? I mean, I'm a cheerleader. That's the most important thing about me at school. I have a lot of friends. I was prom queen last year and would have been homecoming queen this year… if I hadn't dropped out, I mean."

"Why did you drop out? If you don't mind me asking."

"It's dumb, really. Not important."

"Then, if it's not really important, or dumb, or whatever, would you mind telling me the reason a pretty girl like you would drop out of the running for what probably is the single most important competition in your young adult life?"

"Wow. First, stereotype much? Just because I'm pretty and popular and a cheerleader does *not* mean it's the most important thing ever. Did you know I got accepted into three different Ivy League schools? Yeah. Nice move, Jed. And second, the reason it's not important is because it doesn't involve you or your story. Not really. I mean, I guess it involves, well… Never mind."

"Okay, okay. I apologize. I didn't mean to hurt your feelings. But the reason I'm asking about the dropping out is because, whether you think so or not, and I know deep down you know it is, that's why you even brought it up, and stopped, twice, is because you know it's relevant to the story. So again, I'll ask you one more time, Rain: Why did you drop out of the race?"

"*Because*, okay. It wasn't fair. And as much as people all think we're just a bunch of stuck-up kids who don't care about what the other ninety-nine percent of the school's population thinks or cares about doesn't mean we're all heartless psychos like those dumbasses on the football team."

"You're saying you dropped out because of the incident at the dance?"

"Yeah. I didn't want to be sharing a stage with Aidan."

"I see."

"Yeah, I'll bet you do."

More than she knows.

"I know it sounds bad and all, Jed… But honestly? I think Aidan kind of got what he deserved. Him and all those other fuckwits."

There seems to be a pattern forming. But I know I have to dig deeper. Get a real emotional response. Not everyone in Sarah Falls feels this way, and I know just the right question to ask. To humanize the situation. To make it real. To make it matter again.

"Okay, Rain. I want to ask you another question. After the decision to drop out of the homecoming queen race, and that other girl…"

"Edie Montana."

"Yes. After Edie Montana won homecoming queen, what did you do?"

"What do you mean, what did I do? You know, that's why you're asking. Next question."

"For the record, could you elaborate on the details?"

"Not much to elaborate on. I pulled a Carrie."

That seems a little dramatic. And tacky, all things considered. But the Stephen King "kill your classmates at prom" or homecoming or any dance for that matter reference is not only in bad taste, it is perhaps a sign of things that were to come.

"Meaning?"

"Jesus, Jed. I flipped shit. I went to the girls' bathroom, got wasted, went back onto the dance floor, made out with just about every guy that I could get my tongue into that wasn't my date, and called every one of my so-called friends every name in the book. I punched Aidan and went to his car with him and did what we were going to do after we both won."

"Which was?"

"Seriously?"

"Umm... Never mind. I got it. Go on."

"The next day at school I was a legend. They love to build up their heroes, but they love to watch them fall just as much, if not more. You know what I'm saying?"

For some strange reason, I think I do.

"What happened? Why did you drop out and then change your mind?"

"Because. Like you said. It's homecoming."

And it's a crown. *Girls and their crowns.* Go, Wildcats!

"But you thought you were doing the right thing at the time, right?"

She *knew.* She knew what was happening and she didn't say a word.

She nods. Shrugs. The bell rings.

"I gotta go, Jed. Hope this interview wasn't as pointless as I think it was."

She gets up. I say thanks. She starts to leave, and I ask her one final question.

"Before you go. One last thing. What happened the day of the shooting?"

"Who knows? I was sick that day."

"Good luck at Yale next year, Rain. Thanks for the interview."

"Whatever."

And... Stop recording...

CHAPTER NINETEEN

Saturday, October 4
11:00 PM
New York, New York
189 days after the book deal

"You don't believe me," he says, smiling.

But I do. Oh Jesus fucking Christ, I do. Every ounce of courage within me is gone. I am putty in his hands. He could tell me to do absolutely anything and I would do it. And he knows that. Yet, somehow, he doesn't.

"Want to hear a story?"

I know how this goes. He tells me a story. He offers me a deal. I take it. And then I'm fucked.

No, I want to scream. *Absolutely fucking not!*

"Yeah," I end up saying. "More than anything I've ever wanted."

"Before we start," he says, reaching into his pocket, "My card."

He hands me a business card. Apparently even the Devil has a day job. I'm speechless, so he touches my empty glass and it fills itself with the Narragansett on tap.

"I'll spare the setup. It's boring. I'll jump to the... *climax*."

He looks at a beautiful woman across the bar. Lifts his eyebrow. This Al Pacino-looking motherfucker is actually flirting with an NYU woo girl while making a deal with me for my soul.

"His name doesn't matter. The time doesn't matter. Some shlub, some place, some time, boring yawn whatever."

"I think I need to," I start and he touches my lips. They go numb.

"Shhh. Shut. The fuck," his eyes flash white and then return to normal, "up."

I do as he says.

"I tell the guy 'You've already wasted half of your six wishes, friend. Are you sure you don't just want a little help this time? I mean, I am a professional when it comes to this type of thing.'

"I lean in close to his ear and he no doubt smells the stench of a rotting carcass, making his body temperature rise.

"'No thanks,'" he responds, beginning to walk away and distance himself from me. "'But I think I've decided what I can do to change the world for the better this time.'"

"'Sure,'" I say, only slightly showing my disgust for this twerp's abuse of my dirty tricks.

"'Okay,'" he starts, "'I want to save the planet.'" He pauses, takes a deep breath, and finally says, "'I wish I discovered the cure for cancer.'

"I snap my fingers and the next thing he knows, we're in the middle of what seems to be trench warfare. Looking up above the man-made defenses, I pull back by my would-be slave, helping him barely dodge an oncoming rocket.

"'Can't have you die yet, friend. You've still got two wishes left.'

"I walk through the trenches, offering to ease the suffering to soldiers who don't know any better. Poor souls don't even realize the deals they have made until after it's already too late for them. Too late for them all.

"'What happened?'" he asks. "'How did this happen? You rigged it. You warped it again! Why are you doing this?'

"I feign a hurt set of feelings. "'What *ever* do you mean? Are you honestly suggesting that I would be sabotaging your supposedly altruistic wishes? You must be joking.'

"'Honestly. I asked to find the cure for cancer and now the world has gone to complete shit. Enlighten me, Lucius.'"

He stops his story. Points at my full beer.

"That's my *person* name."

I chug the beer and look for him to refill it again.

"You have money," he says. "I'm the Devil, not Warren Buffett."

I order another. And a shot of whiskey, for good measure.

"So I tell the guy, 'It's simple, really. You just don't find a cure like that without any kind of repercussion, friend.'

"'That's bull and you know it!' the whiny little bitch protests.

"'Cures do not exist for everything and everyone… Not without a price. That is the plain and simple truth. Supply and demand are the new fuels for warfare in this day and age. Face it. You just suck at this whole wishing game.'

"'You suck,' he mutters under his breath.

"'Nice retort.' I snap my fingers again and everything returns back to normal. 'Ready for your next wish yet? I've got places to be, souls to steal, you know… All that jazz.'

"'All right," he says. 'I want to warn Janice about the painting. If you won't let me save the world, at least let me save her.'

"'That I can do,' I tell him. 'But I will do it my way. Deal?'

"Little does he know, she's been dead for about a week. She died in the dirty business dealings that culminated in the attacks on the World Trade Center, an event I have people believing was orchestrated by Al-Quaida and some Midwest American mobsters. The painting already got her. Oh, well. At least she died before she could know that he was still alive and had faked his death in prison after he met me and saw the painting. He sold his soul, but he actually thought he did it for the right reasons. Ha.

"'Do I have a choice?'

"I smile. 'You always have a choice, friend.'

"She may be dead, but I can at least avenge her by taking care of the pricks that got her killed in the first place. I owe him that much. After all, he's shown me a good time these last few years, toying with his soul and all. He's made me remember just how much fun it is to be an immortal. Yeah. I'll just ruin everyone's lives who had anything to do with hers. Should be a blasty-blast.

"'Do it,' he says.

"A smile appears on my face. 'Will do, pal. Will do.'"

He pauses.

"So…" he says. I'm confused. "Sooooo…?" he asks. "What do you think of my story?"

I actually don't know what to say. Is this the point where he tries to sell me something? Where he does his deal? Where he threatens me?

"Oh my *Dad*, guy, I don't have all day. What do you say?"

I have nothing.

The bartender leans over the bar and whispers, "Just give him five bucks and he'll go away."

I look at the Devil. He's looking like a little kid now, impatient, bored, somewhat hurt. I reach into my pocket, pull out five crumpled-up ones and hand them to him. He says, "Hrmph," and gets up.

"You kinda suck at this, Jed."

And he walks away, taking my five bucks and smacking the undergrad's ass on the way out the door.

CHAPTER TWENTY

Tuesday, September 27
8:30 AM
Sarah Falls, Kansas
8 days after the shooting

And… Start recording…

"I'm Jed Hollingsworth. But because of the nature of this interview, you can just call me Jed. Sound good? I'm a journalist and I'm going to tell the story of what the papers are calling The Sarah Falls High School Massacre. Alrighty. Let's begin. So, for the record, can I ask your name?"

"Antoine Brown, sir."

"Whoa, whoa, whoa. No sir here. Just Jed, Antoine."

"Sorry, sir… I mean, Jed. It's just, well, my momma always said you should talk to adults with as much respect as possible. And, well, I think since I didn't really listen too much to my momma when I was alive, I should probably start doing it as much as possible now that I'm… You know. Not."

"I see. I'm sure your mother is a real fine lady and I wouldn't want you doing her wrong by breaking any of her cardinal rules or anything. That being said, I think she probably meant your superiors. And those adults you were supposed to be respectful to in the school or work or professional setting. This is significantly less professional of a setting, as you can probably imagine. For a number of reasons."

"Yeah. Me being dead is probably a good enough reason to call it quits on the formalities and shit. Sorry. I mean *stuff*."

"Again, Antoine. Don't censor yourself on my account. Believe me, I've heard worse."

And that is one of my famous understatements that I am so fond of making in the heat of the moment.

"So, let's go ahead and start off the way I like to start all my interviews. Tell me a little bit about yourself."

"Not much to tell. I'm dead. Those white boys killed me."

"I see, but, what I meant was…"

"You know what the worst part about it was? I didn't even know who they were until Aidan came and told me the other day. That's pretty fucked up."

I tense a bit. Not because of the language. Again, I don't really care much about profanity or offensive or as the other journalists at school called it, *colorful* language. No, I'm made uncomfortable by the sense that this was one of the kids on the legendary list. The hit list, if you will. And he has no idea why he was even on it. This is starting to unnerve me.

"You mean you didn't know?"

"Like I said before, Aidan came and told me. He told all of us, he said. I don't know how, because as far as I can tell, we can't see each other. I can see the living people. And I can see myself. But I can't see anyone else. It's weird."

"Why is that weird?"

As if I even have to ask.

"Because Aidan can. What makes him so special?"

I have to change the subject. Have to change it from this to something else. Something that has little or nothing to do with Aidan Montgomery Stockwell III.

"Don't know. Anyway, what about you? I mean, what were you like when you were still alive? What did you do every day? What was your home life like? Anything you want to tell me so I can accurately paint a picture of you in the book."

He pauses. "Anything?" He scratches the bullet hole where his left eye used to be, and yawns.

"Sure. Anything. Go ahead whenever you're ready."

"I played football. Was good, too. Probably going to go play in college, if I could get a scholarship somewhere close. I don't have a car and my momma would die..." He pauses.

There's that word again. That word that makes all of them so damn uncomfortable. Die. Death. Dead. Any and all variations. Understandable.

"You need a moment?"

"Nah, bro. I'm good. It's just... Well... I didn't really have a lot of friends. I was good at football and I was good at lifting weights and I was good at being big and being in the way when my momma needed me to keep all my little brothers and sisters out of her room when she was sleeping between day and night shifts at work. And that was it. Other than my size, I wasn't really good for nothing else much."

"I'm sure that's not true."

"Oh yeah? You're a nice guy for saying that." He leans in close, changing the subject. "Aidan said there's some sort of way you can bring us back. Any plans on how you're going to do that exactly?"

And my heart skips about ten beats. Where did that come from? Why did he have to start asking me questions? This is my interview. Not his.

"Umm..."

"Yeah, that's what I thought. Don't worry, bruh. I gotchu. You're just buying time. But, like I said before, you're a pretty nice guy. I can tell just by looking at you and hearing you talk these last few minutes. My advice to you is to stop telling this damn story. Move on. Let it go. And run. Run as far away as you can. Because if you don't get out of Sarah Falls, or even the state, or this region, Aidan's going to bring a wrath of hurt on you that you ain't never seen or heard about before. I could see him. *Really* see him. I mean, when we were all still alive. He was one scary dude. Believe you me..."

And, suddenly, as if I'm inside a horror movie, Antoine stops talking. There is a loud slicing noise and his neck turns red, a solid line right through the middle. Then he grabs at his throat, gasps for air one last time, and his entire head comes clean off.

Behind him is Aidan Montgomery Stockwell III, holding what looks to be a grim reaper's scythe. He is smiling.

"Interview over, Jed. Get to work on my cure."

He leans forward and lays the scythe on my hand, ever so gently. He raises it and slams it into my right index finger, slicing it off at the knuckle.

He laughs. I scream. Antoine Brown disappears and passes on to wherever it is a spirit goes when it is exorcised or killed or whatever just happened.

There's blood everywhere. Mine. And time is running out. I need to finish this book, even if it kills me. Because there is more to it than I had originally thought. There is more to it that Aidan Montgomery Stockwell III wants kept silent. And he has become Death incarnate to stop me from finding out.

And... Stop recording...

The hospital is fun. It gives me a little time away from Aiden. A little time to my thoughts. A little time to consider those at fault behind the incident.

Who is to blame? I have figured it out. There are many factors that contributed to the downfall of Sarah Falls High School and my beloved hometown. But plain and simple, I blame three people. Jameson Allan, Rick Smith, and Aidan Montgomery Stockwell III.

And I have to get rid of all three of them so the town can move on, I can finish my story, and the ghosts can finally find peace. I need to interview Jameson Allan and find out why he did what he did. I need to interview Rick Smith and see if there was something else he truly wanted out of all of this.

But most importantly, I need to always be mindful of Stockwell. And his threats. And try to figure out a way to get rid of him entirely. Forever. Besides, he's already dead, so it's not like it's actually murder.

After all, he just cut off my fucking finger. He has it coming. Right?

CHAPTER TWENTY-ONE

Sunday, October 5
2:30 AM
New York, New York
190 days after the book deal

"I know that guy," a drunk middle-aged disheveled-looking asshole says as he takes the Devil's seat.

He orders himself a drink, then looks at me. His eyes light up.

"Hey! I know you, too!"

Jesus fucking Christ.

"Ghost guy. Made all that money on those dead kid's stories."

He buys me a beer, so I humor him.

"I got a ghost story for you, ghost guy."

"Yeah?" I ask. "That so?"

So he tells me his story.

"Kim and I met in college and it was love at first punch. Her grandma always used to say that every good love story should have a good beginning, or at least a memorable one. You could definitely put ours into both of those categories. Our story was just full of accidents, some much funnier than others.

"Some not funny at all.

"It all started with a preoccupied Kim. She was on her way to class, not looking much further than a foot ahead of her, when her face suddenly hit the fist of a complete stranger, pointing out the nearest bathroom to a friend. Mister tall dark and handsome was me, Sam."

He stops his story and shakes my hand.

"Nice to meet you, Sam."

"Likewise."

He looks at his phone, then resumes his story.

"'Holy shit, are you okay?'" I asked, genuinely worried that I had killed the beautiful girl.

"She was caught a little off-guard, being punched in the face and all, and literally no words came out when she opened her mouth, just a weird gasping noise.

"'Did I knock the wind out of you?'" I leaned down and picked up her glasses, propping them gently onto Kim's face. 'Sorry about your face. I mean . . . Wow. That was not at all what I meant to say.'

"'Ouch. Look into a mirror, stranger-puncher.'

"'Can we start over?' I helped her up, only slightly copping a feel. I guarantee she didn't mind.

"'You should at least get my number first,' she said, trying not to let her smile show. 'And since you're apparently a fighter, you can call me when you want a rematch.'

"We had a rematch, all right. It was that very night, in fact. I was in love, but she was applying for law school in just a few short months. A sad but realistic ending was approaching in what I thought would most assuredly be remembered as a charming fling, when suddenly, it had been a year and Kim called me, out of the blue, asking me to meet her for dinner.

"There I was greeted with the same beautiful stranger I had fallen in love with . . . plus one. Her name was Kayla, and she was the most adorable child I had ever laid eyes on. I had a feeling right then and there that those child's eyes would spell my doom. Gut feelings are usually true.

"'She's ours,' Kim told me, a forced smile plastered across her face.

"That was when my life ended, and Kayla's began.

"I was a dad now. I hated my job, my wife always complained that she was getting fat, I had an ulcer the size of a grapefruit, I never got the degree in journalism that I so desperately craved, and my daughter was a complete stranger to me. Did I mention that I had an ulcer the size of a grapefruit?

"There was a buzzing noise that kept interrupting my day, but before I could complain or even look up, I remembered that my life was hell and it wasn't a fly, but my boss.

"'Sam! You worthless piece of shit!'

"I looked up, finding the courage to finally speak my mind for the first time in my worthless sixteen years at the company.

"'Look,' I started, a rush of anger and hostility taking over every inch of my body, 'First of all, you will calm the hell down. Secondly, you need to lose some weight, you fat fuck. Just because you outweigh everyone does not give you the right to treat people like shit. I mean, honestly, you're an assistant manager of a piece of crap company and you try to hold it over everyone's head like it's such a big fucking deal and it's really not at all. How did you get the job in the first place? The guy above you retired? Or did he kill himself? That's crazy. You've been here for, what, thirty years? Yeah. So you know what my third point is? Yeah, you got it. You can take your lousy piece of crap job and shove it up your super-sized ass hole!'

"He began to talk, slightly shocked by my not taking his crap, but I immediately cut him off and began ranting again. Realizing that my life had finally taken an interesting turn for the first time in over sixteen years, I also noticed that I had an audience of people who needed to be inspired. I ended my rant with a zinger, knocking over the computer on my desk and telling him to pick it up.

"'What?' I questioned, a look of fear appearing on his face. 'Am I being too condescending?' As he reached down to pick it up, I looked down on him and added, 'That means being talked down to.' I clocked out and heard a loud mixture of clapping, laughing, and cheering as I left my former place of employment. The sun was out and I didn't have a care in the world.

"Then I got home.

"Kim freaked out when I came home early, immediately figuring out what I had done. She told me that I was just a deadbeat loser and that she never should have married me to begin with. I reminded her that I gave up my dream job of working for the *Times* or the *Post* to raise her little accident. Some comment like that should have gotten me smacked, but she was so enraged that she just threw a dish at me. It broke against the wall. She was always a genius when it came to things like that.

"'God damn you, Sam!' she screamed.

"'Yeah, because the broken dish is my fault.'

"We were both silent as I took off my tie and she cleaned up the broken dish with a broom and dustpan that her mom and dad gave her the day they told her to leave forever.

"'I have to get Kayla. We're checking out the dorms at the high school she worked so hard to get into. She's going to freak when I tell her we can't afford a car, let alone tuition for next year. Even with the scholarships. Damn it, Sam. We'll talk later.'

"She left without saying a word, and the next thing I knew, there was a cop at my door. Kayla was fine, the cop kept telling me. My daughter was just fine. She would be alright. There was nothing to worry about.

"'I don't care about my daughter,' I found myself saying,

forgetting that she was right next to me in tears. 'Where is my wife?'

"Over the next few hours, I found myself asking that question. That night was the worst, but I couldn't give up hope. Part of me wanted her to wake up and be fine. Part of me wondered what it would be like if she didn't survive the operation. But part of me, the selfish college student who was robbed of his future and still wanted to travel the world with the love of his life, blamed Kayla.

"A lifetime of accidents, that's all it was. The first introduced me to my wife. The second simply brought about a change in both of our lifestyles. But that third accident, the night my wife hit a truck on the interstate . . . that was the one that finally saved my life. I just didn't know it yet.

He starts to cry.

"Look at me," he laughs, wiping tears from his face. "Blubbering like a big old baby. You need a refill, champ?"

I do.

So does he.

We drink some more and he continues.

"The morning after was the hardest. I had absolutely no idea what the fuck I was supposed to do. I just got up, sat down at the dining room table, and waited. For what? I wasn't sure at first, but Kayla came in and did the same thing. We both just looked at each other.

"'It's Friday,' she told me.

"'So?' I asked.

"There was an awkward silence, not an unusual thing when talking to this stranger who was looking older every day. I waited for what seemed like an hour, not about to make small talk with her or inquire further into why it mattered that it was the end of the school week.

"'Mom makes pancakes on Friday.'

"Another silence.

"Always the one-upper, I simply responded with the boldest statement I could muster all things considered. 'Yeah, well, I quit my job yesterday.'

"She glared at me. I glared back. The morning after was the hardest."

He pulls out an e-cigarette and nods to the bartender, who clearly gives zero fucks.

"I do love my daughter, you know," he says. "She just.... You know."

He continues.

"I got a call that afternoon, saying that Kayla was absent from all her classes. The principal probably felt pity on us, calling the day after Kayla's mom was put into the hospital and finding out that I was also unemployed. He seemed like a nice enough guy, but I wasn't in the mood for sympathy, especially from someone who had no idea what I was going through. How was I going to find the time to go get Kayla? I had much more important things to do, like wait by the phone for the doctors. What if my wife woke up? What if she didn't have any visitors?

"But then I had a horrible realization. Hanging up the phone, I decided that little shit was just screwing things up left and right, breaking everything in her path. I knew she went to see her older friends at that damn private school, probably hitchhiking just to spite me. The only thing I could think about was how much trouble I would be in if Kim woke up without her daughter at the side of her bed. I knew I had to go get her back.

"On my way to get Kayla, one of my tires blew out on the side of the interstate. Never really paying attention to all those times when my dad used to try and help make me manly in the garage, I had absolutely no idea what I was doing and had actually considered starting to walk back home.

"Feeling defeated and beginning to curse the God that I didn't believe in, a sudden set of headlights stopped behind me. The headlights of a white suburban shined brightly on my back tire, and a tall thin man with a seemingly expressionless face exited the vehicle.

"'Trouble, guy?'

"His voice was friendly enough, so I just told him that I was retarded and didn't know how to fix my own damn tire.

"'Easy enough,' he said.

"He walked up to me and shook my hand, saying that I'd be back on the road in less than five minutes. True to his word, he had my new tire on in four and began to put the old tire in the back of my trunk. As he came back, he told me that my left taillight was out. Sure enough, it was.

"'Should get it fixed. Spotted it a few miles back,' he told me.

"'Well,' I said, only a little creeped out by that comment, 'I appreciate the tire change.'

"'No problem,' he said. 'Drive safely.'

"He just stood there, smiling. I put the keys into the ignition and, as my luck would have it, the car wouldn't start.

"'Trouble again?' the stranger chuckled. 'Not your night, is it, pal?'

"It definitely wasn't.

"'I've got jumper cables in my trunk. Want to give me a hand?'

I got out of the car and walked behind my car, noticing the strange out of state license plates. Nebraska. What was this guy doing in New York?

"As I arrived at the back of his suburban, I realized that he had several boxes stacked on top of the cables we needed. He handed them to me one at a time and I set them off to the side of the road as he did so. Glancing into the white suburban of this not exactly normal guy, I noticed something that sent me into panic mode.

"There was a hand sticking out of what looked to me like a black industrial strength trash bag. It was wearing a wedding ring and one of the nails had chipped red polish on it. This guy was transporting a dead woman in the back of his vehicle.

"'So,' he said, 'How do you like New York, son?'

"Jolted back to reality, I managed to answer, 'Fine.'

"'Fine? Just fine? I thought you'd for sure like it better than good old Nebraska.'

"'Nebraska?' I asked, wondering if he knew that I had just seen the girl in the back of his car.

"'Yeah. I teach there, remember? I'm still just a lowly associate professor over in the art history department, but I got the promotion last year to curator of the museum.'

"'Oh,' I tell him. 'Good for you.'

"He drives his car around in front of mine and proceeded to give me a jump. It works, and he even offers to check my oil and windshield wiper fluid, but I tell him I'm fine. I can't get my mind off what I saw in his trunk. But I know that he'll kill me if he figures out that I know.

"'Kind of a Jack of All Trades, aren't you?' I ask.

"'You might say that.'

"'Well,' I begin, trying to shut my door and head off to go pick up Kayla and get her back to town before her mom wakes up from the operation, 'I suppose I was lucky you were here. Thanks again.'

"'No problem,' he tells me, not taking his hand off the door, preventing me from shutting it completely. I look into his eyes and realize that even they are creepy. One looks normal, but the other one is ash gray.

"'Here's my card.' He smiles again, and something about him doesn't seem right. 'You know, just in case you want to come back home some time. Pick up another painting from my gallery.'

"I wave, not even saying anything. The weirdo waves me on, and I'm back on the interstate within seconds.

"As I reach the campus my daughter ran off to, I park my car and get out, inspecting the new tire. Random acts of kindness do not exist. The world is not inherently good. The stranger had helped me out of a jam, but he had also taken my wallet.

"I didn't have much cash in it, and all my credit cards are maxed out thanks to Kim. But that wasn't the point. He wanted to let me know that he knew. I saw the body in his trunk, and he saw the fear in my eyes. The most valuable thing in a man's wallet is his ID. He knows who I am, where I live, and where I'm from. But the thing that unnerves me the most is that I think, for some strange reason, he already knew all that.

"I reach into my glove box and pull out my cell phone, dialing Kayla's number. She picks up and says that she's sorry… She's at the police station. This is just what I need to top off the perfect night. Sitting in the waiting room, I pull out his card."

He nods at me. As I look at the business card on the table, he recites, from memory, the same exact thing: "Lucius Foreman, Curator, Sheldon Memorial Art Gallery, University of Nebraska-Lincoln."

"On the back," he says, "There was a message. 'I'll check up on you from time to time.'"

We take shots, sharing in our strange encounters with the Devil.

"I only see him in bars," Sam tells me.

"Anyway, Kayla had a strange story, too. Mine was eerie and creepy and just all sorts of wrong, but hers was just another plea for attention.

"We made it back in one piece, but we didn't say an entire word to one another. She pretended to be asleep, but I knew that Kayla didn't sleep a wink. We had just gotten done fighting for the last fifteen minutes on our way out of town. The little brat had the balls to tell me that the love of my life was dead and gone. She had no right, and her story, or 'proof,' as she put it, just made me simply despise her that much more.

"She told me a far-fetched tale about being at a college party and then walking home by herself. She was afraid, remembering that her friend's dorm was actually several blocks away and there were very few lights on the campus. Beginning to hear strange and unfamiliar noises, her mind began to play tricks on her and she was suddenly afraid for her life. At this point in the story, I was sympathetic, having a similar inexplicable fear on the side of the interstate with the stranger who robbed me blind. But then she continued her tale, and it left the real world and entered that of fantasy.

"She was being followed now, and she was sure of it, by who she believed to be the serial rapist on campus. First of all, there was no serial rapist, and secondly, I was in no mood for this story. Trying to calm her down, I assured her that there was no one there, or at the very least, it was just some drunk guy trying to get his kicks. That was when the police officer who picked Kayla up at her friend's dorm room interjected.

"'Actually, sir,' he began, 'Your daughter's story has some facts in it that are undeniable.' Intrigued, I listened to the cop. 'We picked up a guy, trying to hide in the bushes outside of the dormitory that your daughter was visiting, waiting for someone to jump out and attack. We currently have him in custody and your daughter has ID'd him.'

"I looked at her, tears forming in her eyes, and began to console her. I felt the sobs of a nearly grown woman, and it chilled me to my bone. For the first time in as long as I could remember, I actually felt something for this accident of mine. But that's when she pissed me off.

"'I want to stay the night,' she said to me.

"The cop made his exit, somehow predicting the ensuing fight.

"'What? Hell no! Your mom's operation is tomorrow morning, Kayla, and you will be back at home with me!' I could feel my face getting red with anger. 'What the fuck is wrong with you?'

"Then she moved in for another hug. I pushed her away.

"'No. Apologize and get your crap. We're leaving."

"Then she shocked me. 'She's dead, dad.' Before I could even react, she continued. 'I know it.' My world began to spin, and for some reason I actually believed what she was saying. 'I was scared walking home from the party and I asked for her. I asked for her help.'

"I grabbed her arm and took her to the car, very nearly throwing her into the passenger seat. The cop followed me out to the vehicle, and he asked me to fill out some final paperwork. 'Sorry about your wife,' he said. 'She would be proud of your little girl. She's very brave.'

"'My wife *is* proud of my little girl. *Is.* She's still alive."

"'Oh,' he said. 'Right. Sorry.'

"Another awkward silence, then he produced a collage of photos of fifteen girls that looked to be around Kayla's age. 'These girls,' he began. 'All of them reported being raped within the last semester here on campus. We believe that your daughter's tip finally brought him to justice.'

"I'm still pissed at her, so I simply nod and tell him that we have to go, and that we're expecting news from my wife's doctor.

"'I understand, but you need to hear this last part. Your daughter is a very smart girl, opting to get those two guys to escort her home.'

"'Escort?' I ask, remembering my daughter's fear. Why would she have been afraid if she wasn't alone? Why would she make up such a lie? Why would she tell me that she asked her mother, who was supposedly already in Heaven, to help her?

"'Yeah. After we caught the psycho, he said that the only reason he didn't touch her was because of the two great big costumed frat guys walking her home to her friend's dorm.'

"I couldn't look at my daughter, but for the first time ever, it was out of shame for myself. I always thought of her as an accident, interfering with my life and screwing up my plans. She was always in trouble, and it wasn't until the cop finished his story that I finally understood the ordeal that my daughter had went through. The psycho said that the big guys were wearing wings and white robes.

"Maybe she was coming from a theme party, maybe they were angels. Maybe my wife is dead.

"I sat at the edge of the bed all night long. Kayla fell in and out of consciousness while sitting at the kitchen table. The operation was going to last eight hours, and it had been twelve since it began. What was I going to do? I had no idea who I was, where I was, and when my life was going to get better.

"Then the phone rang.

"And here I am.

"I'm terrified.

"I run to the kitchen in my bathrobe and put my hand up to grab the phone. It rings again, and I feel a jolt go up my leg that feels like a stroke. I'm paralyzed with fear. What if she's dead? What am I going to do without the love of my life? Am I going to be the guy who spends every Sunday at her grave apologizing for the fight that we had and the mistakes I made and the things we didn't get a chance to do together?

"She can't leave me. Not now. Why does this keep happening to me? Why do the people I love always die? Just like my first wife, Jennifer. She died when we were in the Peace Corps. The doctors there said it was just some sort of fluke thing. She got a virus and it was just too late to help her. She died a painful death. Kim can't die like that. I won't allow it. I won't stand for it.

"The third ring reminds me of the girl I was dating before I met the love of my life. Her name was Constance, and she had the most beautiful poetry. She had a brain hemorrhage while I was at work one day. She had no family, no friends, and no one ever missed her. No one except for me.

"Then there was me. The old me. All my friends and family think I died on 9/11 about twenty years back. For all intents and purposes, I did.

"The fourth ring brings me back to reality. I died at Ground Zero twenty years ago, but Sam rose up from the ashes. A new man. A better man. The answering machine will pick up at six, and the fifth ring is sounding. Time halts and my world stops spinning.

"I feel the warm embrace of my daughter's hand trembling on my shoulder. Turning around, we look into each other's eyes. I get it now, I finally understand. She gives me the courage to be a better man. She gives me the courage to pick up the phone."

He drops three twenties on the bar and walks toward the bathroom, looks back my way, and heads for the exit instead.

I'll never know if his wife made it. I'll never know what his deal with the man from below who teaches in the heart of America was all about. But his sadness is only outweighed by his hopefulness.

The journalist in me likes to think that everything worked itself out after a few years and they all lived the life they were capable of living. The fiction writer in me thinks there's so much more story to be told and I feel completely cheated by his Irish exit. But the part of me that somehow might make it out of this whole crazy thing with my soul still intact likes to think that it sometimes a story is just a story and a couple of drunk kooks in Manhattan near closing time just like to spin a yarn.

Regardless, I'm shitfaced. And tired. And the road has me seeing how weirdly connected we all are. Some mysteries are best left unsolved.

CHAPTER TWENTY-TWO

Tuesday, September 27
8:30 PM
Sarah Falls, Kansas
8 days after the shooting

And… Start recording…

"I'm Jed Hollingsworth. But because of the nature of this interview, you can just call me Jed. Sound good? I'm a journalist and I'm going to tell the story of what the papers are calling The Sarah Falls High School Massacre. Alrighty. Let's begin. So, for the record, can I ask your name?"

"Why are we here, Jed?" they all ask.

Valid question. I made them come to me because I wanted to get this over with. But I can't tell them that. That's way too insensitive. Even for me.

"Because I felt that a diner was more… Homey. It just felt right."

"Fair enough," their teacher says.

But the main reason is because I can't go back to that school. Not after the cops started asking me what my business was there. And not at this hour, especially.

Dr. Martin Goldman is my psychiatrist. He got word of what I was doing and has been calling me all day, leaving several messages on my voicemail. To be honest, I know I should answer him. He just wants to help.

But I don't. Because I'm busy. I simply don't have time.

"Jed. This is Dr. Goldman. I just got done having lunch with my secretary, Mrs. Rothstein. You need to stop this nonsense. Remember your condition. Call me back at my office as soon as you get this message."

My *condition* is under control.

"Jed. It's Dr. Goldman again. I know you think you've got this under control. I know you think you're just fine. But Jed, you haven't been filling your prescriptions. You need to take your medication. Don't make me get a court order again. You remember what happened last time you went off your meds. Call me. I'll be in the office working late tonight."

He's all talk. He knows that bar fight in college was an isolated incident. He knows I'm not really a violent guy.

"Jed, please. It's Marty. You really need to call me. I'm leaving the office for the night, but please call my cell. You have the number. I'm worried about you. I just heard you were at the high school the other day. And the Stockwells said you talked to Aidan… ?"

If only he knew the extent of my Aidan problem.

I also received another fun voicemail in between my frantic messages from the good doctor. This one was from my boss at the *Times*.

"Where the fuck *are* you!? Needless to say, you're fired."

Straight and to the point. Oh, well. It was a shit job anyway. I have much more important work to be doing. I can't afford to be distracted by mundane human interest pieces every other day for a paper that will most likely be going under within the next couple of years.

I interview Amy Hester, a girl who Rick Smith shot three times in the chest before asking her if she would give him a blowjob in front of her mother, Jackie, the Home Economics teacher. When Amy refused, he asked the distraught teacher and mother the same question. She considered it, she told me, after her daughter faded away. But he just laughed and shot her in the face, yelling "there's your money shot!" The rest of the Home Ec class chimed in with similar horror stories about how Rick systematically asked them for crude sexual favors before executing them. Male and female alike. But when it came down to the last six students, Jameson Allan whispered something into Rick's ear and Rick looked like he could have smacked him.

"And that's when he said it, Jed," Ariel Effken told me.

"Said, what? What happened in that room?"

"Rick told Jameson that he didn't *care* that they were in the wrong room. He said, and I remember this, because he was waving the gun around and it looked like he was going to kill Jameson along with the rest of us, 'Fuck your list, loser!'"

"I see. And then what happened?"

"He pushed him to the ground, took the gun out of his hand, and killed the rest of us without another word."

All of this happened in less than three minutes. Fourteen students and one teacher. Humiliated and murdered for no reason at all. And you can't even say for being in the wrong place at the wrong time, because they weren't.

The diner is now empty, and the staff is all looking at me.

"Jed," one of the waitresses says. "I just called Dr. Goldman. Honey…" She looks at me with such pity. It feels terrible. "Jed, honey… Before he gets here, can you please tell me something? Just *who* is it you think you're talking to?"

"Yeah, Jed." A voice I have come to know and fear interrupts my train of thought.

"Aidan." I whisper.

His face is now yellow, his lips are cracked, his eyes are sunken almost completely into his head, and his smell causes me to gag a little bit.

"That's what we thought you'd say," the waitress blurts out.

She walks away from the table and goes behind the counter with the rest of the busybodies she works with. Nosy losers with nothing better to do than start drama with their best customers.

Aidan sets his scythe down on the table. "Nice."

"What do you want?" I ask him, not really wanting an answer.

"Life. Any more questions? Or do I have to lop off another appendage to prove my point again?"

I look down at my bandaged hand. The one without an index finger now. I immediately assess the situation and realize he might actually attack me in front of these people, even though they can't see him.

I nod.

"Good dog," he says. "So where are we at with my situation, exactly? Do I need to take matters into my own hands yet?"

"To be honest with you…"

"You haven't done jack shit." He puts up his black hood and begins to resemble the grim reaper yet again. The skin from his mouth droops almost completely off his face as he picks up his scythe and starts to fade. "Final warning, Jed. You're safe this time, but it really is too bad about old Coach Lester."

"What do you…?"

And before he fades away completely, he whispers, "Wanna race?"

I don't hesitate, just like Coach taught me. Before I know it, I've grabbed all my equipment, without bothering to even turn it all off.

And I'm out of the booth and running past the just-arrived Dr. Goldman and his assistant.

"Jed!" he yells as I push my way through the diner doors, "Stop! Son, this has to end now!"

Again with the understatements.

I run past the parking lot, which has two cop cars waiting in it. Their lights go on and they follow me into the nearby neighborhood where David Lester lives. When I arrive at his house, I see the lights are all off and the driveway is empty. I ring the doorbell frantically, as the cops show up right behind me, one parking in the street and one parking directly in the driveway. Coach opens the door.

I push past him, shut the door, and lock it. By now, I'm covered in sweat and out of breath completely. Out of shape. He would be less than proud. If I got him to safety, that is. And that was my first priority. Screw the rest.

"What in the hell are you doing, Jed?"

He was wearing a Sarah Falls High School baseball t-shirt. He looks as if I've scared him half to death. Half was as far as I ever want it to go.

"This is going to sound crazy, but someone wants to kill you, Coach. And it's my fault."

And, before he can even ask me to elaborate, Coach David Lester is spitting blood into my face, looking down at his chest, and not comprehending because he's not seeing what I'm seeing. He sees a gaping wound, ending his life. I see a long scythe blade coming through and almost touching me. I back away.

Aidan removes the scythe. His lips and the skin below fall to the ground and burn into nothing as they hit the carpet. "Maybe you can take me serious now that you've got a little bit more stake in this."

The cops break the door down. Coach takes his final breath. His wife comes downstairs to see him dead on the floor and me covered in his blood. Needless to say, Aidan, who simply walked *through* the arresting officers, has my attention.

"Your move," he says, laughing all the way down the street and past the audience which will undoubtedly become a jury of my peers.

And... Stop recording...

CHAPTER TWENTY-THREE

Saturday, October 3
11:30 AM
Kingston, New York
the day of the new book

So here I am. Drake's house. His ghost meets me at the door and instructs me to follow him to his Panic Room, which is the room no one could get into after the massacre. It's full of drugs because it's Drake and of course it is. He makes me drop acid and chug a beer. And then he starts.

"So it's one, right? And the Halloween party to end all Halloween parties is tonight. I'm making some last-minute preparations and going over the guest list one last time."

I guess we're just starting. I don't even bother recording as he goes full-on Drake and takes over the storytelling duties. This isn't so much an interview as a trip. And yes, before you can even ask, it's a bad trip.

"Let me pour some T, Jed. You listening? The strangest part about living life to the fullest each and every day is that you technically have a lot of friends. But not really. What I mean is that I know a lot of people. And because of the way I have chosen to live my life, I make it a point to only know people who are actually interesting. But I've never really been very close to anyone. Not since the day I lost my family.

"Okay, so you know how I actually said that it's one? Well that puts me way super behind schedule. That's another reason the real world doesn't have time or room for a person like me. I am literally nothing without my schedules, plans, and lists. I remember every single conversation I have ever had with every single person I have ever met. Ever. I've had this for most of my life. Ever since I can remember, really. Forever.

"Anyway, I'm getting off subject. I do that a lot."

He stops talking, for the first time in about five minutes, and gives me a look I don't like.

"What the fuck are you doing, Drake?"

But I know that look. And I know Drake.

He walks into me, smiling as he does it. And by into me, I mean *into* me. As in possession. He's driving the vehicle of my body and let's just say that Drake was never a good driver, even when he was sober. Especially when he wasn't dead.

"What I'm trying to say is this: I wanted to wake up at one, start working, and get on with the rest of my day. But that didn't quite happen. Last night was crazy and if that's not the understatement of the century, I just don't know what is, to say the least, and I'm a little off my regular routine. Routines, like schedules, and lists, and memories, are everything for me. I have what my doctors have always lovingly referred to as a severe obsessive-compulsive personality disorder. This dictates what I do, how I do it, when I do it, where I do it, and every single thing I ever think or act on in my everyday life. Literally.

"Some people just say that this is a person being anal retentive, which is the classy Freudian way of saying that I have a preoccupation with details that results from an issue I had back when I was learning not to poop myself as a baby. But I say that's bull shit, no pun intended. OCD is literally a huge part of my life. It's the basis for every single thing I do. Being anal about some things is pretty bad for a lot of people, but I'm anal about everything. There are something like seven commonly accepted signs of a person having OCD, and I have all seven of them. In my daily routine. Not just signs, but actual big, huge contributing parts of my daily routines and schedules.

"They say that something like less than one percent of human beings have true OCD, yet everyone always says that they have it in passing. Borderline schmorderline. They joke, and I forgive them, but they just don't get it. When something like this drives your very being, it controls you. It owns you. People say I'm fucked up because I watched my whole family die. I say I would have been this way regardless. It's in my DNA.

"And while we're on the subject of OCD and DNA, my two favorite acronyms for things that thoroughly describe and secretly destroy me daily, let's talk some more about statistics. Out of those less than one percent of people out there suffering from some sort of obsessive-compulsive personality disorder, do you know how many of those end up in mental institutions at some point in their lives? Almost all. It's also said that over ten percent of the people who have

OCD commit suicide at some point in their adulthood. Good thing I'm still young, I guess. And dead."

He looks in the mirror. Or, rather, I look in the mirror, but I can't control my face, let alone laugh at his terrible joke, so he frowns and continues.

"I am afraid to look into the statistics that say how many of those patients end up there permanently. I'm guessing the odds are not in my favor."

He does a line and opens up the door, leaving the panic room for the first time since everyone died in Suicide Mansion.

"But who gives a flying fuck about statistics. Whenever people are throwing out stats to back up their supposed facts or even their over glorified and somewhat pompous opinions about the world and how it should be and how it would be if they were in charge, I always jump in with one of my favorite quotations. Did you know that seventy-five percent of all statistics are made up? Well, they are. How do I know this? Because I literally just made that up.

"So what I'm trying to say is simple. I'm saying that schedules, and by schedules, naturally I mean my schedules, are important. And mine's a little off. I need two hours to wake up and get ready every single day, otherwise the whole day is ruined and I will be off for the rest of the day. Possibly even week. Hence my issues with everything that everyone else around me considers to be normal. Whatever the hell that means.

"Speaking of routines, you smell like shit, Jed. Let's fix that."

He walks me up the stairs and into the bathroom, turning on the lights and the shower and getting me naked. He looks me up and down as he does so. Something tells me he always wanted to do that.

"My morning routine is simple to me, but complex and somewhat daunting to everyone else who has ever been fortunate (or would that be unfortunate?) enough to see me in action. Keep in mind this is every single day of my life. Ever. Not much changes, but even though I am literally the exact definition of a creature of habit, I can change. I just prefer not to. I don't like it. And why should I? I mean, after all, I am awesome. I have everything. I know everyone. And to be honest, when you've got no commitments, no ambition, and more money than the Bill Gates, who the hell really cares if you've got a few minor character defects?

"So here's an average morning for me. And by average, I mean this is more or less the same exact morning routine that I have had every single day for the last eighteen years of my life. Not kidding.

"Get up to same Offspring album on alarm every morning. Music is a very important part of the routine. Let the song finish while waking up. Must reach the other side of the room before next song starts. The playlist will continue throughout the morning workout, starting with stretching. Counting begins and will continue through the rest of the morning wakeup routine as well as the rest of my life whenever I get overwhelmed, underwhelmed, or just plain whelmed, whatever that may mean. The song and now the stretching routine comes to an end. Work out time. Counting continues. Three hundred is the magic number for the workout routine. Like the *300* workout. Yes, I am very vain, but that's just part of my OCD. A benefit is that I am a creature of habit and working out is a must, so I am always healthy. Unfortunately, this is also a bad thing sometimes, such as when I take drugs or drink alcohol, I am a *beast* as the kids would say, but I am almost always about to die whenever I party. Every single time. Hence the panic room full of drugs. The songs go throughout the workout routine. Which gets us to now. And why you're all naked and awkwardly looking like someone who needs to go to the gym and stop eating like a college student.

"Shower time. Twenty-five is the magic number for the shower routine. Everything must add up to twenty-five for some reason. Twenty-five on each arm pit. Twenty-five on each under arm. Five on each angle of the head, repeat five times, totaling twenty-five. Five on each angle of the crotch, repeat five times, totaling twenty-five. Twenty-five on each side of the back. Twenty-five on each butt cheek. Two sets of five before the soap is applied and three sets of five after the soap is applied, totaling an additional twenty-five.

"Now it's time to show you my closet."

He again looks at the mirror, winking, all but confirming my suspicions about Drake's sexuality. He walks me into the second bathroom connecting to the master bedroom. Because of course he has two bathrooms to himself. Fucking rich people.

"Getting ready. Fifty is the magic number for the getting ready routine. Toweling off. Brushing teeth. Combing hair. Shaving. Putting lotion all over the body. Second shower, repeat the whole showering process again. This can take a while. I could go on. And on. There are obviously some other parts of a daily routine, but I can tell I'm losing you fast.

"Why I count. When I count. Where I count. How I count. Some other nervous ticks other than the counting. Constantly. Even when I'm just sitting and waiting, I'll start. There are three types of counting. The first type of counting is the quick count, which is literally counting as fast as you can, sometimes up to three numbers at a time and going to as high as you can before you pass out or calm down. The second type of counting is the long and drawn out type of counting that is really slow and very calming. This is done to surprise yourself that you got that high and makes time seem to move a lot faster because you are slowing down. This is done to fall asleep. And the third type of counting, which I hardly ever do is the type that most people do and are very familiar with. The third type of counting is the actual counting. It is useful for most people, but ironically it is terrible and hardly ever used by actual counters."

And somehow, I pull through. And push him out of me.

"Fuck, Drake!"

He's laughing hysterically.

"Boundaries!"

I take his shirt off and put my own back on. I don't feel like myself. I don't even smell like myself. I fucking *hate* possession.

"Then there's the journaling and near photographic memory, although that is hardly ever the case or what people like me call it. This is when you constantly record, whether physically or mentally, the surrounding areas, conversations, and feelings of literally anything and everything around you at all times. This is a taxing, but a very valuable skillset to have. There are some famous people with photographic memories.

"So anyway, let's get back to what I was talking about earlier. The guest list. I've invited literally everyone of note who I have ever met throughout my years, knowing damn good and well that almost all of them are going to jump at almost anything to get here. This is, like I said, going to be the Halloween party to end all Halloween parties. Not only is it going to have anyone who is anyone in attendance, but it's also hosted by me, the most interesting person any of these people have ever met. Oh, yeah. And there's the other interesting thing. It's in my mansion out in the middle of nowhere. Which just so happens to be haunted.

"If they ever decided to make a movie about me, they'd probably sum this whole experience up into one nice little blurb, like they have on the back of the movies or a cover flap of hardcover fiction novels. Of course, they'd make it much more exciting than it really was, add a love interest, and then hint at something ridiculously over the top that redeems me as a character. Whatever.

"It would all probably sound something an awful lot like: After Drake's entire family is killed in a senseless shooting at a family reunion, he inherits their billions. Living each day to its fullest, he has become a world traveler, socialite playboy, professional student, and small-time con artist. But when a life so full of adventure and intrigue becomes dull and meaningless, he decides to buy a secluded mansion out in the middle of nowhere and throw one last party. The Halloween party to end all Halloween parties. The catch? The mansion is haunted."

I shake my head.

"Yeah. Right. That's exactly how they'll talk about me. Not to be bragging or anything, but I have had a pretty interesting life. And this party that I'm about to throw? It isn't just going to be a party. I mean, think about it. Would I title it the Halloween party to end all Halloween parties if it wasn't really the biggest thing ever to happen in not only my, but everyone else who is invited and no doubt coming's lives? Of course. I have a horrible feeling about this, but whatever. It's going to be so fucking *lit*, you don't even know, bro. Like, I'm talking straight *fire*.

"I just have an uneasy feeling. You know what I mean? I mean, of course I'm going to have those types of feelings, but then again, it's just a feeling. If I can get through this last night in the house, it'll leave me alone and I can move on with my life just like everything was before I moved in. Easy enough, right? Sure. But still. It's just that feeling. In the back of my mind. And in my gut. It's just like the day I moved in…"

"Here, Jed. Take a shit-ton of these and let's get this shit rockin'. You're gonna want to be loaded to see the wild ride I'm about to put you through."

CHAPTER TWENTY-FOUR

Tuesday, December 1
9:00 AM
Sarah Falls, Kansas
73 days after the shooting

It's been two months since Coach Lester's murder.

Aidan stopped killing when I got arrested. And because there was no actual proof, no physical evidence, they couldn't hold me as a criminal. But after they read my journals and started watching the tapes of the interviews, they could justify holding me as a dangerous crazy person. So I've been institutionalized for the last two months. Stuck. With the ghosts. Begging me to finish their unfinished business. Haunting me.

I could bore you with the details, but quite honestly, after the actual arrest, they put me back on my meds and it was all a little blurry after that. Just like it was the first year or so after my parents' death. Just sort of going through the motions, not really in control.

I could bore you with recounting the therapy, the first escape plan, the first escape attempt. But I won't. Just know it didn't work. And the only thing it did was make things harder for me. More medication. More time. More guilt. And more fear.

I could bore you with recounting the ghosts and how they visit me even though I'm on my meds now, the second escape plan, the second escape attempt. But no. You know how it all went down.

So they moved me. And I stopped plotting. Because, after all, rumor had it they were actually going to let me go.

Anyway, Aidan started killing again, and I was the number one suspect, so they started to look bad. Yep. They. The all-powerful "they." But not me.

I know I'm not crazy.

So there was no proof of what had happened and the Sarah Falls Reaper murders were ongoing. Aidan was actually getting powerful enough that he was being seen. On purpose, no doubt. He couldn't come at me, though, because this is a Catholic institution and it wasn't within the confines of Sarah Falls. For some strange reason, I found through research, ghosts cannot leave city limits of where they died.

I thought about the idea of a third and final escape plan. I thought about the last escape attempt. I thought about its inevitable outcome. So I got smart. And I made a decision. And that decision was simple. I knew I had to play the game, by lying and getting back on medication voluntarily. And it worked.

"They" became Dr. Goldman again. And Dr. Goldman released me.

So my mission continues. And I need, now more than ever, to finally finish what I have started and complete this damn book. Even if it kills me. Or gets me put back into the mental hospital. Or jail. Or prison. Or worse. If there is such a thing.

The interviews must go on. For the sake of my very sanity, they have to. This is no longer Sarah Falls' story. This is mine. And theirs. And it has to end. Because I'm sick and I'm tired and I'm almost done. I'm almost dead. It's been months, but I'm still here. With them. After all, they're not going anywhere.

I've fortified my house. My parents' old one. I have an exorcist on order. I have several ghost hunters on speed-dial. Everything in my name is protected against ghosts, demons, and spirits alike. I was allowed to secure all this through the internet access I had in the Catholic nuthouse. Part of my "therapy," as Dr. Goldman called it.

I played Goldman's game. Now he's playing mine. And even though he knows I'm lying to him and I know he's humoring me, we both know we're being used by something more powerful than we understand. He calls it a secret psychopathic copycat serial killer. I call it the ghost of Aidan Montgomery Stockwell III. But history will call it something else.

We are pawns of Death. And we are completely and utterly powerless.

Since I can't go onto school property and the town is afraid of me, I'm going to have to get creative here. All interviews with ghosts will have to be at my house. All interviews with the living will have to be in a public place. I'll be safe from the ghosts. The living will be safe from me.

But none of us are safe from Stockwell.

And that leads us to right now, my first interview upon release. It's only fitting that it should be with someone I trust completely. Someone I respect.

And... Start recording...

"I'm Jed Hollingsworth. But because of the nature of this interview, you can just call me Jed. Sound good? I'm a journalist and I'm going to tell the story of what the papers are calling The Sarah Falls High School Massacre. Alrighty. Let's begin. So, for the record, can I ask your name?"

"James Berkhardt. I teach... Taught... English."

"Yeah. That's right. I always knew you would, James. Even back when we were in school together, I knew you were going to end up teaching here."

"That much of a nerd, was I?" he laughs.

"No, I just meant you were pretty much teaching our AP Comp class anyway. Mrs. Denninger was such an idiot, and you just couldn't take it. It was great. We all liked you, man. You made that class worthwhile."

"And to think, I was worried my students wouldn't like me."

But that was obviously a lie. James Berkhardt was voted "most likely to succeed." He was the homecoming king. He was president of the debate team. He was probably the most well-read human being I ever encountered. And it's sad, really. Because he was probably one of the biggest "losing touch with friends" regrets I had when I went off to college. All in all, he was just a nice guy.

"You know," he interrupts my train of thought, "This actually almost happened about a year ago."

"The incident?"

"Yeah. That one didn't make the news, though. It was actually my classroom. The only people who even knew about it were the handful of security guys, the cop who arrested the two kids, and the principal."

"And you."

"And me."

He laughs. I'm not sure why, but I let him finish his story.

"So this kid starts causing shit in my remedial senior English seminar and I think the kid's armed, so I try to deescalate the situation before he can rile up another kid who I know for a fact has a weapon. I failed. They start going at it. The class circles the fight and I can't get through. A teacher's nightmare is an incident that is out of control and there's no bigger reminder that we're outnumbered than a fight that breaks out in our own classroom."

"What did you do?" I ask.

He smiles again. It's weird. Almost like he doesn't even think this is a big deal. Like it's just an everyday occurrence for teachers nowadays.

"I push my way through and somehow get in the middle of the crowd and physically separate the kids... a big legal no-no. If you so much as touch a kid, you get fired. I don't even hug my seniors at their graduation parties because I'm not about the unemployed life. But not that day. That day I was trying to literally save lives. And I think I did."

He pauses for a minute and then whispers a name that I can't make out.

. "What was that?"

"Oh, I was just thinking about what happened next. Tanya. There was this little white girl that shouldn't have been in that class. There was a glitch in her schedule and our counseling department had totally dropped the ball, but she was cool with it and just wanted her credits. I think she had a crush on me, so she stayed. Anyway, Tanya was the closest person to the intercom, so I yelled over the crowd as the kids are swinging at each other over me for her to push the panic button. Which she did. And when the voice over the room came on, she screamed 'Send everyone!' Which is funny now. At the time, not so much."

"So what happened?"

"They sent everyone. And they carried the instigator out of the room while I escorted the real dangerous kid myself. As he realized that we were alone in the hallway and no one could do anything to help me, he lifted up his shirt and flashed his knife at me. I nodded at it. I dared him to grab it. And when he reached for it, he was tackled by Coach Lester. Lester and I both had a special meeting with the principal, a police officer, and a member of the school board. We signed papers. We updated our resumes. And then we waited for a phone call to tell us why we were both fired."

"But you weren't."

"Nope. And when I walked out to my car that night, I honestly questioned quitting the profession."

"What kept you here?"

He smiles. Then wipes the tears from his face. I don't know when he started crying, but I can't blame him.

"The Coach. He said to me as we walked to our cars, 'Jimbo, how many kids ruined your day today?' And I thought long and hard. The answer was two. One would be suspended and would not return to my classroom and the other was going to be expelled and most likely serve jail time. Then he patted me on the back and said, 'And how many kids didn't ruin your day?' And so I went home, kissed my wife, got some sleep, and went back to school the next day. And every day after that. Every day until my last one. And when I heard gunfire that day, I wasn't even scared. I was ready. Because I knew it was the same thing. Two kids were ruining a lot of people's days. But there were over a thousand who weren't. And I was here for them. The majority."

Sarah Falls High School truly did lose their best and brightest. I wonder if James Berkhardt will ever be replaced? Somehow, I doubt it. What happens when a dying breed dies off?

"So what keeps you here now?"

"Sorry to push you on this, Jed, but I have a request to make."

"Sure. Go for it. These interviews are for you guys."

"Yeah. Well, I don't need to be told what to do or how to do it, like some of the other victims. I completely sympathize with them, but I also feel a little guilty. Because, well…"

So I tell him what I think he needs to hear.

"Because you matter, too."

"Exactly!"

He keeps stroking his left hand. His ring finger, to be more exact. It looks like he has a tan line in the place of where his wedding band should be.

"What do you need, James? You don't just need to be told that you were loved. You know that. You've known that your whole life."

"Yeah. It's… Something else."

He looks down again for his missing ring.

"It's… The ring. Rick Smith took it when he shot me. And, I guess, as far as I can tell, I can't move on without it. Or at least, I can't move on without knowing it's safe."

"I've heard of this type of thing before. A physical item, or totem, links the dead to the world of the living. Usually this is found with poltergeists or even malevolent spirits, but in your case…"

I stop. Malevolent spirits. Demons. Monsters. Are they made?

Or do they just become that way in death? He looks at me, with that teacher look. And when he speaks, it sinks in just how much this school, this *world*, lost when James Berkhardt was killed.

"No. I'm not like Stockwell. I'm just not wired that way."

He knows what I'm thinking. And it's not supernatural. It's not magic. It's because he's great at what he does. Even in death, he's still trying to teach. Trying to help others heal and learn and be their very best. Even me.

"I'll find your ring."

"Thanks, Jed. That means more to me than you can ever imagine. But I think I know why the ring's so important to me. It's… Well…"

So he talks. He gives me a story, where I didn't expect one. We talk about how he has given his widow the blessing to move on. He says she should get married to another man. Not now, but when she's ready. And he wants me not only to find the ring, but to give it back to her. And tell her what he said.

"I'll tell her."

"I can't move on because I've got unfinished business with her. And because the ring that ties me to this realm is missing. She can't move on because I can't move on. And I can't move on because of some crazy outdated rule about the afterlife. I could write an entire novel about what I've learned. Too bad no one could read it."

"I could," I suggest, only slightly kidding.

"I'm sure you would, too." He laughs. He gets up and starts to walk away. "Thank you for doing this, Jed. I want her to know it's okay. I want her to know it's okay to love again."

"I'll tell her."

He walks through the wall of the public library, pops his head back into the building and looks as if he wants to say something else. "I may be out of line, Jed. But…" Then he says it. What I've been avoiding for months. "You know that goes for you, too, right?"

I act as if I don't hear him. He shrugs. Waves. And goes back to wherever it is he has been staying since he was killed in the halls of Sarah Falls High School.

And… Stop recording…

You know how I said some ghosts had unfinished business? And how I said that was full of shit? Well, I lied. I know, I know. I'm starting to sound like a bit of an unreliable narrator, but hear me out. Please.

It's not like you have a choice. You've stuck it out this long, so bear with me. I may not be the best guy for the job, but I'm the only one who can do this. So here it is. Another little nugget of wisdom courtesy of crazy Uncle Jed.

Some of them do have unfinished business, but not in the traditional sense. Some ghosts need to actually hear that they're dead. Some need to acknowledge it. And most just need to have their story heard. And felt. They need to be told they matter. And for some strange reason, they need to hear that it's going to be okay. Wherever they're going, it's going to be okay. I never lie to them. I never say that it's going to be better. Because how the hell would I know? I haven't been there. I don't even know if it *is* a there. Or a *when*. Or whatever.

But that's beside the point. When it comes to the term unfinished business, that's a cheat. An easy way out. One out of ten or so ghosts have something they need to be reunited with. Something physical. A totem. And sometimes I'm the one who needs to find it for them.

Especially if it's out of the zone or region where they died. You see, ghosts can do a lot of neat tricks. But they can't leave the area they died. Whether it's a town or a building or even a room is entirely dependent on how powerful the ghost is. Or rather, how powerful they were before they died. And let's face it. No one is powerful at the moment of their murder. No one.

CHAPTER TWENTY-FIVE

The New York Times
The Past

Perhaps the education system is to blame.

Between nonfiction best-sellers like *Fires in the Bathroom* and *Lies My Teacher Told Me*, everyone and their mom knows the education system, as a whole, is broken. There are countless titles out there, and documentaries, that acknowledge the problem but simply look the other way when asked for a solution. Now, I'm not going to say I'm better, but seriously... Why bring up the blame without a solution? I have some problems with the education system. Hell, if everyone didn't think I was crazy, I probably could have been a teacher at some point. But that's neither here nor there.

Let's talk about the state of education. There are teachers who aren't paid enough. There is special education. There is mainstreaming. There is solution after solution and even my own plan to fix the state of public education. And here's mine.

The age old battle between making the high school diploma worth more and the push for college is one of the biggest problems out there. College. It is the most important time of one's young adult life. Don't believe me? Consider this. The Bachelor's degree is now the new high school diploma and the Master's degree is now the new Bachelor's degree. You can't get a job without skills. And you can't get skills without an internship. And, well, you do the math. Something needs to change.

Or maybe we just need teachers who care. All of them. So here's my simple solution to those who are thinking about becoming a teacher: If you don't care. Don't teach. If you can't teach, but you care, you can maybe even pull off more of an impact than the ones who can't. After all, they do say those who can't do, teach. What does that say for those who can't do or teach? What is their purpose? And why are so many of them working in schools?

CHAPTER TWENTY-SIX

Tuesday, December 1
8:30 AM
Sarah Falls, Kansas
73 days after the shooting

And… Start recording…

"I'm Jed Hollingsworth. But because of the nature of this interview, you can just call me Jed. Sound good? I'm a journalist and I'm going to tell the story of what the papers are calling The Sarah Falls High School Massacre. Alrighty. Let's begin. So, for the record, can I ask your name?"

"Allison Johnson. My friends call me Ally. So I guess, everyone calls me Ally."

"So you were pretty popular, Ally? Is that a safe assumption to make?"

"I've learned that making assumptions is a terrible way to begin a friendship, Jed. But in this case, you are forgiven. Because yeah, I guess that would be a good place to start. I'm a pretty likeable gal, I guess you'd say."

"What did you do to deserve what happened to you?"

"Excuse me? Deserve? I don't think any one of us deserved what happened to us. You might want to rephrase your question, Jed. Again. Assumptions."

"Yeah, sorry. I've been out of the game for a while."

"Yeah. We know. But we also all know that what doesn't kill you makes you stronger. And when you assume. It makes an ass out of you and me."

"You're right. I'm sorry, Ally. I'll rephrase. Why do you think Rick Smith and Jameson Allan targeted you specifically? It doesn't seem like anyone on that list died at random that day several months ago. It doesn't seem like the Sarah Falls High School Massacre or the Sarah Falls Reaper cases were random at all. So, again, why you?"

"Because. It's simple really. I kind of gained a conscience of sorts in the last few weeks of my life."

"What do you mean?"

"No, it's not like that at all. I wasn't a bully, if that's what you were wondering."

"Okay, I'm lost. Go back a little bit. To the beginning."

"No way, Jose. That's too far back for my liking. I'll just go back to the beginning of that school year. Deal?"

"That works for me. Go for it."

"So as you probably already know, I had a bit of a reputation."

I nod, knowing. But I wanted her to bring it up. And I never thought in a million years it was going to be that very reputation that got Ally Johnson killed that fateful morning in Sarah Falls.

"So yeah. I wanted to be popular. And I was pretty and nice, but I wasn't anything else. I wasn't a jock. I wasn't a cheerleader. And I wasn't smart. I was just... Me."

"Wasn't that enough?"

"You were a Wildcat, Jed. You know something like being attractive isn't ever enough. You have to have something else. Money. Fame. A reputation to uphold. So I had to get a reputation. And as a freshman, I knew exactly what that was going to be. You see, I was a lot more *experienced* than most of the girls at school. If you catch my drift."

She flashes a flirtatious look my way. I try to ignore it.

"Yes, I suppose I do."

"I had pretty much slept with anyone and everyone who was popular at Sarah Falls High. Boys and girls. And teachers. And coaches..."

She trailed off, started listing names. All sixteen of the boys on the now infamous list were on the top of her *own*. Very different contexts, but when you got right down to it, the outcome was the same for all three of them. Rick Smith wanted fame. Jameson Allan wanted revenge. And Ally Johnson wanted respect.

All three of them wanted to be seen.

"And that's why I got killed, I guess."

"What do you mean? How did your reputation get you killed?"

"Simple. Rick Smith came to town. He creeped me out. He tried things. But I wouldn't let him because, A, he was creepy, and B, he was a *nobody*."

"I see."

"And three weeks later, when the shooting happened, I was an easy target for his rage."

Among many others.

"I'm so sorry, Ally."

"It's whatever. I just have the strangest feeling in the bottom of my gut. I replaced the itch and the desire for popularity with something that just won't go away."

"What is it?"

"That's just it, Jed. It's... the reason I can't move on. Or pass on. Or over, or whatever the heck you professional ghost talkers call it."

"What is it, Ally?"

"It's guilt. That's what this feeling is. You see, out of all the people I used and let use me, I never once thought about *her*."

Her who? I almost question. But I don't need to ask. I just check the school files at my fingertips. Ally Johnson missed almost half of the school year when she was a junior. She has a child.

"I didn't even get to hold her. And my unfinished business on this world is to do that. Or at least see she's okay. You see, part of me wants to move on and forget. But a bigger part of me, the part that slept with damn near everyone, wants to see the child I gave up for adoption last year."

So I turn to her and I say the one thing I know I have to say.

"We'll find her."

And I'm not lying. If I finish this book and stop Aidan Montgomery Stockwell III, I will do just that. I will help her pass over.

All the love she had to give wasn't enough in the end. And I think she was just too young to realize that.

"Part of me gets it, you know?" she says. "A sick, twisted, broken part."

"Yeah? How so?"

"They weren't just killing people who crossed them or embarrassed them or for any other plain reason than revenge. No, Jameson and Rick killed us because they had to. Sarah Falls was out of control. And they knew it."

I don't know if I agree completely. Hell, at all, but I keep listening just the same. "Go on."

"Think about it. What are you doing? You're looking for answers. For you. For your victims. For your survivors. For your town. For Sarah Falls."

"I'm still not exactly following, Ally."

Either she's smart or crazy. Or both. But hey, who am I to judge?

She goes on. "Why do you think we all stayed around after we died? Deep down, in our tummies, we knew. We weren't ready to leave. We all had unfinished business to take care of. Just like me. Just like everyone else, I'm assuming. Am I right? Did anyone pass on?"

I look around the room at all the lost souls, waiting, some less patiently than others, for their time to tell their story and find the closure they need. Months of doing this. They are all here. Some have left, but most have chosen not to. Why? Because. They aren't done yet.

"Atonement?"

"Sure, Jed. You can call it that, if you want."

She never cries. She's strong. Part of me thinks she can't cry anymore. Not after what she had been through. Besides, she was dead long before the incident. Whoever killed Ally Johnson was probably still alive and well in Sarah Falls. Whoever killed her years ago, killed her spirit, broke her completely, was probably looking for that very same atonement, that very same peace, that all the ghosts of Sarah Falls are so desperately looking for.

"I promise you, Ally..."

"Don't promise, Jed."

But I do. And I have to. She deserves it. She's been hurt enough. And... Stop recording...

Sometimes, just sometimes, they stick around for another reason entirely. Sometimes ghosts stick around for the living. They can't move on because the people they left behind can't move on.

CHAPTER TWENTY-SEVEN

The New York Post
The Past

This is more than just about their role models. I have a better question for you. Have you spoken to your kids at all recently? Parenting. Or lack thereof. That's where a majority of America places blame when something like this happens.

Parents nowadays are more concerned with being cool or a friend than a parent. Drinking is a nonissue with some parents. "They're going to do it anyway," some argue. And popularity. Boy oh boy, don't even get me started on this. I heard a parent admit, almost *flaunt* the idea that he was going to live vicariously through his kid. He said, and I quote, "If my kid isn't popular by the time they are in junior high, I'm sending them to private school." He's going to buy popularity. He's going to force that kid to be something he might not want to be. Might not even be capable of being. And for what? You guessed it. For himself.

But what do I know? I can't ask my parents what they thought about stuff like this. I can't ask my parents what they think about school shootings. I can't even ask my parents if they're disappointed in the man I've become.

CHAPTER TWENTY-EIGHT

Tuesday, December 1
9:00 AM
Sarah Falls, Kansas
73 days after the shooting

And... Start recording...

"I'm Jed Hollingsworth. But because of the nature of this interview, you can just call me Jed. Sound good? I'm a journalist and I'm going to tell the story of what the papers are calling The Sarah Falls High School Massacre. Alrighty. Let's begin. So, for the record, can I ask your name?"

She smiles. Doesn't answer.

"For the record," I repeat.

"It's only fitting that you would come back."

"How so?" I try to play it cool.

"Oh, Jed. Darling."

She lights up the room. Just like she always did.

"Kristy," I start to plead.

"Shh..." She raises her fingers to my lips. I can almost feel her. Almost. "You don't want this interview. You don't want to know what happened. You just need to know that I'm okay. I am. I'm just here because of you. For you."

And just like that I'm crying. I can't control the tears. Can't hold them back. It's all coming so fast and it's all rushing over me like a tidal wave, and I just want to get away. I want the voices to stop. I want her to go away. I want her to be here. For real. With me.

She was staying to check on me. She says she doesn't want to leave without me. She'll wait, she says. She has always loved me. She never got over me. She waited and waited and waited and it's only fitting that I came back all these years later to let her go.

She recounts a brief love affair with a man who was but a boy. She says it isn't me. She laughs and tells me to get over myself. But I know better. I know her. And I know us. Without saying a single word, I nod and acknowledge that she is talking about me.

I recount a brief love affair with a woman who was anything but a girl. Same game and dance. Same response. But she does the thing

I never could do with a pretty girl. She calls bullshit. She knows it's her. She knows it's me. She knows. She always knows.

"I died at the hospital, Jed. I made it all the way to the parking lot."

She had been shot in the stomach, protecting three girls who were hiding behind her when Rick Smith was down to one bullet before he had to reach into his bag. He let the other three girls live because, as he said, they "got the picture."

"And that's why you're here. In my hotel room."

"Yeah. I died close enough to the outskirts of town. I could try to stretch my powers to their limit and see you. But only when you wanted to see me. Only when you absolutely *had* to see me."

If only she knew just how much I needed her.

"But I want you to know, I have been here the whole time. Watching. Waiting. Hoping you wouldn't need me. Hoping, for some strange reason, you would just pack up your things and get back onto the bus that brought you back here in the first place."

How did she know I came via bus? What else did she know? "I still can't believe the timing. You know?" I act like I don't. "Oh, Jed." And she's smiling again, making me weak with just one glance. Looking at her now I start to believe in a higher power. But then I remember the details. And I question it all over again.

"Stop it," she says, interrupting my train of doubt.

"Stop what?"

"Doing that. Thinking. Overanalyzing. You always do that and I hate it when you do that." She isn't smiling. But even when she's mad, she's still glowing. She still cares.

Overthinking has caused me a lot of grief in my lifetime.

I remember being at that bus stop, sitting next to strangers and waiting to return to a strange land, my hometown. And I remember waiting and knowing that this time, things were going to be different.

I fumbled the tiny box around in my pocket as I silently, patiently, waited for the car to come and pick me up, taking me back to the town I wrote off so many years ago. I wondered what would have changed, but the people standing around me wondered the very same things, and it made them all feel special. Made them all feel important. But they weren't special. They weren't important.

Miles away, the bus had yet to leave the station and would not do so until the driver got the "all clear" signal. He thought he was special, just like I did. He was not.

The reason for returning home was an important one to me, of course, but I had no idea just how important until I got a text message from one of my old college buddies.

I let go of the small engagement ring, letting it slip back into its tiny box. And when I read the text message slowly, methodically, everything changed. Forever.

"OMG – Sarah Falls shooting. U OK dude? C/M ASAP!!!"

The world stopped. Sarah Falls, the town where I grew up. The town I wrote off when I went to college. The town I thought of only when I thought of her. Taking her away. Sarah Falls was now changed. It had become suddenly something very different.

I remember thinking, *I've walked those halls. I've run and driven those streets. I know those people. How could this have happened?*

Calm down, I remember thinking. *You don't even know what has happened yet. Not for sure. It's got to be a simple mistake. It has to be. Just has to be.* Right?

My hands were instinctively back in my pocket, fiddling with that ring again. I grabbed it tight. I held on to something physical. Something real. I knew that no matter what, nothing mattered. Nothing mattered but her and me, together, forever.

And the world started to spin again. The bus stop came back into focus. I was back. *I just have to wait a little bit longer*, I remember thinking.

But I couldn't. How could I? So many fears. So many questions. So many things I needed to say. Where was the God damn bus? What was the hold up? Didn't they realize I had to get to Sarah Falls? Didn't they know that I was here? The prodigal son, Jed Hollingsworth, was finally back.

And the bus came. It stopped. People all filed in, one at a time. The driver asked if everyone was on board. He looked at me strangely. Did he know what happened in Sarah Falls? Did he know me? He shut the door. I looked down at my feet, and the bus pulled away, off to the town I now more than ever had to return to. Without me.

"You came back to town after the shooting, Jed. Why?"

Because I was late. Because I got a stupid text. Because I knew no matter what I did, no matter how much I wanted to fix things, I couldn't. It was too late. I was too late. But I don't have to tell her this. She knows. Somehow, some way, she knows. She always does.

I gave up literally everything to leave Sarah Falls, I returned for nothing. My parents are dead. My career is in shambles. And the one person I ever let inside, the one girl I ever truly loved, died. And that's why I have to finish this story. Not for my sanity. Not for my pride. Not for my career. Not for the victims. Not for the survivors. And not even for the town of Sarah Falls, which has brought me nothing but misery and pain all my life, hence why I left. No, I have to finish this story for her. For Kristy DeGraw. I love her. I always did. I always have. And I always will.

I pull out the ring I've been carrying since the day I got back into town.

She laughs.

"Put that silly thing away, Jed."

She starts to fade and tells me to get rid of my death wish.

I say I will. "I will." For her. "For you."

I don't ask her to wait, but she says she will. "I will." For me. "For you."

We kiss as she fades away. And I swear, for the first time in years, I feel something.

The ring drops onto the floor and the room is silent. But not empty. Not anymore.

I miss her so much.

And… Stop recording…

So you're probably wondering. About a lot of things. First and foremost, yes. I'm okay.

That's a lie. But I will be okay. Eventually.

Second, I've been moving further and further away from city limits. Aidan's getting more powerful and who's to say that framing me for murder and cutting my finger off is where he'll stop. So yes, I've temporarily moved from my house to a hotel by the hospital and, most recently, to a pretty sketchy motel on the outskirts of town.

Aidan's story is also getting worse.

Turns out, his dad was into some pretty heavy stuff. Like Salem Witch Trials heavy. Supernatural stuff. Devil worship. You know, typical rich asshole interests worsened only by the loss of a legacy and an only son.

He's killing about one per day now. Picking off the survivors one by one, hinting that he's going to make Rick Smith and Jameson Allan a footnote in not only Sarah Falls history, but American, even world history.

He doesn't even want to come back now. He's just killing.

Wait a minute… What was that?

I walk over to the door and notice that something white has appeared on the floor. A note. A note slipped under the door.

I open up the unmarked envelope. The words inside the folded note read "Drop it. We don't want you here." The outside is just as straight-forward: "Last warning."

I interview the motel night manager. I tell him about my story. He already knows. Then I tell him about the note. He suggests I go back with him to my room, pack my things, and he'll move me to the other side of the motel. The one next to the main office. It has a camera and everything.

He's not being nice to me. He's not even taking into consideration the age-old adage "the customer is always right." No. He just knows that Sarah Falls isn't a place people want to stay. Not anymore. And he needs my money.

It scares me that ghosts can hurt the living, if they're powerful or, as Aidan would suggest, *important* enough. It also scares me that this whole town is beginning to hate me. But which is really scarier? Homicidal ghosts? Or average folks who are a bit unhinged? I'm not super thrilled to find out.

As I move all my stuff into the new room, get my new room key, and make sure that there are no intruders inside, I can't help but wonder how much longer I'll sleep with the lights on. Even after all of this, there are some things you cannot unsee. Some things you shouldn't even try to unsee.

"That note," the motel night manager asks, as he walks toward the door.

"What about it?"

"Can I see it?"

I hand him the note which he examines.

He laughs, crumples it up, and tosses it into the trash can next to the nightstand. "Kids," he says. "Just messin' with you. I wouldn't worry about it. Not like they can get into your room."

He waves, shuts, the door, and I lock it behind him. I close the blinds and turn off the lights.

"Right," I say.

The thing that scares me isn't the fact that there was a note slipped under my door. The thing that scares me is that there was a note slipped under the door... of the closet.

CHAPTER TWENTY-NINE

Saturday, October 3
2:30 PM
Kingston, New York
the day of the new book

"You passed the fuck out, Jed! Now, I'd love to give you more 'hashtag sad girl summer' playlists from my past to keep you up at night, but truth be told, my life was pretty fucking cool. Until, you know, I died. That sucked anal beads."

My head is splitting. Drake's still in my body. He's controlling my actions. He's controlling my body. He's controlling my... brain...?

So here I am, or rather, here Drake is, moving into the mansion against all my various advisors' wishes and suggestions. The price is just too good to be true, I know it is, but it's just such an amazing place. I mean, it's a risk, sure, but what's life if not one big string of risk after risk?

You know how people always say "I wish I had done this" or "I wish I had done that" all the time? I did those things. I always have. I always will. That's right. I'm "that guy," if you will. I have to be. Being as I have no one, I've always tried to live my life to its fullest, at every single point in every single moment. And when it all comes right down to it, I've done it all for one person. Myself. I mean, why shouldn't I? I'm twenty-two years old, have an unlimited cash flow, and no one to share it with. I can't even remember the last person I actually had a meaningful conversation with. No family. No loved ones. No friends. Just me. Me and my adventures. And that's what led me here.

I went to eleven different colleges in five different states in the last six years of my life. Never got a degree. Come to think of it, barely passed most of the classes I took. But it wasn't about the knowledge. It wasn't about the degree. It was always about one thing and one thing only. It was about meeting people. And not just any certain type of person. All kinds. Anyone who could hold my interest.

When that got old, I decided to become a low-level confidence man. It was fun for a while, but that got old pretty quick. Screwing people over is only fun if you get credit or acknowledgement. Otherwise it's just a waste of time. Pointless, if you will.

Then I traveled. Don't get me wrong, I didn't just travel after all that. I've been traveling since the day my family was all killed. I mean, I get the notice that I've been given literally millions of dollars to do whatever the hell I want for the rest of my days when I'm only eighteen years old. That's way too much money for one person to have. Especially such a jaded and easily bored kid. So I blew it. And have been ever since. Money is literally no object. I can buy my way out of or into anything. Why the hell not, right?

Which brings me to this really nervous-looking realtor dude. He's a quick talker, but I kind of like that. Like I said, I was a con artist once upon a time, and what are realtors when you get right down to it? I can dig that. I know he's leaving a lot out, but this house is quite literally a steal, even by my definition of the word.

He's telling me some last-minute story about the mansion. Some more history about the house itself. It's kind of like *The Shining*, but a little creepier because this stuff that he's so nervously filling me in on actually happened. That stuff's all boring, so I'll just skip over it and tell you that I told him that I don't care and I just want a big quiet place out in the middle of nowhere to be left alone. How long? Who cares, I just need this. Need to get my thoughts straight. Need to fix things, you know, in my head. For a while.

He tells me that his cell phone is always on and gives me what I think might be the twentieth business card he's given me since we started talking about this place. Then he looks up after hearing a noise, wipes sweat from his forehead, and shudders. He offers some final comment about ghosts or something like that. Then he leaves.

As he leaves, I see that there is a dog, not mine, not his, not a neighbor's out here in the middle of nowhere. At first, it just sits at the end of the driveway. Then it starts barking. The realtor looks skittish, as usual, and scurries past it and into his car. He doesn't even look when he gets back onto the highway.

The dog barks the rest of the day and well into the night.

It's two in the afternoon and I'm talking to the catering company people and waiting for the DJ to come and set everything up while also trying to get all the decorations set up.

People don't realize just how much effort it takes to put together a great party. At least this one has a good theme that is already taken care of. Halloween. Costumes. Drunken dancing and walking failures. Should be amusing.

It reminds me of my fraternity days. That's right. A few of my days in college, I was a part of a fraternity. Actually, don't tell anyone because they're all really big on their secrecy and would probably have me killed if they knew any better, but I was actually in a few different fraternities. Like I said, live each day to its fullest.

So as I already said, I have a college story. Just like everyone else. The only differences are that I actually remember my college days, I didn't really learn anything, and there are literally hundreds of memorable stories to tell. After all, I went to several colleges for experience only. Learning is lame and boring, so I went for the parties.

The only friends I ever made were while I was in various pledge programs in fraternities. Hell, I was even the pledge class social chairman back in the day. I always kept in touch after I left, but I never really cared. Those guys sure knew how to party, but there's a time and a place for that. And for me, it was years ago. I don't see a reason to stay in contact with people if I don't have anything in common with them. And besides, if they were truly my brothers, as they all several times claimed to be, they would have known why I am the way I am. And they would have accepted me. Or worse, tried to help me. And that's just not something that interests me too greatly at this point in my life.

I speak with the DJ on the phone. Things are not going as planned. Then I text the party decorator. She is only slightly less of a pile than he is. I am overwhelmed and begin counting. After 743 paces in the kitchen, I still can't shake the feeling that this is all going to go horribly wrong.

Which is the exact same feeling that took me completely over the first night I stayed in this mansion.

The first night alone in the mansion, I was so excited that I couldn't sleep, so I started unpacking my stuff, but that seemed monotonous, so I started doing exactly what I'd been doing ever since I inherited millions of dollars. I started exploring.

The way I figure it, I can tackle the whole right wing of the house in a night and do the rest tomorrow. There's no way I'm sleeping. There's just too much stuff to look at. Oh, I forgot to mention. All the stuff of the previous owners? Yeah, that's right. It comes with the house. Free.

I hear that dog barking outside again, but don't worry too much about it. I ask a lawyer friend about former owners, mostly out of a weird desire or need to ask about the court case that made it one, legal, and two, *famous* to disclose about a house being haunted when it is being sold. It depreciates the value significantly apparently.

Then I feel something wet on my ear and realize that the phone starts bleeding. Not exactly sure what's going on right now. I throw phone across the room, pulling it out of the wall and breaking it against the wall. The phone starts ringing.

I run away. Go outside to smoke a cigarette. Smoke the whole pack. I can't just do something once. I have to do it full-on. This is good for workout and narcissism purposes, but not for health and risk-taking purposes. I don't do anything just to do it. There is a reason for everything. And everything is always done in excess. Smoke whole pack. Drink whole case or bottle. Do whole score of whichever drug. Always the same. Almost always ends in me almost dying.

I get ready to go back inside but notice some strange stuff going on upstairs. I should to go upstairs sometime soon and investigate the attic. The windows go to a room I didn't know I had in the house before just now.

Right before I go inside something else happens. I realize the dog isn't barking but staring directly at me. He's about twenty feet from my front porch, panting.

I slowly go back inside as I hear him start to growl. I plug the phone back into the wall. Clean off the blood, decide that it is paint or something reasonable like that. But where is the paint? Not important. I check for messages on my cell. There are two. The first one is from the lawyer. He explains the house is haunted and more about the Suicide Mansion, as the locals call it. He apologizes and seems not just nervous, but downright desperate this time around.

The second one is from a cop. The realtor just killed himself. He wants to talk to me about the incident and the house. I'm not a suspect, but there is some strange stuff going on and he wants to get all the information he can get as soon as he can get it. The cop is on his way over right now.

I start counting. It's what I do, whenever I get scared, or agitated, or irritated, or basically anything. I count. I look outside. The dog is gone. But the cop is still coming. I'm okay. I'm okay. Everything is going to be okay.

It's three. And the Halloween party to end all Halloween parties is tonight. In order for this party to be considered a success, it has to make me a lot of money. And by a lot, I mean enough to actually pay this dump off so I can sell it and be rid of it forever. And it has to be remembered (whether through actual peoples' memories or photographic evidence is another story entirely) as a rager.

To be considered a rager, a party must fit certain criteria. So now we're straight on what it is to be classified as a rager. I would know. I've been to a lot of them. Hell, I threw a lot of them. It reminds me of better days. Not better, maybe just different. More innocent times. Just like the last few ragers I was involved in (whether directly or indirectly is unimportant and trivial) while in the fraternity back in my college days.

At the World Leaders Conference, informally titled "Suck My Dictator," I went as Saddam Hussein. It was a blast. We all made shirts for everyone who wanted to remember the fun they had. The front had a picture of the late dictator Josef Stalin, photoshopped into a party and holding a beer bong, and it simply said "Quit Your Stalin," on the front, followed by "And Get to the Party!" on the back. An Asian kid went as Kim Jong Il. A black kid went as Obama. The shirts were pretty sweet. They had a picture of Hitler's face. Instead of a mustache, the words "come join the party" were present. Great shirts, funny costumes, offensive jokes, but there was still something sort of, I don't know… Missing.

Then there was the two-night shenanigan festival known as the double header costume extravaganza weekend. On Friday, we had a superhero theme and it was called "Somebody Save Me (A Beer)." I went as Clark Kent and had a girl go as Lois Lane. Halfway through the night, I transformed into a Superman costume. It was legit. It had fake muscles and everything. I even had the stupid curl in my hair. Then, when everyone recovered in the afternoon, we went over to the party house and cleaned everything up and started setting up for the Saturday night sequel, the super villain theme party called "Do Me Deadly." I went as the Carver from *Nip/Tuck*. Remember that show? So fucking cray. What can I say? It was a blast, but I think almost everyone there remembered the whole event, so still, though very fun and ridiculously illegal in more ways than one, it was still not officially a rager.

I was always fond of the Jungle Party. Not because of the outfits, but because it was already a guaranteed rager in the making, just when it was in the planning stages. Let's just say that before the party even started, everyone was already nearing blackout levels. We made Jungle Juice, which is the most dangerous mixed drink you can serve at a social gathering, especially when it is full of half-naked men and women. I started the night out dressed in a giant gorilla costume and ended up in bed with bruises all up and down both of my legs, a broken arm, and three naked strangers I had never met before going to work on me. One of them was a guy. Rager.

Another favorite is always going to be the St. Patrick's Day Party. Green beer. Green outfits. No responsibilities. Random hookups. It's seriously like a poor man's version of New Year's Eve. So many bad decisions happen when there is Irish music playing over and over on loop and everyone is getting shitfaced right before we go back from Spring Break. Not to mention the times that we were actually still on Spring Break. St. Patrick's Day is a holiday that is only celebrated or appreciated in either Ireland or the United States, but let me tell you, every time our group was out of the country on Spring Break, the country that we were visiting enjoyed St. Patrick's Day. One highlight of my past St. Patty's Day during Spring Break? I'll give you a preview. Just imagine me jumping from rooftop to rooftop, not spilling a single drop of beer while doing so, and hooking up with a girl who not only didn't speak a bit of English, but might have actually been a serial killer. I know. Fratty. Super fratty. TFM, as some would say. Total Frat Move. Is that website still going? Can you believe that book made it on the *Times* best-seller list? Pretty sure it sold more than your book, Jed. And yours was fucking sweet.

Then there's February's slew of parties that girls all love and guys all hate. There's the Valentine's Day Party. Then there's the Anti-Valentine's Day Party. And then there's the Valentine's Day Massacre Reenactment Party. They all share a common thread. They are for fat girls to cry and eat a lot of food and then try to get laid by guys who are too drunk to say their own names. I've always had a theory that if a relationship can survive a rager that takes place on or near the Hallmark created holiday of Valentine's Day, those two people are definitely destined to be together forever.

I've heard about the Employee of the Month Party. Not sure what that one is all about. But I know I went to one once. I woke up inside the back of a taxi. No recollection after beer pong tournament number four.

I have also always enjoyed the occasional Tour de Franzia Party. Everyone dresses up like they are doing the Tour de France, bike outfits are always hilarious. Especially for those who are even remotely out of shape or have a huge package. Let's just say that drunk people wearing ridiculously tight clothes and playing wine pong is always a recipe for disaster. Rager, guaranteed, every single fucking time.

Then there's always the ABC Party, also known as Anything But Clothes Party. It's pretty self-explanatory. You essentially wear anything but clothes. You try to get as fucked up as quickly as possible and get laid as many times as possible. I know many unexpected surprises that led to young parents after a good ABC Party.

The Rubix Cube Party. Another personal favorite. Only six colors are worn. Shirt, pants, hat, and you have to switch clothes with other people to become one solid color. Nakedness is always good. Especially when it's a little colder outside, if you know what I am hinting at. Which you do.

Just like the Match Party. Sometimes this is referred to as Dynamic Duos. Usually taking place at a huge house, this is a larger party consisting of at least two fraternities and two sororities. And not to mention all the other random GDIs and friends of friends of friends that will no doubt show up and try to mooch free drinks off strangers. This is when you or someone else in charge sends out a list of preselected couples or duos costumes and have one person dress as one person and another person dress as the other person and then they each try and find the pair, partner, or couple at the party. This is your date for the night. Pretty self-explanatory. Not always a rager, because of a number of reasons. Sometimes the pair doesn't show up. Sometimes it's an ex. Sometimes it's worse. Sometimes it creates an ex. This usually leads to a fight, which is raging, but not a rager. Unless you're into that type of thing. The only thing raging about fights are the raging boners some bros get when the blood flows from the fights.

Then there's the good old Stoplight Party. You wear red if you're taken. You wear green if you're single. And you wear yellow if you're a slut. Rager.

How about the Ginger Party? This one usually ends badly. And by usually, I mean it ended badly the one time we were brave enough (or would that be dumb enough?) to pull it off. It's simple really. A recipe for comic gold. And a little bit of disaster added into the mix for fun. You invite a girl. Each guy does this. The trick? They have to be a redhead. Once the girls figure out that we're essentially making fun of them, the joke is over and the chaos ensues. This usually leads to many fights, which are always funny.

Viagra and Sweatpants. CEOs and Office Hos. Four Loko AKA Black Out or Get Out. Speakeasy. GI Janes and Army Hanes. The Formal. The Anti-Formal. All ragers.

Cases and Cuffs Party is where I met the one girlfriend I've ever had. We were handcuffed and had to finish our case before we could unhook ourselves. Needless to say, she had to pee after about four beers, so we went to the bathroom. We fucked right there on the floor. We lost the case race, but we won something far greater. I'm sure this probably wasn't a rager, but it was definitely a very memorable party for me. I should call her some time.

The glorious Heaven and Hell Party. Upstairs is heaven. Downstairs is Hell. The stairs (or the garage) is going to most likely be GDI land, also known as Purgatory. Alcohol everywhere. Lots of slutty costumes. Perfect combination. Rager? I would definitely think so.

So what exactly is this whole party before the party concept, you are probably wondering. It's pretty simple. They fit into two categories. One is for the Friday only and one is for the party before the party on any given day of the week or weekend. Priming and FAC are the formal titles. Our group was getting sick and tired of actually organizing and scheduling the primers and the Friday Afternoon Club meetings so to speak, so they simply just started saying fuck the time, just come (or don't) whenever you want. We just started calling this "Ish," meaning to come around four-ish, or five-ish, or six-ish, or whenever-ish. It was called "Ish" by most of its famous participants, or the FAC by the classier of its participants, or simply the party before the party or primer by those who simply didn't know any better.

You get the picture. You bankrolled a few of these. And you're probably wondering where the fuck I'm going with all of this. Let me tell you. All these parties were tame compared to what happened at the Halloween Party to End All Halloween Parties. I should have listened to my gut. I knew something wasn't quite right with this place back when I woke up and explored the house after the first morning I ever stayed here.

The cop never showed up last night, which was weird, but whatevs. I wake up the next morning to the most bizarre thing ever. The house is unpacked. I mean literally completely unpacked. I walk around and notice that some crazy things happened while I was out like a light, and this was going to be the first of what would probably be classified as hauntings. What happened to me last night? The last thing I remember was exploring this wing of the house and being super excited about all the awesome stuff I found and then, out of nowhere, nothing. No memory at all whatsoever. Crazy.

I apparently fell asleep in the right wing, and I've been woken up by a loud crash. No, not a crash. The front door closing maybe? I don't know. Can't be too sure what all the noises in this house are. Maybe it's just the pipes or something. Or what is it that all old people who are too adult to believe in ghosts say? It's just the house settling. That's right. I'm sure it's probably just that.

I'm getting up and wiping the sleep from my eyes when I get somewhat of a minor shock. I close my eyes and shake my head a few times, yawning as I do so. There's no way I didn't see that before. All the drawers, cabinets, and doors are all open on this floor. Literally every single one. And all my boxes are neatly stacked and packed up with one another. And here's the weirdest part of all. All my stuff is neatly put into the rooms, spaces, and drawers. And I didn't touch a single thing. But even stranger is the fact that it's all in places that make perfect sense for me. It's like someone read my mind and put everything away right where I would have put them all away as if I had done it all myself. Maybe the maid service and the movers all came and started early and thought I was a drunk and didn't want to wake me up? I highly doubt that, but it's possible. Weird.

But as I am walking toward the stairs, I glance at the other wing of the house. The left wing. The one I'm going to explore later. When I'm looking over there, more of just a glance really, is when I notice something even weirder. The walls are all painted a different color. When I moved in, the whole house is either dark wood colors to match the really expensive and old looking floors or just good old plain white. But these are red. And I mean dark red. Blood red. How long did I sleep? Were there workers that let themselves in, worked around me, and were decent enough to not even wake me up? No way, it's only been light outside for a couple of hours. Strange.

Then there is the most shocking of all the discoveries. As I get down the stairs, I look and see what the loud crash was. The back door is broken, shattered really. But the fact that the back door is broken and someone has obviously been in here while I was sleeping is not the immediate concern. There's something else that catches my eye before I can even process the home invasion. Outside, directly in the back yard, there is a really old swing set that is set up as of this morning in the backyard. This is actually kind of creepy when I think about it. What the hell is going on?

So I call an old paranormal investigator friend of mine. I know this house is supposedly haunted and all, but the dog thing is new to me. I wonder if that has anything to do with all the supposed ghosts and crap that they were all warning me about when I moved into this place. I'm not sure, but I'm sure he'll have something to tell me, especially at his discounted friends and family discounted rate that he'll no doubt charge me for the phone call long distance.

According to the research of some English dude in the late 1980s, dogs, cats, animals, and, get this, babies, are all significantly more susceptible to hauntings and or residual effects of ghosts and paranormal leftovers, if you will. So what this guy is saying, and I could be wrong here, is that if you've got a dog at your front door that is barking every time there is something wacky going on inside your house, say, a haunting for instance, that that dog in particular is going to be seeing what you think you're seeing. Only amplified.

The dog's barking, as usual, and the power keeps surging on and off, off and on. It's been doing this ever since my call to the paranormal investigator. He would be having a heyday with all this nonsense. I guarantee if he was here right now he'd be telling me that it's my own damn fault for telling them to bring it on. I'm alone in this house, I know, but it's still kind of pissing me off. Old houses do weird stuff. Hell, new houses do weird stuff. But this is getting a little out of hand. I'll have to just add the plumber and electrician to the list of people who need to come and fix this place up, oh, say weekly for the rest of my life. The joys of being a ridiculously old mansion owner.

I also did a little research today. It turns out that the past sixteen owners of this place have either been murdered or committed suicide within, get this, fourteen days of living here. Great news, right? There is a really creepy story to go along with each unfortunate past owner of the mansion, and they're all over the newspapers. Funny how almost all this was either glazed over real quick-like or just completely ignored altogether by the realtor and the lawyers that sold me this place. There were a few words spoken in passing, but it's starting to make sense why the realtor was so nervous. And why he offed himself. The best ones, dead previous owners, I mean, were the ones who took others with them. Yep, they either killed their entire family or butchered a stranger or just offed themselves within the two-week maximum stay limit.

Now, a normal person would be worried. Hell, scared shitless, even. But, as you are starting to gather, I'm as far away from normal as they come. Me? I'm just intrigued. And a little pissed off. But what the hell, right? The house was a steal. Of course there's going to be a story that is equally crazy and unbelievable attached to it as the price it was itself. It only makes sense.

The papers and the journals and the blogs and all the busybodies and nosy neighbors all call this place the same name. They call it Suicide Mansion. Night two alone, here I come. Let's see if I can beat the world record and not go crazy and kill someone or someones, or, more importantly, myself. I'm pretty confident that I'll do quite okay.

So I decide to look around the rest of the upstairs. Last night, I looked all over the right wing of the mansion. Tonight's agenda is simple. I'm going to start the exploration of the left wing.

Not much of note at first, a lot of empty rooms full of, literally, nothing at all. Pointless really, but whatever. Then I make a discovery. The one that sold me on the house entirely in the first place. That's a lie, the price and the seclusion were what did it for me, but this was a close number two. I walked the halls the first time and immediately fell in love with this room. And now I'm back. I've found the library again.

But there's something different this time. There's a pile of, oh, I don't know, not dust. You know, cleaned area. I look further into this weird occurrence. Cleaning crew? No, they haven't been here yet supposedly. Must have been whoever broke in while I was sleeping this morning. Go ahead and clean away, potential breaker-inners. Feel free.

Then I find something strange. A secret passage.

Room full of strange things. Unpublished books. Writer? Could I have possibly found a new meaning to my life? I've always wanted to be a writer, or a musician, but never had the drive. Or the talent. Until now. This stuff is brand new. All of it. And it's all great!

I start reading from the diaries and journals of the previous owners of the mansion. No one has ever lasted for more than three weeks in the house.

Until now... Hopefully. Some of the books start falling off the shelves, which is pretty much par for the course today, so I take the journals downstairs to read. I get a few pages in and make the mistake of looking outside and see something. Oh my god. There's a, what looks to be a, oh my God. There's a clown on the swing set outside. Just staring at me.

I run as fast as I can to the front hallway, hear something move across the wood floors in the living room. Was that the piano bench? The piano begins playing louder and louder and louder. The piano continues to play louder and louder and louder, even in the closet upstairs with a pillow over my head. I don't even remember running upstairs. It's so loud!

The piano stops.

Banging on the walls. And then... nothing.

I get up. Start exploring again. Inch out into the hallway, look around. I don't see anything out of the ordinary, so I keep walking around and then try to head for the steps, but something catches my eye: I see a group of dead girls applying makeup to their decaying faces.

One. Two. Three. Four. Five... Fuck this. I run down the stairs.

Every mirror I go by, it's strange. It's as if all the mirrors in the house, which are all uncovered now, somehow, even though I haven't touched them and they were all still either covered up or packed away just minutes ago, are starting to show different faces in them.

Then I hear walking noises upstairs. In the locked attic.

I look outside the window and the clown is gone, but the swing is still swinging on the swing set though, and the back door is open.

Time to call someone. Time to fix this. Now. But the phones are dead. My cell has no reception. The power is out. I'm starting to rethink this whole thing.

I run to front door and open it to find hundreds of dogs. Silent. Staring. They start to growl. I slam the door shut and pass out inside, waiting for them to go away.

Next thing I know, it's eight. And the Halloween party to end all Halloween parties is tonight. I'm losing track of time. Not very many people are here yet, then the crowd grows.

Some costumes of note include: Gumbi, fucked up on acid. "Sheet," the brown ghost. The ghost of Bill Cosby's career, Ghost Dad. The Genie from Aladdin. Batman and Catwoman. Dildo. Taco and Hot Dog. Twin Towers with plane sticking out of them. "This is My Costume" Shirt guy. Used Tampon. Power Rangers. Pikachu. Ghostbusters. The Devil and a Pregnant Nun. Jason, Freddy, Leatherface, Norman Bates, Michael Myers, Ghostface, and the Strangers are at odds with the "Cereal" Killer. The Teenage Mutant Ninja Turtles are, of course, the drunkest ones at the party.

Can't stop thinking about the journals I found and the story of the writer possessed by the house. He killed his family and friends at a big costume gala they threw for the town elite. Then he turned the gun on himself. His final words are in the blood-soaked journal and they are very clear. They all deserve to die. Everyone.

This is the house that the guy was writing from. The pit that he was talking about is in the backyard of this property. He was the clown. He killed all these people and put up a swing set over the grave. Oh my God.

This family is a bunch of psychos. And their leader, the grandfather, was a horror novelist.

Or was he was right? That's it. They all deserve to die. All of them. They deserve it. They deserve to die. Die. Die. Die. Die. Die. Kill. Kill them, Drake. Kill them all. KILL THEM ALL. KILL THEM NOW!!!!!!!!!!!!!!

And when Drake, in me, is possessed by a memory, I see my shot. And I take it.

I pull him out of me. He laughs. But before I can disconnect, I see a glimpse of something. Something Drake didn't want me to see.

Drake is connected to the guy in Indianapolis from earlier, Drake's mom is tattooed lady, Drake is exactly like his dad, what with the show gloves and watch being left after each murder, good killers have no fear of ever getting caught.

Drake was the kid in the van. His parents and family members are dead because of a car accident. Like mine. They made their millions robbing banks and being high profile con artists.

Drake inherits everything.

The haunted house's last owner was the father of modern horror. He was a famous novelist.

"But I can't just tell you his name quite yet, Jed. That's too big of a reveal."

"You've been inside me, Drake. I think we're past shocking."

He laughs.

"Grow up, Drake," I say, realizing he actually can't do that.

"How about I tell you something better first? Build up a bit."

So he tells me about the night of the exorcism and the ghost hunters. The exorcist becomes possessed. And how the exorcist grabbed an axe and killed everyone. Then himself with a shard of glass from the broken window in the attic. Drake decided to hide the bodies. The house had to sell, but how? And that's when the journals gave him an idea: throw a party. The Halloween party to end all Halloween parties. It would be perfect. He'd invite everyone he knew and charge a butt load of cash to enter. Then he could buy the house flat-out, sell it, and move on to his next adventure. It was perfect.

They all deserve to die. All of them. They deserve it. They deserve to die. Die. Die. Die. Die. Die. Kill. Kill them, Drake. Kill them all. KILL THEM ALL. KILL THEM NOW!!!!!!!!!!!!!

Drake? Who's Drake? Not me, he yelled to himself. Have the party. Invite them all. And kill them all. I'm not Drake. I'm the original owners of the mansion. All of them. Drake is us. We are Drake.

I try to slap him, remembering too late that I can't. He looks hurt.

"Stop. Fucking. Around." I tell him.

"Fine," he says as he sits down on the barstool. But you're not going to like the rest of this story, Jed. Yours truly isn't just the quirky protagonist from this point forward. Shit's gonna get real dark, real fast."

"Try me," I say. Setting up all my equipment one last time.

He smiles. And I can't quite place my finger on why, but the smirk he gives reminds me of Stockwell right before he changed into the Sarah Falls Reaper.

CHAPTER THIRTY

Wednesday, December 2
12:30 PM
Sarah Falls, Kansas
74 days after the shooting

And... Start recording...

"I'm Jed Hollingsworth. But because of the nature of this interview, you can just call me Jed. Sound good? I'm a journalist and I'm going to tell the story of what the papers are calling The Sarah Falls High School Massacre. Alrighty. Let's begin. So, for the record, can I ask your name?"

"Stop calling, Mr. Hollingsworth. This is ridiculous."

"I'm sorry, sir, but I have to get your comments. Your son, what he did, it changed a lot of people's lives. Forever. If I could just get you to..."

And Rick's father cuts me off, which is a warm welcome compared to what he usually does. Which is hanging up. "My son killed a lot of people, Mr. Hollingsworth. I get that. And I feel terrible, I really do. But let's get a couple things straight. My ex-wife and I don't talk. I remarried when I left her years ago. I haven't spoken with my son since he got into that death metal crap. He was a disappointment. She was a loser. And you know what? I have a new family now."

"Mr. Smith, if I could..."

"No, Jed. You can't. What my son did was unforgivable. End of story. But it had nothing to do with me and I'm not about to let you or anyone like you use this story to further your own agenda and make me look like the bad guy. I tried. For years. But I just couldn't take it anymore. The drugs. The alcohol. The fights." He pauses. I think about asking a question, but stop. Is he talking about his son? Or his wife? Or both?

He begins again. "Leave me alone, Mr. Hollingsworth. Let me live my life. It's hard enough without people like you digging up the past. I've moved on. So should you."

He hangs up.

And... Stop recording...

Aidan is coming for me. He's getting closer.

As I've said before, I've already left the house. I figured I had to get out of city limits, at least during the nights. I can always run from him, but I have to sleep. My house isn't protected anymore. He's getting stronger with each and every spirit he destroys. And his power grows exponentially as soon as he takes a life.

That's right. Aidan's killing again. Of course, I'm the number one suspect, which makes finishing my work that much harder. But everyone in town, the cops included, know my deal with Dr. Goldman. They all know that it's part of my "therapy" to continue my quest and write my book. Of course, a lot of them think I'm a crazy writer, not an actual schizophrenic, which is what all the doctors think I am. But I know better. You know better.

And Aidan certainly knows better. He's getting closer.

After killing more and more, he can stretch the limits of his boundaries. He's literally breaking the rules of the undead. He's crossing over, little by little. Even in death, he thinks he's in charge.

He's at the edge of the highway. Watching me. Waiting for me to screw up. Waiting for the time when he can slip into my motel room and slit my throat. I don't think he even wants to be alive anymore. Being undead is too much fun.

He's getting closer.

His death toll is rising. And it's just adding fuel to my fire. It's just adding material to my book. But it's also adding to the sadness of Sarah Falls. You see, Aidan isn't just killing random people. There is a pattern. But the cops are stumped! There's word they're about one murder away from bringing in the big guns. The FBI wouldn't get any further, though. It's still the work of a mysterious serial killer, picking off survivors of the Sarah Falls High School Massacre... One by one.

He's in the parking lot now. Watching me. Waiting.

He started with Coach Lester, the social studies teacher, baseball coach, and student council advisor. And my friend. At first, I thought it was just to "motivate" me to help him come back. And I think I'm right. I really do think that Stockwell originally planned to simply scare me into helping him. But I got arrested.

And he developed a bloodlust. He got more powerful every time he exorcised one of his own, but the power that surged through him, the abilities that he attained after taking a life? He went crazy. He went mad.

And so he kept doing it. Now, unfortunately, he can't get enough. It's the one thing he didn't really have in life. He had power. He had connections. And he had the ability to lead, manipulate, and control by fear. But he didn't have the ability to take life.

He's killed more. He's trying to be remembered. He doesn't want to be overshadowed by the school shooting. He's going to kill even more than Jameson Allan and Rick Smith did that fateful day not long ago.

Since the Coach, he has taken the lives of nine more victims that survived the original ordeal. He killed Nancy Fleming, the photography and journalism teacher and cheerleading sponsor. He killed Ingrid Appleton, the school's Vice Principal. He killed Floyd Fleming, the social studies teacher and head varsity football coach. He killed Ron Claussen, the campus security office. He killed Randy Chen, the art teacher. He killed Katheryn D'elacroix, the English teacher. He killed Simone Madison, the French teacher and key club sponsor. He killed Cal Niles, the math and economics teacher and junior varsity wrestling coach.

And he killed someone else, too. Someone who threw the police for a curveball. Someone who, unfortunately for me, was personal and seemingly unrelated to the school shooting.

Reaper victim number ten was Dr. Martin Goldman, my psychiatrist. He told me this in person. That's right. He's outside my motel room door. Right now.

Aidan's here. With my doctor.

And they want to talk.

And… Start recording…

"I'm Jed Hollingsworth. But because of the nature of this interview, you can just call me Jed. Sound good? I'm a journalist and I'm going to tell the story of what the papers are calling The Sarah Falls High School Massacre. Alrighty. Let's begin. So, for the record, can I ask your name?"

"Dr. Martin Goldman."

So I interview my own doctor. He tells me his version of the story. He tells me to stop this at once. He tells me he originally thought I could have a brain tumor. But I'm not going to tell you the specifics, because he would only be scientifically planting the seed of doubt into you as my readers, and that helps no one.

"Let me tell you a story," I say to him.

So I do. Aidan looks bored, as he fades away, probably going to go take another life. It's out of my hands, so I have to help Dr. Goldman pass over, get him off my back. Make him understand.

So I tell him a story with absolutely no plausible explanation.

"This is my story, so bear with me."

He does.

"When I was younger, I was always terrified of my grandfather, but for no real reason other than just plain stupidity. Never seeing him just added to my fears, fueling them with the ideas of horrible things, and trying to explain why I never saw him. Only later in my life would I realize my grandfather was not only one of the most achieved men, but also the most loving in my entire lifetime. The reason I had never seen him until my twelfth birthday was because my mom and him had a bit of a falling out when she moved to New York. He was diagnosed with cancer and given only a few months to live when mom decided it was about time she put aside her grudge and let me meet him.

"When I walked into his room, I realized he was lying on his bed, trying to reach for something. I asked him what he was doing and he replied, 'What are you doing?' At first, I didn't know what to say. Was he just kidding around or was he actually senile? He laughed and said, 'Just giving you crap, kiddo,' explaining he was reaching for his TV remote. The first couple of times I went to his house, I didn't really do anything but sit there and watch old M*A*S*H episodes with him. What was it with old people and that show? I had nothing in common with this old fart, but it was making my mom happy. The only thing that kept me going was the idea he would be dead in just a few more weeks. What a horrible thing to think, I know, but it was the truth. Give me a break. I was twelve.

"So one day, when I arrived at his house, I realized the TV wasn't on. I rushed upstairs, thinking he had died or something, but I was wrong. He wasn't in his room at all. I heard a loud crash above me and realized he had gotten out of bed and was in the attic. Walking up toward the stairs, I saw a whole bunch of photo albums. I took one from the pile and dusted it off. 'Memories,' it said.

"He walked down, almost falling and potentially breaking bones, like old people do all the time. And when he saw me, his face lit up. Not like it had ever done before. 'Have I ever told you about the war?' he asked. Come to think of it, he never had before. So I humored the old fart and sat down on the couch with him. We talked for hours about the war he fought in. I saw a picture of my grandma. She was very pretty and she looked a lot like my mom when she was younger. She died in a car accident before I was born. I wish I had gotten a chance to meet her."

Dr. Goldman cuts me off.

"Jed, this is a pleasant story, but why don't you get to the point?"

So I do.

"Later on, after I had entered high school, I had to watch a movie in Coach Lester's class about World War II. When he assigned our class the interview project, most people were mad and immediately began to complain. But I was secretly excited and rushed over to my grandpa's house immediately after school let out that very day. I spent the next four hours asking him more questions about his youth. Who would have thought such a grumpy old man would be able to tell such great stories?

"I got an A on the paper and also got out of having to worry about what to give him for a Christmas present. On Christmas Eve, when we gave out presents, I asked my mom where grandpa was. She started freaking out and yelled for him. My dad picked up the phone and called the ambulance. Grandpa had had a stroke. I honestly thought he was dead. The only thing I could think about was my first thoughts of him day we first went up into the attic. I couldn't stop thinking about the awful thing that was running through my mind that day. I couldn't stop thinking about a world without this stranger who had become so important to me. I couldn't stop thinking about living without my grandpa in my life."

"Did he die that night, Jed?" Dr. Goldman asks.

"Let me finish the story, Doc."

He nods. I continue.

"We all rushed to his hospital room. He was fine, but he was crying. A former soldier and football coach of thirty years bawling like a baby. He was looking at my report. I'll be honest with you, I might have cried a little bit as well. All I could think to say was, 'I got an A.' God, what an idiot he must have thought I was. But it didn't matter, though. Grandpa was happy to be alive and I think he was even happier to have a reason to live. You see, the doctors had given him only two months to live, and that was almost six years previous.

"When graduation day came along, I scanned the audience. I saw my mom. She was crying, of course, and next to her was a very bored, but very proud dad. The thing that really shocked me, though, was the man sitting next to my mom. A man in a wheelchair, wearing our school colors and one of my athletic pins from baseball season. I was ecstatic to see my grandpa out of his nursing home for the first time in over a month. After the ceremony, I walked over to my mom. Dad was gone, and so was grandpa. I was a little emotional, as was she, but with good reason.

"'Where's Dad?' I asked. 'Did he have to take grandpa home already?' My mom looked me in the eyes, and I saw her begin to cry again. But after a few seconds, I realized they weren't tears of happiness. I was getting a little bit concerned as she hugged me and said, 'I'm very proud of you, son. I didn't want to ruin your special day with any bad news.'

"I asked her what she was talking about. And her response made me believe in a higher power. Her response was what made me realize I was different. She told me my grandpa had passed away earlier that morning. But I knew. Deep down, it all made sense to me. He wasn't ready yet. He wanted to see me graduate. He had one last thing to do. And once he did it? He was gone. Forever."

My former psychiatrist doesn't say anything for a while. He just nods and scratches his head. Then he tells me a story of his own, with a plausible explanation.

"That's nice, Jed. But you cannot honestly expect me to believe you. And even if I did, and let's say, for the sake of argument, I do, your mind was obviously just playing a trick on you. It was a highly emotional time for you. You were moving off to a big scary college. You were leaving Sarah Falls for the first time in your young adult life. You saw your grandfather there because you needed to see him there. You can believe in a higher power if it helps you, but I think you're just grasping at straws. I'm sure there is a rational explanation."

"So? What's your point."

"Let me tell you a story, Jed."

He's dodging.

"In other words..."

"You got it. My turn."

So he tells a story of his own. One from when he was working with the police in New York City, years before he moved to Sarah Falls, the town he would eventually be murdered in.

"Ted was the new cop. It's common knowledge that the newbies get the crappy cases no other cop wants. The case wasn't just a typical homicide, though. It was a serial. For some reason, this guy was getting away, and had racked up a death toll of four single white males. The only thing the men had in common was that they had some kind of relationship to the local theater. The first victim was an actor, the second and third were both set workers, and the most recent was the director. Most cops would have a criminal profiler give them what they were looking for, but the guys at the precinct had no intentions of making things any easier for Ted.

"This guy was good, and judging by how many he had already killed and gotten away with, he wasn't stopping any time soon. Three weeks had passed since the first body was discovered, turned upside down with two bullet holes in his back. Every case had occurred on a Tuesday night, after a performance. The first one was the lead in a local production of *The Phantom of the Opera*. When the lead was killed, the cops before Ted investigated the usual suspects. Jealous actors were immediately questioned, but they all had alibis and all of them checked out. No one knew the two stagehands, and the director had a list of enemies longer than a little girl's Hanukkah list. The only thing they had in common was their place of employment, at least, as far as Ted could tell.

"After a night at the computer, he took a shower and went into the office. Ignoring the everyday jokes and pranks of his juvenile coworkers, he began cross-referencing all the victims. Two hours went to their phone bills, another hour went to attending a lecture on the human condition, for which he was forty minutes late, and two more hours went to going through their last weeks' expenses. A rookie would have missed it, but Ted was getting pretty good at his job, and noticed a similarity. Possibly even a break in the case. Not only did all four of the victims eat at Vincenzo's, a popular Italian restaurant, before their last performances, but they were all last seen with the same woman."

"Of course," I say. "There's always a woman."

The late doctor laughs and continues his story.

"Connie Binders was her name and she had been the mistress to countless others. She was a bored housewife and her husband was out of the picture. She said they might as well be divorced and they hardly ever even saw each other. She was a suspect, but the only thing linking her to the victims was the fact that she had slept with all of them the night before the murders. Ted had to let her off after twenty-four hours, due to lack of evidence placing her at the crime scene.

"He was about to give up when something dawned on him. What if the husband was the one picking them off? What if this was revenge? Stephen, the husband, was immediately brought in for questioning. He came in carrying a long box and refused to let it go. After the officials at the front desk checked it out, they said it was okay and he could bring it inside with him. And let me tell you, Jed, this guy, in my professional opinion, was a nut.

"Ted asked him where he was on the four nights in question. After two minutes of beating around the bush, the suspect got aggravated and instructed Ted to quit the small talk and just listen to him. 'I knew my wife was cheating on me,' he explained. 'It's been going on for years. You see, I encourage it. She has never loved me, and I have always been repulsed by her. But we signed a prenuptial agreement and I don't want her to have anything.'

"Ted couldn't figure this guy out. He wouldn't even allow him to ask questions. Apparently, he had made it real big in Vegas back in the eighties. He invested well and purchased the finest model he could find after he moved to Los Angeles. A few years passed and he wasn't interested anymore. But while Ted was lost in thought, Stephen Binders did something strange. Something... Crazy.

"He pulled his long box onto the table, opened it, and what he pulled out was the single most bizarre thing Ted had ever seen. It was a dummy."

"Wait a minute," I ask. "Like a puppet, dummy?"

"Exactly. He was a ventriloquist by trade, Ted was now finding out. 'The rest of the interview will be conducted with Mr. Bibbavi. Stephen is gone at the moment, but Mr. Bibbavi would be more than happy to tell you what is going on here.' Ted later told me that the look in Stephen's eyes was eerie. It was almost as if he wasn't even there. Apparently, he was utterly and completely insane. 'Stephen is a killer, detective. He killed those men because he couldn't stand the thought of them performing in his theater. You see, detective, when Stephen returned with his new wife, the Actors Guild kicked him out, saying he was a no-talent hack who got lucky. Stephen blamed his wife, but deep down, he knew. He still knows. He's nothing without me. He's just a pathetic little...'

"And then Stephen's eyes regained life and he screamed, 'Stop it! Shut up! Don't listen to him! He's only trying to deceive you!' Naturally, Stephen Binders was arrested right there on the spot. The poor fool never really even cared about his wife being unfaithful. He was simply jealous that she was unfaithful with better actors than him. Better performers. So, naturally, he created an alter-ego in Mr. Bibbavi. He used his own past life to destroy his current one. And his future.

"Two months passed, a promotion had given Ted just what he needed to gain the respect of his fellow coworkers and everything seemed right in the world. He was going to be getting married in three short weeks and the trial of the century was underway. Stephen was going to be put away for life, due to the fact that his lawyer pleaded insanity on his behalf. He still thought the dummy was the one killing those men. As for the dummy, it was donated to the local theater and was put up in a memorial hall for the theater's founder, Stephen Binders, with a plaque saying, 'the greatest director and performer of our long and esteemed history.'

"But that's not the end of the story. Before Ted could tie the knot, he was called back in on one last assignment. It seemed there had been another murder in the theater. When they went to the crime scene, they found another actor. A young white male with two bullets in his back. It was the same signature, but the only thing was, this time, there was an extra clue. They followed a long trail of blood down to the basement of the old theater. Upon entering the new museum dedicated to the serial killer, what Ted saw on the floor shocked him. They had found Mrs. Binders, dead, her own blood covering the floor.

"At that exact moment, Ted received a call from the District Attorney. Stephen had just hung himself in his cell. But what was even more puzzling was the way Mrs. Binders was killed. She wasn't shot, like the previous five victims. She bled to death, presumably after killing this newest victim, due to a large hole carved into her back, almost as if she was a human-sized, well, puppet.

"As the coroner ran to the nearest bathroom and the chief was making sure the crime scene was secure, Ted got the final shock for the night. He found a shard of glass near the body and picked it up to examine it closer. There was blood covering the jagged piece, more than likely Mrs. Binders', and as he walked over to the middle of the museum, he noticed the case holding Mr. Bibbavi was broken. Rumor had it, years later, it was actually broken. From the inside."

"So you *do* believe me, then! I can't believe you, doc. You've understood the supernatural all along!"

He offers an explanation.

"No. Stephen Binders was crazy, killed four actors, and hung himself in jail, rather than spend the rest of his life in a mental hospital. Connie Binders didn't stop sleeping around, and her infidelities caught up with her. She and her lover killed each other in a lovers' spat. The end. Case closed."

"No fucking way," I say.

He starts to quiver. And that's when he does something that he always used to do when I was his patient. He gives himself away. He always tried to lie to me when he thought it was what he was supposed to do, but every now and then, I would catch him and he would have a tell. His whole body would quiver, and he would look at his watch.

He looks at his watch.

"Wait a minute. What was the cop's name again?"

"Ted, but that's hardly..."

"And what's your name?"

"Jed, you know this. My name is Martin Goldman."

"Martin *Theodore* Goldman?"

He looks down at his watch again.

"That's why you're still here. That's your unfinished business. You were that cop. That's why you moved to Sarah Falls. That case."

"No, Jed."

"I'm right! Aren't I?"

"Stop this nonsense right now. I really must be going. I can see that our session has gone nowhere."

"Where are you going, Doc? You're dead. You can't exactly go about your business as if you aren't."

"Goodbye, Jed. I'll come back tomorrow when you're feeling more rational."

"Rational? Fuck you, Doc! I'm trying to *help* you! Why can't you just admit that some things exist that cannot be explained! Why can't you admit my grandpa showed up to my graduation the afternoon *after* he died? Why can't you admit one of the Sarah Falls High School Massacre victims has become a *grim reaper*? And why can't you admit a demonic ventriloquist puppet killed a bunch of people twenty years ago?"

"Because, Jed."

"You have to at least admit it's *possible* I saw my grandpa, right?"

"I suppose, but..."

"And you have to at least admit it's *possible* Aidan is a demon, right?"

"It's a stretch, but with his father's affiliations and extracurricular, err, *memberships*, not entirely out of the realm of possibility. But, Jed..."

"So why is it so hard for you to believe a possession didn't occur and make you give up your career for another one?"

"Because I made it up!"

And I'm shocked. Speechless.

He calms down. He elaborates. "I took advantage of a crazy person and framed him. I killed those actors because I wanted a case to solve. I wanted to matter. I wanted to help people so much that I was blinded!"

And the truth comes out.

"Ted" was the killer all along. He invented the idea and separate persona of the possessed puppet to justify the murders. As an officer of the law, it was easier to ignore he was just as vile as the criminals he killed than to admit it to his colleagues, his followers, and himself.

But I call bullshit. He knew, all along, that what he was doing was wrong. He was going to spend the rest of his life getting a psychiatry doctorate and helping solve mysteries and save peoples' lives, but...

"But, how did you get away with it then? Why weren't there any prints or actual physical evidence to use against you? No one is that careful, Doctor. No one is that good."

He shakes his head.

"I was."

And with that revelation, I no longer believe in the people or the town of Sarah Falls.

"Fine," he says. "You win. But at least do me one favor, Jed. At least finish *your* story. If nothing else, it could serve as a form of cognitive reconstructive therapy. You need to finish this now or forever be lost to the whole thing. You need to interview the two shooters. Then you need to interview the parents of the two shooters. Then you need to publish your novel. As a piece of *fiction*, not nonfiction. Then maybe, just maybe, you can move on. And recover." He pauses. Looks around him. Remembers he's dead, and starts to fade. "I remain hopeful, Jed."

Even in death, he still doesn't entirely believe in the afterlife. Even in death, he's still a skeptic. Heaven would have been a challenge for Dr. Martin Goldman. Lucky for him, that's not where he's going.

And with that, the last person capable of breaking what little my heart had left to offer does just that. This story has taken everything from me. And I simply do not believe in good anymore.

And... Stop recording...

A reaper, by definition, is a ghost that has taken a form that is harmful to the dead. A grim reaper, by definition, is a ghost that has taken a form that is harmful to the living.

Aidan did this because of his father. He dabbled in the occult. It was no secret in this city that the Freemasons were in charge. But this was ridiculous. Whether he did it on purpose or not, Aidan's dad made a deal with the Devil for his son's soul. Now he's more powerful than ever. Not because of his power. Not because of his prestige. Because he is damned.

Maybe he was made that way. Maybe he simply became that way over time due to abuse and neglect. But I am starting to think maybe Aidan was always destined to be this. A monster. A demon. A grim reaper.

CHAPTER THIRTY-ONE

Saturday, October 3
6:30 PM
Kingston, New York
the day of the new book

And… Start recording…

"I'm Jed Hollingsworth. But because of the nature of this interview, you can just call me Jed. Sound good? I'm a journalist and I'm going to tell the story of what the papers called The Suicide Mansion Massacre. Alrighty. Let's begin. So, for the record, can I ask your name?"

"Shit, this is great. I can't believe I'm actually being interviewed by your egocentric flawed-yet-handsome ass."

I shake my head.

"Fuck. Sorry. Right. My name is Drake. But you know that. I have a last name, but maybe you can make me like Madonna or Cher or Prince or something and just give me a first name and call it good. Make it more mysterious, you know?"

"Tell me about the last night you were alive in the mansion. No more fucking around."

So he tells it straight. For the first time in his entire existence, there aren't any more games or lies or tricks.

"Gary Kaspera used to take off his watch at the end of a chess match, you know? That's how the audience, and his opponents, knew that he had won. My dad did that, too. And I guess the jig is up, so, yeah."

He removes his gloves. I didn't even realize he was wearing gloves.

Then he touches my forehead and shows me the truth.

"I took my gloves off before the murders. I wanted to feel the life slip out of their bodies. I wanted to feel something. Just like Kaspera and his watch at the chess match, my dad did the same with his watch at each crime scene. I took off my gloves after each murder, good killers have no fear of ever getting caught, I guess you can say I finally became my father's son in the end.

"My dad was the leader of the gang of bank robbers from the

earlier story on your road trip. The ones who killed that kid's family. All in all, we were all destined to either die in a horrible tragedy or become insane. So yeah, I'm the killer. Not the ghosts. This is exactly what the house wanted. All along.

"The clown ghost story and a lot of the supposed hauntings are actually an elaborate trick played by the grandson of the family we took out in Indianapolis. He's about our age. He blamed me for the death of his grandfather, a famous deceased horror novelist.

"The stories I told you? They're all just unpublished manuscripts from someone you know quite well. The ghosts are simply manifestations of the last emotion or thing that happened to them. I lied. Some of this is coincidence. But most of it was planned the second this place went up for sale."

And as he says this, world-renowned horror writer, recluse, and founding father of Sarah Falls, Aidan Montgomery Stockwell Sr. appears, showing me the image of Drake taking the shotgun to himself all those years ago, covered in the blood of every friend he ever had. Every friend, that is, but one. Me.

CHAPTER THIRTY-TWO

Wednesday, December 2
3:00 PM
Sarah Falls, Kansas
74 days after the shooting

And... Start recording...

"I'm Jed Hollingsworth. But because of the nature of this interview, you can just call me Jed. Sound good? I'm a journalist and I'm going to tell the story of what the papers are calling The Sarah Falls High School Massacre. Alrighty. Let's begin. So, for the record, can I ask your name?"

"Jameson," he coughs. "Jameson Allan."

"Okay, Jameson. I'm going to cut to the chase here with you. As you're no doubt aware, I'm on a bit of a time crunch because you made the mistake of killing someone who is hell-bent on killing me. So you'll forgive me if I skip over the backstory and simply ask you one question."

He nods. Clears his throat.

I begin. "Why?"

He shakes his head, as Aidan shows up and puts his hands on his shoulders, taunting him. Teasing him.

"Even in death," Jameson begins. "I can't really escape."

I notice the anguish in his voice.

"I'm sorry, Jameson, but..."

"You don't really care. I get it, Jed. You shouldn't. You can't. Because, well... You aren't me."

"Boohoo," Aidan mocks, disappearing into the wall behind them. Probably off to go plot my next nightmare.

"I was bullied every single day of my entire life. I got tired of it. I drew a line in the sand. I made a plan. I know, it's so stereotypical and ridiculous that you can't possibly even feel bad for me. I'm not asking you to. I'm just asking you to listen."

"I'm listening, Jameson. I asked *you* here, remember?"

"You know my *backstory*, as you put it. There's not much more to it than that. But the reason I can't pass on isn't because of what I did. It isn't even because Aidan continues to torment me and won't let me leave. No, it's much simpler than that."

"And what's that, Jameson?"

"No one knew me. Not really. My parents, even though they loved me very much, didn't really ever even know me. But it wasn't their fault. Hell, Thad didn't even know me and he was my best friend." He pauses again. Clears his throat as his voice cracks. "Thad was my only friend, come to think of it."

"What do you mean, Thad didn't know you? Weren't you two... Close?"

"Yeah. No. Not really. I mean..."

He looks as if he's going to cry and I reach out to him, forgetting we can't actually touch. He pulls away anyway.

"I'm not going to cry. I can't do that anymore. I've done enough for the rest of my existence. I swore to never shed a single tear again after the homecoming dance. And even to my own shock and horror, I can't even cry for all the innocent people who died."

"They didn't just die, Jameson. You killed them."

"You know, the funniest part about this whole thing is the fact I'm not even gay. I just didn't have the heart to tell Thad that. Or my parents, not that they thought I was anyway."

This struck me as odd, but when I corrected him yet again, saying that nothing about this incident was funny, he laughed. Literally. Aloud. Like, a big belly laugh.

"What the hell's wrong with you, kid?"

"You really don't get it, do you, Jed? I'm not gay. No one knew that but no one really cared. I didn't kill anyone. I just wrote a fucked up plan that I was doing as a form of self-therapy. But yet I'm still a *faggot*. I'm still a *monster*. I'm still a *murderer*. And I didn't even *do* anything." And then he says something that changes everything. "I didn't kill a single person."

"But..."

"Rick Smith did. He took my list. He threatened to kill Thad and my parents. I tried to stop him and..."

And he shot him.

"So there it is. The big secret I had to tell, but I had to get Aidan off my back long enough to tell it. I had to get you alone to tell it. I had to make sure you survived long enough to make the world really know. The truth. Originally, everyone wanted to know the motive. I get that. They just assumed my motive was revenge. But that's not true. I didn't have one. Never. Because to have motive, you have to act. And now you know."

"But Rick...?"

"Rick Smith wanted to do it because he wanted to be famous. The only thing left to do anymore to be famous is to have really fucked up shit happen to you or to cause chaos and disorder on an astronomical level. He wasn't going to wait. And he sure as hell wasn't going to let any fucked up shit happen to him, so he went a step further. And *caused* some fucked up shit. Period. Fame is a powerful motivator, especially when you are a clueless, boundary-free, spoiled rotten, ignored, latchkey sociopath in a backwards and unforgiving small school."

He wants to cry again. He still can't.

"What can I do?"

He starts to fade. Hopefully going to the right place, he laughs again, wiping away his nonexistent tears. "Take down my fucking Facebook page."

And... Stop recording...

So the story is almost done. But will anyone believe it? Two shooters, but really only one who pulled the trigger? This is truly a story for the ages. It isn't just Sarah Falls' story now. It is the world's. This is important. More important than I could ever have even imagined. This is the type of journalism that might actually get my career back.

If I want it. And if I survive long enough to tell it.

I can't stop now. I have to move on to the next interview.

And... Start recording...

"I'm Jed Hollingsworth. But because of the nature of this interview, you can just call me Jed. Sound good? I'm a journalist and I'm going to tell the story of what the papers are calling The Sarah Falls High School Massacre. Alrighty. Let's begin. So, for the record, can I ask your name?"

"Nick Allan."

"And your relation to the incident, Mr. Allan?"

"Jameson is... Was... No is... My son."

"Jameson Allan."

"Yes."

"One of the two shooters." He looks at me as if I have just punched him in the stomach. "Sorry. I'm not very good at the whole subtlety thing when it comes to the starts of these interviews. To be honest, Mr. Allan, I don't really know why I'm even still doing this. Going after the truth, I guess."

"The truth? That's what you want?"

"Yeah, I suppose it is what I want."

"No. That isn't it, Jed. If you wanted the truth, you would have gotten it by now and written your damn book. You want to live in the past. You want to relive the pain and misery of other people. Why? I don't know. But I know people like you. I've known them my whole life it seems. They've just been popping up out of the woodwork more and more often after my son died. And they won't leave me alone. I'm doing this because I want you to write your damn book. I want you to finish your work. And I want you to quote me. Word for word. Are you listening? Is that thing recording? Good. Because you won't want to miss this."

He pauses again. He takes a big drink of water from the glass in front of him as his wife, Candace, comes up behind him. He reaches back and touches her and looks me deep in the eyes. Looks at me. Really looks at me. Looks *through* me.

Then he says it. The quote he was waiting months to say. The quote that will end his pain and suffering. The quote that, God willing, will finally allow his son to pass over and move on to whatever was waiting for him on the other side.

"I love my son. Love. Present tense. Always have. Always will. He was a good kid, no matter what others say about him. My wife has different thoughts and fears and wonders every now and then, but the fact still remains that he is my son. And you cannot understand that for two reasons. The first being you have no children of your own. And I understand that. But the second is your own fault. Whether it's partially genetic or has something to do with a chemical imbalance or whatever doesn't matter to me. It's the fact you don't seem to even care. These are not just people you are messing with, Jed. This town has been through enough, what with the school shooting, the media frenzy, the myths of the Sarah Falls Reaper, and now this damn book of yours. The one you just can't seem to finish."

"Sir, all due respect…"

"Do not interrupt me, boy. I'm not done yet."

His wife's grip tightens on his shoulder. He waves her off. She backs away. And he continues his statement. And that's when I understand that this is no longer an interview. It's his life's work. It's his child's pain. It's his marriage and his philosophy all rolled into one nicely-worded speech. For me. For him. For his wife. And most of all, for his son.

"Finish your book. It's over. The deaths are over. The healing has to start now, because if it doesn't, it's never going to happen. I've been trying for months to move on. It almost cost me my marriage. It almost cost me my job. But I sat back and realized I had already lost the worst thing I could ever lose."

"Your son."

"Exactly. Please, interview my wife and get out of my house, Jed. I'm not trying to be rude, I'm just trying to do the same thing you should have done months ago."

He doesn't say it. Neither does his wife. And I'm not going to either. It goes unsaid, but that doesn't mean we don't all know what he was talking about. It's time to move on. And when I ask his wife about an interview, she says it's too late. She's already heading off to bed. She had taken her nightly sleeping supplement and wasn't going to be ready to talk to anyone, especially the man her husband viewed as demonizing and profiting off her only son's final days here in the land of the living. I would have to leave.

So I walk home.

This interview, though powerful, is just another dead end. That isn't supposed to be a joke. I'm very obviously not a comedian. I'm a journalist. Or a writer. Or a crazy person. Pick one. Mix and match. I don't really care.

And... Stop recording...

I got an exorcist and a bunch of protection from the ghost of Aidan Montgomery Stockwell III, but nowhere is safe. He's too powerful. So I tried to get rid of him. I tried to expel him. Long story short, it didn't work. So I'm going home. I can't live in fear forever. I have to face him. What's the worst he can do?

Right?

As predicted, Aidan is waiting for me when I arrive home. But before I can even begin to plead for my life, something strange happens.

The grim reaper raises his scythe and begins to chase me through my own home, when suddenly, he stops. He disappears. He's...

Gone.

And that's when I realize I've somehow, inexplicably been saved by another supernatural force. After all, a ghost can apparently only be destroyed by another ghost. Rick Smith apparently got tired of being one-upped by an elitist prick like Stockwell. So he simply popped up out of nowhere, in the nick of time, and killed him. Again.

He sits down. Points to the notebook and the pen on the table. I sit down with him. He is ready for his interview. He wants to tell his story now. Is he tired of being overshadowed by the Sarah Falls Reaper? Or does he actually feel remorse? Who knows...?

Let's find out.

And... Start recording...

"I'm Jed Hollingsworth. But because of the nature of this interview, you can just call me Jed. Sound good? I'm a journalist and I'm going to tell the story of what the papers are calling The Sarah Falls High School Massacre. Alrighty. Let's begin. So, for the record, can I ask your name?"

Aidan is dead. There is only Rick Smith now. His eyes are blank. Steam is rising from his body. He sits and the chair starts to burn. All the while, Rick Smith is silent.

"Okay, fine. If you want it that way, I'll do the talking. Sound good?"

Nothing. But the chair is now ashes, so he is standing. Panting. Staring.

"You're Rick Smith. You had no friends. And then you made one. And together, with Jameson Allan, you killed a bunch of your classmates."

Nothing.

"And then yourself."

He smiles.

"You think this is funny?"

He nods.

"Fine. I'll read the police reports. These are basically tactless versions of the obituaries. You don't mind if we get tacky, do you, Rick?"

No response.

"Of course you don't."

He crosses his arms. While still staring. He doesn't even blink.

"Victim number one was named Dan Scott. He was an aspiring

guitarist and liked playing music with his band and dreaming of making it big someday. He never will. He was eighteen years old when you killed him. Why did you kill him?"

I lay a picture of Dan at his feet. He shrugs.

"Victim number two was named Annie DeLucco. She was a straight A student and liked the idea of leaving Sarah Falls to go to Dartmouth and experience the rest of the world. She never will. She was fifteen years old when you killed her. Why did you kill her?"

I lay a picture of Annie next to the photo of Dan. He shrugs.

"Victim number three was named Gavin Armstrong. He was the president of the speech and debate team and liked planning his future. He never will. He was sixteen years old when you killed him. Why did you kill him?"

Gavin's photo sits next to Annie's. He shrugs.

"Victim number four was named Aidan Montgomery Stockwell III. He was a football star, Yale bound senior and liked pretty girls, fast cars, and wanted to buy everything that wasn't for sale. He never will. He was eighteen years old when you killed him. Why did you kill him?"

Another photo. Another shrug.

"Victim number five was named Antoine Brown. He was a football player and wanted to go pro and make his mother proud. He never will. He was seventeen years old when you killed him. Why did you kill him?"

He shrugs. Yawns.

I continue naming names, spouting facts, and placing photos around him, forming a circle.

Amy Hester. Ariel Effken. Suzanne Gerard. Adrienne Balogh. Sue Scheel. Stacy Marshall. Liz Gambino. Rochelle Albertson. Natalie Grantham. Cherise Reeves. Nonny Brown. Betsy O'Bannon. Gary Boyd. Sam Moats. Ally Johnson. Tegan Mumford. Alex Kennedy. Terry Akin. Phil English. Cam Innes. Todd Maguire. Seth Bartels. Grady O'Hara. Paul Swanson. Miguel Cisneros. Eddy Gilbert.

"Students. Sons. Daughters. People without futures."

He watches me, turning ever so slightly each time I place a new photo on the ground in front of him. Eyes black. Smirk permanently etched on his mouth.

I continue, moving onto the teachers, some of them just kids themselves.

Tyler Jacobson, social studies teacher. Jackie Hester, home economics teacher killed along with her daughter and entire classroom. James Berkhardt, English teacher, my friend, who was planning on renewing his vows this summer.

I almost lose it when I set down James' photo, but I'm only thirty-four names into the list. I'm not done yet.

More teachers. More professionals. More innocent lives unfairly snuffed out too soon. Ben McFerrin. Tom Albrecht. Keith Tanner. Kelly Ernst. Samantha Ferryman. Heather Rhodes. Don Butler. Jake Watson. Patty O'Brien. Kent Harman. Arnold Palladino.

"Victim number forty-six was named…"

I pause. His ears perk, his smirk becomes a smile.

"No! You don't get to smile!"

I throw a glass of holy water at him, which immediately causes him to scream in a fit of rage. That actually worked. He's hurting.

Good.

"Victim number forty-six was named Kristy DeGraw. She was a journalism teacher and the newspaper advisor and liked living a long-distance relationship, much like that of all her favorite creative writers did in the past. She was waiting for me. She wanted to marry me. She wanted to live forever… with me. She never will. She was twenty-five years old when you killed her. Why did you kill her?"

He groans a little, stretches, and resumes not caring.

"Why did you take her away from me?"

He shrugs.

"Fine."

I have reached the conclusion.

"Victim number forty-seven was named Jameson Allan. He was a scared kid and liked boys and wanted revenge. He got it all right. He was sixteen years old when you killed him. And for some Godforsaken reason, you killed forty-six other people in Sarah Falls. Why did you kill him?"

He's looking at Jameson's photo as I place it on the floor, completing the circle around him. There are no spaces left. I have completed the circle.

He turns around, slowly at first, piecing together what I have done. What I was doing the whole time. Yes, he needed to hear the names and the people behind the names. Yes, he needed to put a face with the lives he ended. But most importantly, he needed to think I was just trying to make him feel guilt.

People like him don't feel guilt. *Things* like him don't feel at all.

"And *'victim'* number forty-eight was you. You were an evil piece of shit. You were a *famous* evil piece of shit for a little while. You left behind no one. No one cares about you. You're dead. Move on. Why are you still here? Why did you kill them?"

He looks at me. He unfolds his arms. He starts panting. His eyes ignite in flames.

"Last chance."

He tries to walk out of the circle... But can't.

He starts screaming, low guttural noises that don't even sound like something a human would be possible of making.

I pull out Danny's lost wedding ring. I pull out a postcard from Ally's baby's foster family. And then he gets it. All the promises I made. All the unfinished business that was left in Sarah Falls... is over.

"You're the last one here. I'm the only one who can see you. And you're trapped. As soon as I leave, you're alone."

He composes himself. Closes his eyes.

"So tell me your story. Or I'll leave you here."

He opens his eyes again. They are no longer black. They are red. And there is blood coming out of his ears and eyes. He opens his mouth.

"Why?" I finally ask. "Why, God damn it. Why? Is this doing anything to you? Anything? Do these names mean anything? Are you listening to me, you sick little fuck? Why? Why? Why?"

Silence. "I'm not afraid of you," I whisper. Silence. "WHY!?"

And he smirks. I know why. His entire body ignites into flames and he doesn't even scream.

"Because you could."

He burns until there is nothing left of him.

And... Stop recording...

I'm almost done.

CHAPTER THIRTY-THREE

Saturday, October 3
6:30 AM
Kingston, New York
the day of the fire

"But that's too easy," Drake laughs. "The the final reveal? Aidan Montgomery Stockwell is not the ghost... It's his grandson, Aidan Montgomery Stockwell III."

The little shit smirks and puts on his hood.

"Hiya, Jed. How's this for a final act super-villain team-up?"

Drake is removing his gloves, grabbing a scythe out of the ether and standing next to Stockwell. "When a Reaper is vanquished," he says, "He is deposited in with the family estate, which is this here Suicide Mansion that once belonged to his grandfather. He took advantage of the house's power and used it to get his final revenge against you, Jed."

And that's when Drake reveals that his unfinished business is not that he's innocent, but rather, that he didn't get a chance to kill me.

He talks about what it means to be unfriended, both emotionally and psychologically and what it did to him, a man who would spend hours a day scrolling through his various social media accounts and friending, adding, and essentially stalking everyone from his entire life, dating even as far back as grade school.

He cuts Aidan in half, ending the Stockwell nightmare before it can even begin again.

"Sorry to crap in your cornflakes, Drake, but you lost. I'm not dead."

"Right," he says, spitting up blood, realizing that the cocktail that I had made him was laced with holy water.

"And you know why?"

"No idea. Why?"

"Because I never unfriended you. I never friended you. I don't use Facebook. Because of two reasons."

He's coughing and writhing in pain on the ground, looking up at me, seeing a family portrait that I somehow never noticed until just now of three generations of Stockwell men.

"One, because I'm not an old person."

He laughs.

"And two? I try not to use social media beyond research purposes. Because it's filled with monsters.

He stops laughing.

"Because it's filled with people like you."

"Oh," he says, as he starts to fade. "Well, fuck my shit."

And he's gone.

And… Stop recording…

"I'm gonna go ahead and call bullshit," I tell my agent, who's on his way, no idea what he's going to encounter when he gets here. He's talking about my love life. Or lack thereof.

"She can talk to whoever she wants to talk to," I continue. "She can meet (or not), drink with (or not), dine next to (or not), and even fuck (or not) all God damn day as far as I'm concerned. I couldn't 'give two shits,' as the grim reaper once infamously said. The agreement was that we just wouldn't talk about it."

I can't believe I've just lived through this nightmare for a second time and he wants to talk about my this nonsense.

"Meanwhile," he says, "You just keep ghosting people."

"I keep *what*?"

He laughs. "Jesus fucking Christ, Jed. Ghosting. You match, you meet, you fuck, you disappear. Ghosting. How do you not know these things?"

My agent clears his throat.

"What?" I ask, ready to jump into another long diatribe about how this whole thing is his fault anyway.

"Well," he sort of half-whispers, "You did say you loved her."

Silence.

"Go fix things, Jed. It's all worth it if you have someone to share it with."

What am I doing?

This has all been worth it because it'll be another best-seller. I'm going to publish it as a novel, of course, because no one would believe me anyway. And America loves a sequel.

I delete the pending friend request from Drake, the one that caused the whole ordeal. And then I do something I should have done over a year ago. I check the "remembering" page for Jameson Allan.

A few nice memories, but they're outweighed by the death threats meant for his mom and negative, mean, angry comments about his sexuality, his perversion, and his murders. Still so much hate.

The world will never change.

I don't even remember lighting the match. Or signing my name on the deed. There are sirens in the background.

So I go. The one person to ever survive the night in Suicide Mansion.

I'm done here. I'm done with all of this.

CHAPTER THIRTY-FOUR

Thursday, December 3
1:00 PM
Sarah Falls, Kansas
75 days after the shooting

I broke into the house that Rick Smith used to live in late last night, after I sent him and Aidan Montgomery Stockwell III back to hell. And then I did the most important thing I've done for this town since I started this crusade.

I stole Rick Smith's journal.

But I'm not even going to read it. I don't have to. It will become part of my book, yes, but I don't need to read it to end this. That will all just be fluff to this already nearly complete dark and macabre masterpiece.

But that's for later. Not now. Not yet. I've still got one last person to talk to. One more interview left and I'm done. Which brings me to here. Right now. The final talk before I'm done.

And... Start recording...

"I'm Jed Hollings..."

"I know who you are, you fuck."

"Umm... Huh?"

"Don't you fucking dare '*Umm... Huh*?' me, you piece of shit. I'll answer your questions. I'll take your punishment. But you have to do one thing for me when it's over. You have to answer one of *my* questions. And you have to do it honestly. Deal?"

No sense in arguing.

"Deal."

"Okay, Jed. Go ahead. Let me have it."

So I do. I tell her the story.

The whole story.

She lights up a cigarette. Hand shaking.

"That it?"

"No. No, it certainly isn't it."

So I tell her the stories behind the stories. I read to her actual excerpts from interviews. From the survivors. And I lay it on thick. I tell her the rest of the stories. Of the victims. The ones who *didn't* survive. I let her know what type of life I live because of people like her and the monster she helped raise.

I'm sweating. She's crying, but not sobbing. Just letting the tears collect at the bottom of her chin. Dripping onto her beer- and filth-covered shirt.

"Assuming you're the one who broke into my house last night, too?"

"You bet your ass I did. And you know what? I haven't even read your son's journal yet. I don't have to. I know what it's going to say and frankly, I don't care. That's going to be for everyone else in America to read."

"Uh-huh," she says, starting to shake uncontrollably from withdrawal from God knows what. She puts out her cigarette and starts scratching her arms.

I'm almost sick. I have to end this. But I can't just let her off the hook. She *had* to have known. Evil isn't just born. Not like Rick Smith. It has to be raised. Or at least *noticed*.

"You could have stopped this, Mrs. Smith."

She shakes her head.

"You know what? Here's the deal. There's no easy way to say this, so I guess I'll just start by saying no, I'm not sorry for stealing your son's journal. You lost all rights to protecting your son when you failed him so horribly he had to do what he thought he had to do to get your attention. So there's that. No apology from me."

She just sits there. Motionless. I continue.

"In fact, I think the town of Sarah Falls needs, no *deserves*, an apology from *you*. What your son took from us was much more personal, much more valuable, than any single item I could have ever taken from you."

Again, nothing. Just like her demon spawn.

"I'm not an idiot. I understand that you will probably not be apologizing any time in the near future, but know this. You may not feel guilt now, or five years from now, or even on your death bed, but all of us... We'll never stop apologizing for not saying goodbye, making things right, or fixing something that will now always and forever be broken."

I'm yelling now.

"If you want the fucking journal back, fine. You can have it. Word for fucking word. In my book. But you'll have to share your son's words with every single family in Sarah Falls. And every single reader in the nation. So without further ado, I'm going to end this pathetic attempt at an interview by *accepting* your apology. You know, the one you never gave, never will give, and don't understand why or how to give me, the families, and the victims of Sarah Falls."

I stop. I catch my breath.

"I forgive you."

"Fine," she finally says. "My turn."

She rifles through her purse for another cigarette.

"Is he in hell?" she asks. "My son. And don't you *dare* fucking lie to me."

Without any hesitation whatsoever, I let her know.

"Yes."

She lights another cigarette.

"Good. Now get the fuck out of my house."

And... Stop recording...

I leave. And the last of the ghosts of Sarah Falls leaves with me.

So. Here we are. I know you have questions. But that's tough. I'm the interviewer, not you.

Did I learn anything? Did I finally get my life back in order? What happened with the engagement ring I always carry with me? And speaking of rings, how about Mr. Berkhardt's lost wedding ring? Or Ally Johnson's baby? Did I ever find her? And what about the other ghosts and survivors and their testimonies?

I'll be honest. I'm tired. And I've almost died a lot these last few weeks. So I'm going to save this to my computer. Email copies to my former colleagues at the magazine. Maybe make a call to my old boss and beg for my job back. And sleep. For a month.

As for the rest of the story? I guess you'll just have to wait for the book. The one I'm writing when I wake up. The one I'm dedicating to the people of Sarah Falls. The one I'm writing for Kristy DeGraw and all the other victims of Rick Smith. The one I'm writing for Coach David Lester and all the other victims of Aidain Montgomery Stockwell III. But most of all, the one I'm writing for Jameson Allan. Because he deserves it. He's paid enough. And so have I.

So yes, in the end, I'm writing it for myself.

Please. Buy it. Read it. Talk about it. And learn from it. God knows I have. I hope it keeps you up at night. Like it keeps me up at night. Like it's going to keep all the ghosts and walking ghosts of

Sarah Falls up each and every single fucking night for the rest of their lives.

I'll close with a final testimony. A story of sorts, not taken directly, but overheard as I watched in horror as the first responders walked out of the high school and emptied their breakfasts onto the chalk-covered pavement.

The ghosts will stay with me because I deserve it. The survivor's stories will stay with me because how could they not. But this one. This tale will haunt me until the day I die.

One paramedic is still reeling from the bloodbath to this very day because of what he saw. And what he heard. That's right. Heard. He could still hear cell phones going off on the corpses of the students and staff members as he tried his best to keep his cool. He was young, but he knew what that meant.

They don't know yet, he'd thought to himself. *Their loved ones still think there's hope.*

I don't know anyone who could have kept his or her cool in that situation.

Even me. Especially me.

I heard him telling a reporter a few weeks later that he put his cell phone on silent after that day. He said that he has a panic attack whenever he hears one go off in public. Can you even imagine? Never again being able to hear something as simple as a chime or a preselected jingle or even a text message ding ever again?

The answer is no. You can't. And that's why it's so important I'm telling you this right now. Because you have to realize that this not only ruined the lives of the victims and their loved ones. It ruined everyone in this town's lives. Forever. And, if I've done my job right, maybe it's ruined a little bit of yours.

This is a call to action. I *hope* you feel bad, because I do. And these people do. And to be completely honest with you, that's good. We can take it. But if we spread it out a bit? Maybe, just maybe, we can get past it.

So buy my book. Silence your phone. And delete your Facebook, X, Instagram, Snapchat, TikTok, and whatever-the-fuck accounts right now. Reach out and touch people, while they're still alive. Out of some sign of respect, if nothing else. Before it's too late.

Or don't.

Either way, I'll see you soon.

CHAPTER THIRTY-FIVE

Now

When I was on my way back to Sarah Falls, I was going to figure things out. I was going to propose to Kristy DeGraw, the love of my life. I was going to start taking my medication regularly. I was going to write for the Sarah Falls Gazette, fix up my parents' house, and start a family.

Then the worst school shooting in American history occurred. And Kristy was one of the victims. But I still had a chance to prove myself, to fix things, make things make sense again, but I didn't. And I fucked everything up.

When I left Sarah Falls to go sign my first big book deal, I texted Kristy's cell phone, still in service because her mom and dad couldn't bear to cancel it, what with her adorable little voicemail greeting still on the account and all.

"I love you," was the message I left.

Obviously, I didn't get a response. Part of me actually kind of expected one. And not a "Who is this?" because it was someone else's number, but an actual "I miss you and I love you, too, Jed." From beyond. From her. From Kristy.

When I was there briefly before I went on this insane road trip that somehow ended up being connected to Sarah Falls in just about the most cinematic way imaginable, I thought, what the fuck, why not send her another text.

"I miss you," was the message I sent.

Again, I got no response. And again, it hurt. She would be so disappointed in the man I have become. She would be so sad for me.

So when I told my agent that of course I'd write another novel, and of course I'd be loose with the facts and ramp up the Stockwell scares to the max on this sequel that I didn't know was a sequel until I lived it for myself, I thought, I don't *deserve* a response. But I texted her again anyway.

"I'm sorry," was all I could come up with.

And then, the universe sent me a response. Two, actually.

The first was a notification on Tinder from Cali. "Hey, Jed. I'm super sorry about how we left things. Want to try again some time?

Maybe that beach we talked about? I'll understand if you're not interested… being all famous and stuff."

The second was a text from my agent.

"Big things, Jed. Big money."

But it wasn't the sign I needed. Not until I checked my outgoing texts to the only woman who ever really knew me.

First: "I love you."

Months later: "I miss you."

Just now: "I'm sorry."

And then she did it. Somehow, she sent me the message I needed.

Directly below the message from this morning, in tiny bold print: "Read at 11:42 AM."

In her own way, Kristy forgave me. And she told me, again, to move on. To take the plunge. To have faith.

So I did just that. I drove to the beach spot Cali and I had joked about before I went to Suicide Mansion. I parked on the side of the road. And I went to find her.

It's a little after noon, slightly overcast, and I can hear the ocean waves as I see there's a little cabana with a margarita bar and hardly anyone on the beach. I stroll past the guy in the shack, no customers on the stools, and give him a wave as I notice Cali on the beach. There is a blanket big enough for two people, but she is alone. She's on her stomach, reading the new Nicholas Sparks novel. On her right, there's a bucket full of ice and a couple of empty beers. On her left is a large amount of space on the beach towel and books by James Patterson and Stephen King.

"Hey," I say, always one with the great opening lines.

She puts her book down, lowers her sunglasses, and smiles. "Well hey there, stranger."

She turns around and sits up, patting down the spot next to her. But I freeze, like I used to freeze with Kristy.

She laughs. "Go get some liquid courage and come join me."

She points back at the cabana.

I walk up and order two Narragansetts. I pay the guy in cash and let him know that I'll probably be back. He offers to let me start a tab if I want to do the credit card thing and as he starts to trail off about the weather and how he can't believe that we have the beach to ourselves this morning, it hits me.

By "we" he means him and I. Not Cali and I. Because, of course,

Cali isn't *really* here. She's dead. She's a ghost.

And worse, she knows it. This is my penance. She's been lying to me all along as I road trip my way to a comeback. The finest form of ghosting there is usually ends up being committed by actual ghosts. She's not a flight attendant. She's a reaper. She died and lives on the wire, transferring her consciousness to wherever she needs to go and suck the last little bit of life force out of her every single victim. All male. All stupid. And, like me, all deserving.

I wave the old man off, saying I'm good with cash. And I think about sitting at one of the bar stools, but what the hell. I might as well go sit on the blanket someone left behind and enjoy one of those books while I drink alone.

On my way back to the beach, I hear him say something that I can't quite make out. Before I can turn, I notice Cali is watching us. Watching me. She's waving, smiling.

"What's that?" I ask him.

"I said you two make a cute couple."

And there it was. Not a sign from the universe. Just a nice comment from a guy trying to make a good tip.

And as for the end of this particular story? Let's just say that I'm done being a piece of shit. I'm done telling you other people's stories. And I'm done telling you all of mine.

Let's just say I'm going to go ahead and start that tab and see where this goes.

THE END

JH, 2024.

ACKNOWLEDGEMENTS

This book would not have been possible without the support of so many people. I want to take a moment to highlight a few.

The guidance from my writing mentors, David Hollander, Scott Wolven, and Shanna McNair has been unmatched over the last decade. My colleagues and professors in the Walt Whitman Archive and University of Nebraska-Lincoln English department have offered so much support since my return to academia. Thank you to Timothy Schaffert, Stacey Waite, Chigozie Obioma, Debbie Minter, Shari Stenberg, Ken Price, Kevin McMullen, Brett Barney, Amelia Montes, Robert Brooke, Adrian Wisnicki, Ashlynn Stewart, and Samantha Gilmore. I am grateful to my former coworkers at Lincoln Public Schools. Pam Davis, Kristen Friesen, Matt Gerber, Kim Davis, Pat Hunter-Pirtle, Diane Brodd, Shirley Roeber, Michaela Hahn, and Kurt Glathar all played a vital role in the educator I have become. My former teachers, or as I like to call them, my "formative" teachers, deserve some praise. Cheryl Rauch, Nancy Bargen, Kathy Stewart, Ann Quinlan, and Paula Damke all taught me to be creative and paved the way for me to inspire others to do the same.

Thanks to the various lifelong writerly friendships forged at The Writer's Hotel, the Sarah Lawrence College Summer Writers Seminar, the Chicago House of Two Urns Writers Residency, and Team Comic Booked. Parks Kugle, Greg Renz, Grace Carpenter, Claudia Lux, Travis Tyler, Cameron Njaa, Jon Serri, Vivek Sharma, Scott McDaniel, and Julie Carpenter are all wonderful friends and even better writers.

My New York family gets a lot of love, too, for letting me spend so much of my time justifying the east coast life about one-fourth of the year... for a few years longer than planned. Kevin Hagen, Kevin Lesser, Nate Skaggs, Johnny Kou, Jordan Forcier, Fausto Wilson (who gets a special shoutout for taking my super-duper serious author photo at the infamous Hotel Empire in Manhattan), and my favorite adventure buddy of all time, Kristie Hagen. Thank you for making me feel at home, but also making me actually go home every time I had a contract to honor.

Thank you to John Doan and Larry Lorenz for giving me my first job, my backup job, and my current job at Trade a Tape Comic Center in Lincoln, Nebraska. May the next 50 years in business be as exciting as the first.

So many countless thank yous for the gracious, careful, and supportive eyes and words from the entire Poe Boy team. Graeme Parker, Derek Schneider, and Carole Bulewski have been so welcoming and I truly feel like I've found a new writerly home. Do yourself a favor and check out the other books available from *Poe Boy Publishing*.

It goes without saying, but still shouldn't not be said, this one goes out to my former students. There are somehow thousands of you now. I hope you learned something from me, whether it be in an English or a leadership classroom at the high school or the college level. But mostly I just hope you are well. I'm proud of all of you.

I am thankful for the words of wisdom from my parents, Bill and Diane, and my grandparents, Larry and Carol, as well as the support from my brother and his family, Jim, Erika, Sawyer, and Sebastian. Extended thanks go out to all the extended family of aunts, uncles, cousins, and to the chosen family we've lost and gained along the way. And of course a shoutout to my hundreds of brothers in the Bond from Phi Delta Theta fraternity.

Lastly, this book is dedicated to those who won't be here to hold it but will undoubtedly find a way to read its pages. Larry Hill, Larry Schulze, Gene Eckel, and Dustin Niemeyer. I think of all four of you every day. And I hope this book makes you proud. Especially the Larrys, for whom this entire book is dedicated.

RESOURCES

There is help. There is hope. To reach the Suicide and Crisis Hotline, visit 988lifeline.org. To register to vote, go to vote.gov. To help stop domestic violence and bullying, visit both thehotline.org and stopbullying.gov. You are not alone. And you are loved.

ABOUT THE AUTHOR

Jeff Hill is a writer who helps others tell their stories. Currently pursuing a PhD in Human Sciences and a graduate certificate in personal leadership at the University of Nebraska-Lincoln, Jeff holds a BS in education, graduate certificates in both digital humanities and the teaching of writing, and a MA in English, all from UNL. He became a college lecturer after teaching high school for a decade and currently serves as a chapter advisor for Phi Delta Theta fraternity. He has over 100 publications for various literary magazines, available both in print and online. A former research associate for the Walt Whitman Archive and faculty member of the Writer's Hotel writing conference in New York City, Jeff is also a freelance writing tutor and has worked part time in a comic shop since he was a kid. *Dead Socials* is his first novel. You can find him on Instagram, Twitter/X, and Patreon as jeffhillwriter.